C000049387

All the Little Secrets

A Novel by
D. Thrush

Copyright © 2020 D. Thrush
All Rights Reserved
Copyright law prohibits the reproduction,
copying, scanning, or distributing of any part of
this book without permission from the author

Cover design by Bukovero
Title page heart from Shutterstock
Drawings by D. Thrush
Author photo by David Peters

ASIN: B08QGBW7FB
ISBN-13: 979-8580771946

Praise for All the Little Secrets

"A thought-provoking, emotionally-tugging novel which will keep you interested to the very end." *Shebb*

"A great story and a 'best-friends heroine' who is really worth getting to know." *constant reader*

"...I really loved the ending." *Sally*

Novels by D. Thrush

Literary & Women's Fiction

Guardian of the Light

Whims & Vices (Book 1)
Fate & Flirtations (Book 2)

All the Little Secrets (Book 1)
Little Secrets Revealed (Book 2)

~*~*~*~*~*~*~*~*~*~*~

Chick Lit

The Daughter Claus (Book 1)
The Claus Cause (Book 2)
Merrily Ever After (Book 3)
The More the Merrier (Book 4)

Fairy Tale Karma

~*~*~*~*~*~*~*~*~*~*~

Contents

Chapter 1 – The Present

This is not a love story, though it's about love. The many illusions and delusions, the glittery facades and mutations, the nicks and flaws, when you're convinced with every fiber of your being that you're in the midst of it. But that excitement in the pit of your stomach, it isn't truly love, is it? It's more often longing or loneliness or hope. Or a simple case of lust.

The myth of love. We build up this ideal image to which we stubbornly cling. It has to be true or life isn't worth living. We know in our hungry hearts that a grand passion awaits us, that it hides in mere mortals, that we must recognize that diamond in the rough, that toad waiting for our kiss.

We search for that perfect person who will fulfill our every wish and desire granting us all that is possible. Yes, we ardently believe, but it more often cruelly taunts us, rarely bursting out of its cocoon into a glorious butterfly fluttering in our hearts.

What we do for the dream of love. The deceptions we accept, the humiliations we endure, the lies we tell ourselves. Reality is mostly bitter, or sometimes we find someone who comforts us with their affection. For a while. But is it what we dreamed of and aspired to? Is it the transcendent experience that fills our hearts, lights the darkness, and warms our souls?

No, this is not a love story. This is about my search to find it.

~ ~ ~

I'm at the LAX airport with my head tilted back in an uncomfortable gray plastic sculpted chair, pondering the huge ductwork snaking around the cavernous ceiling. I admire the intricacy of it and marvel at the skills some innately possess. If only I were gifted enough to invent something useful or create something beautiful that would shift the world. Having a consuming sense of purpose would temper the emptiness and yearning that sometimes afflict my days, but I'm just an average person. Filler on this planet as most of us are. Drag on this spinning globe.

I've closed my tablet and stuck it in my carry-on shoulder bag. The warm yellow puddle of sunlight spilling through the window while I was reading had made me sleepy, and I can't stop yawning as I wait for my flight back home to northern California from Los Angeles. I adjust the tortoiseshell frames on my nose and tuck my dark hair behind my ears as I stand to stretch my stiff back and legs.

A frazzled mother endeavors to corral two small children who whiz by. I smile at her with sympathy. My kids are adults now, thank goodness. It hadn't been easy being a single mother. I remember how rambunctious my kids had been, often draining me of energy and patience. I dig in my bag and pull out my last power bar. I hold it out to her as she herds the kids by me, and she smiles and gratefully accepts it. I watch as she seats the kids and breaks the bar in half.

My stomach lets out a rolling growl, reminding me that I won't be home for hours. There's a newsstand across the way past the relentless flowing mass of travelers toting suitcases and hurrying to their destinations. Everyone is always in a hurry. Time is forever ahead of us, mocking us as it zips into the past. The days melt together and suddenly years have gone by. Where did the last year go? The last decade? And now time drags as I wait for my flight and my stomach growls.

Heaving the strap of my heavy bag onto my

2

shoulder, I weave my way through the gaps of rushing people into the narrow confines of the newsstand. With mild interest, I browse the rows of magazines and displays of mugs, T-shirts, and neck pillows in the claustrophobic space, bumping and apologizing as I go. A packet of mixed nuts will tide me over until I get back home.

I squeeze past a guy pulling a small suitcase and bounce into a carousel displaying postcards. Scenes of sun-drenched beaches and curved palm trees tilt closer as I reach to steady the metal display and stagger backward into someone coming the other way.

"Excuse me," I mumble.

How embarrassing to be so clumsy. Graceful I am not. At least I didn't knock over the carousel. That would've been worse. I can see myself on my hands and knees scooping up postcards. I just need to get my packet of nuts and get back to my seat in the waiting area if someone hasn't taken it.

"Vera?" says a male voice.

I look up. It takes a few seconds for my brain to register who is standing before me like an apparition from the past.

"Brad?"

My heart gives a little lurch, and I wonder if I'm dreaming. I had never expected to see him again. Not after the way things had ended. Not after I'd moved away. Funny. I hadn't thought about him much in a long time, and I used to think about him all the time. Sometimes I still did. A song or movie would trigger fleeting memories, or I'd lay in bed in the darkness and my mind would go to that desolate place of regrets and what ifs. Why hadn't I done things differently? I'd handled everything all wrong. At one time, we'd been happy together. He was happy too. I know it. But I'd gone and blown it. I can feel myself revert to that insecure person I'd been in his calm

3

presence. Opposites we were.

He looks the same, though a little heavier, a little older, and without his mustache. I stare for a moment at his upper lip. He has the same light brown tousled hair that curls up by his collar and the same blue-blue eyes that transfix me. I remember that irresistible cleft in his chin, the dazzling smile, and those expressive eyebrows. Now smile wrinkles fan out from the corners of his eyes and make him even more appealing. He's dressed in light gray slacks and a white dress shirt with the sleeves rolled up on his forearms like he's serious about getting busy. He clutches a black briefcase. How does he manage to always look so put together and professional?

Of course, I'm wearing loose, light gray sweatpants and a Rosie the Riveter T-shirt that proclaims, "We Can Do It!" A plum colored hoodie is tied around my waist, and I'm sporting purple sneakers with pink shoelaces. I dress for comfort when I travel, not that I travel much. I also like to be comfortable when I run to the grocery store or go anywhere nowadays. There was a time when I wouldn't have left the house so disheveled, but, somehow, I've morphed into an unkempt hermit. I feel invisible anyway. No one ever notices me anymore. Not like when I was younger and attracted male attention that I had no clue how to manage. If I could go back, I still wouldn't know how to react any better.

Brad pulls me toward him, away from the errant postcard rack and out of the way of a throng pulsing toward the checkout. He's only inches taller than me, and I gaze into his mesmerizing eyes.

"What are you doing here in L.A.?" he asks.

"I had to go to a training seminar for work. What are you doing here? Do you live here now?"

"No. I still live down in San Diego, but I had a

meeting with clients here. Are you on your way back? I could give you a lift."

Alone in a car in proximity with Brad for a few hours. I waver for a millisecond. As tempting as that is, I shake my head.

"No thanks. My flight's leaving soon. I live up north now."

I can't stop staring at the flash of his white teeth when he speaks. He must've had them whitened.

"That's right. You moved away." He nods and studies me. "Your hair's shorter."

"I cut it."

I self-consciously flip it over my shoulder, but it falls forward again. Gray hairs thread through the dark, straight hair that falls just past my shoulders. I should've colored it. My thick hair had been at my shoulder blades when we'd been together years ago. He'd called it my mane and had often encouraged me to cut it, saying it was too wild, but I had liked the sensuous feel of it on my shoulders, upper arms and brushing down my back.

"How long has it been? Fourteen, fifteen years?" he furrows his brow.

I reach back into my memory, but my thoughts are unfocused and erratic. It's the Brad effect. I've always been weak within the vortex of his presence.

"It's been a while," I agree.

I try to do the math. It seems like forever, yet it feels like no time has passed standing here with him. The nearness of him can still affect me.

He lifts his wrist to glance at his watch. When did people start wearing watches again? Funny how things come back around.

He looks me up and down. "You look exactly the same."

"So do you," I say, despite his weight gain. He always appreciated good food.

"I wish we had time to catch up, but I'm driving

back to San Diego, and I have to get going."

He sets his briefcase against his leg and pulls out his wallet. The glint of a simple gold band on his finger catches my eye.

"How long have you been married?"

He shrugs with a beguiling smile, as though I've caught him doing something wrong.

"About fourteen years, so it must be fifteen years at least since I've seen you."

"I guess so," I answer now more fervently attempting to do the math in my head. "Kids?"

"Yeah, two. Like you." He holds out his business card. "Call me so we can catch up. I'd like to talk when we have more time. We should talk."

I shake my head. He's married now, and I can't let myself get sucked back into the Brad vortex. It took me a long time to get over him. I don't want to risk my heart again. It had never been safe around him. No, I've learned my lesson.

"It's nice to see you, though." I quickly turn to flee back to my seat before I have the chance to hesitate.

It always amazes me when I have the mettle to walk away from him. Leave the past in the past, especially when it's painful. Don't open up old wounds. Run, Forrest, run!

"V." He grabs my arm using the nickname he'd called me, which causes a trace of affection to surge through me. "Why can't we be friends? Give me a call. Come on. We need to talk, V."

His touch feels familiar, yet strange, and I resist the automatic impulse to respond. Like a magnet, my body is drawn to his. It had always been like that with us. It had always seemed beyond our control.

How often do you feel that with someone? For me, Brad was the only one. No one else came close. Not even my ex-husband. But Brad isn't mine anymore. It didn't work between us and now he has a wife, a family. *Walk away*, I tell myself urgently. I take the card he proffers because I know he's tenacious and give him a weak smile. He always gets what he wants.

He glances at his watch again and leans into me. "You're still sexy." His words tickle my ear and send a rush of exhilaration through me.

Yeah, right. In my baggy sweatpants and T-shirt. But I believe him because our chemistry is still undeniable.

The crowd parts for him, and he disappears into it. Like he'd never been there. Like a mirage. Like a flash of lightening straight into me. Brad. Brad. Brad. Those blue eyes. That teasing smile. My every breath sighs his name. How can he have such an effect on me in just minutes? Thus is the power of Brad.

I return to my hard gray plastic seat by the window in the puddle of yellow sunlight, forgetting to buy a snack. On the way, I fling his stupid card toward the garbage receptacle that sprouts fast food wrappers. It flutters stubbornly to the ground. I snatch it up and look at it as I sit, my heart beating his name.

Fletcher Construction & Renovation
Bradley Fletcher – Director of Sales

That charismatic smile and ability to bedazzle and persuade make him a born salesman. I'm curious if his parents are still investing in properties with him. They'd completely financed him in the beginning–when he was with me. They'd propped him up and given him a financial cushion. They'd indulged his little hobby to buy and renovate houses, probably never expecting him to build it into a viable business. They'd assumed he'd tire of the grueling physical labor and uphill battle of sales and

7

follow his brothers into college, into actual careers, but they'd underestimated his ingenuity and charm. He could influence people to do what he wanted them to do. He relished the challenge of it, the wheeling and dealing, the negotiating. It was a skill set he naturally possessed. He had the cool confidence and affability that made it easy for people to trust him and made it hard to say no.

His parents had never approved of me. They thought I wasn't good enough for him because I didn't have a degree or impressive job. Neither did he, but they wanted someone who would elevate his status. Definitely not me–a divorced woman with kids, and five years older at that. Someone who would never provide him with his own biological kids, though he wasn't sure he wanted any. Does his wife meet their criteria? I don't think he would've married anyone who didn't. She must be educated and accomplished, most likely from a notable family, probably gorgeous because he could interest a woman who checked off all the boxes. But does he feel the same magnetism we'd had? Does he really have it all?

I stare out the huge plate-glass window at a plane taxiing up to the gate. The seats around me have filled, and I clutch my shoulder bag in my lap like a life jacket rescuing me from sinking into an undertow of the past.

I can't focus on the math, but I'm certain he's wasted no time getting married after our breakup. I'm disappointed, but not surprised, that he'd gotten over me so fast. Could he have married the same woman who'd left him that breezy message on his answering machine one Sunday morning after I'd quietly slipped out of his king-sized bed?

My stomach still knots at the memory of hearing a chirpy female voice making plans with my boyfriend. Had that one instant changed everything?

8

If I hadn't heard it, would things have turned out differently? Would I have happily persevered in that obviously dysfunctional relationship until it had crashed into reality? Or had I been too hasty? I could've been wrong. Maybe things would've worked out if I'd hung in there longer.

"She's a friend," he'd immediately asserted, brushing it off. "Really just a client."

But I knew him by then. Deep down, I knew he could easily lie or bend the truth to benefit his own ends. That's the way he was, and that could be why he always got what he wanted. He was ambitious and dogged and ruthless, and I found it kind of sexy and admirable at the time because I didn't know how to get what I wanted.

I get out my phone and text my friend, Marcy. She knows the whole story, and it will blow her mind that I ran into him.

OMG! I ran into Brad at the airport. Crazy, huh? I wait a few minutes for her response and smile when I get it.

Tell me!

I text back the bottom line. *Looks great. I hate him. Married. Kids.*

She texts. *What a jerk. Don't you even.*

I frown at the phone. *No way. Married!*

There's commotion around me. People are lining up to board hurriedly, pulling luggage and kids behind them. I stand up, shift my bag on my shoulder, and send one last text. *Boarding.*

After I find my cramped seat on the stuffy plane, I curse him for still being in my head. Brad. The perfect man who got away. The one I lived and breathed and wrapped my life around. The one I'll always compare others to. The one who swept me up like a hurricane, swirled my senses, and never gave me quite enough of himself.

An overweight man plops down in the seat

beside me, emitting a whiff of cigarettes. I turn my face to the window and watch the baggage handlers tossing luggage haphazardly onto the upward moving ramp, disappearing beneath us into the plane's hollow girth. It's blindingly sunny, and I switch to my sunglasses and lean my elbow on the narrow sill of the window, resting my chin in my palm.

Why did Brad have to look so enticing and give me that mischievous smile that invites the type of musings that make me blush? The thought of him causes a little tingle of excitement. He always had that effect on me. From the moment we met.

The Past

Chapter 2

We met online. I resisted the idea, but Marcy pushed me to place an ad, even helping me write it when I couldn't think of anything to say about myself. She clicked my picture for hours, arranging me in different poses, brushing my hair this way and that, making me change my clothes, trying to get me to smile in a flirtatious way for my profile photo. It felt forced and stupid. I couldn't smile naturally, but she finally got a good photo when she made me laugh. I didn't expect to get any responses to my ad and was hoping I wouldn't so Marcy would get off my back because then I could say, oh well, we'd tried.

I was reluctant to jump into dating again after a series of disappointing attempts following a painful divorce. My ex had long since moved back to Arizona where he was from. He'd never been interested in being a father when we'd become surprise parents and quickly married. I hoped he'd come around, but he never did. He just announced one day that he wasn't happy and was leaving. And that was the last of him. I hadn't bothered pursuing him for child support. He would've dodged it somehow, and it wasn't worth the trouble. At least I'd divorced him.

To my amazement, I got immediate responses to my ad. I set up meetings with a few guys in the same restaurant bar where I was required to ask them questions Marcy had deemed significant. She always wanted me to call her immediately afterward and give her a full report and was more disappointed than I was when I didn't feel any attraction. Maybe I was too picky, or maybe I just didn't want to subject myself to yet another bad relationship. That was clearly my pattern, and it was getting old.

Then Brad answered my ad saying he liked my picture and could we meet. He'd gotten right to the point, and that impressed me. No wasting time on the phone or emailing back and forth. He said he wasn't interested in flirting if we didn't have chemistry in person. He was pragmatic. That appealed to me. I didn't want to waste time either. I was a single working mother with little time to spare and was already annoyed that I'd spent so much of it meeting the wrong men.

His photo showed him with longish hair and a trim mustache which gave him an appealing masculinity. He was short, but I was shorter. Height was probably an issue for him, and he must've had trouble meeting women who weren't taller. I was five years older, but that hadn't bothered him. Even the fact that I had two teenagers didn't deter him. That was encouraging.

I'd been single longer than I'd been married and had gone on many first dates over the years, never much interested in second dates. I felt numb most of the time. No one sparked my interest, though sometimes I briefly dallied.

I was usually calm before a date, though a shred of hope always clung to me. One day can change your life. One person can change your path, leading you down an entirely new one than the one you'd been blithely following. But, more often than not, it was just a date. Just a blip in my life until another blip came along.

But before I met Brad, I was a wreck with butterflies careening around my stomach. Something in me *knew* this was different. *He* was different. I fluffed up my long, dark hair. My eyelashes were naturally dark, and I had thick eyebrows that I trimmed into arched lines. Clear nail polish, dark heels, and a short-sleeved cream sweater with dark slacks completed my appearance. I remember because he complimented me on how my dark hair looked against my light sweater. I later learned he wasn't generous with compliments. He was too logical to think in sentimental terms.

I usually met a new guy for drinks or coffee so as not to commit to too much time in case I wasn't interested, but Brad suggested dinner in this lovely restaurant, the inside of which I'd never seen. People who didn't fret about prices went there. He was investing time and money in this date. He was serious, and we hadn't even met. I felt the pressure of his expectations and a bubble of optimism swelled within me. I feared it would pop and drench me with disappointment because, I decided, this was the last one. I was going to close my profile after this, no matter how it turned out.

Brad's seated in a chair right inside when I pull open the heavy door and stumble slightly as I enter the restaurant. Darn rug. I glance around and immediately feel out of place. I tell myself I *do* belong here. I know that I'm pretty, as evidenced by all the male attention I've been granted over the years. I just never knew how to deal with it and gravitated to men who showed less interest and were less attainable.

My parents had high aspirations for their pretty daughter, and my looks could've been a great asset if I'd learned how to use them, but I'd always aimed low and, despite assessment tests in school revealing that I was bright, I'd always lacked the capacity to use my assets to my advantage.

I muster my dignity after my brief display of clumsiness and adorn my face with a smile.

"Vera?" He stands, and I notice our heights are compatible. He wears a white dress shirt and dark gray slacks, which I later learn is his usual attire.

"Brad." We shake hands. His is warm and his grip is firm and business-like.

He gives me a quick grin and approaches the hostess to let her know we're ready to be led to our reserved table. A server instantly appears, and Brad places his hand on my lower back, giving me the signal to follow the server to our cozy table by the window. The server pulls out my padded chair and places the white cloth napkin across my lap.

White tablecloths are draped over orderly round tables, each with a crystal bud vase containing a single rose. Simple and elegant. Well-dressed couples and families fill the tables around us as skilled servers weave gracefully between them. It's all so very opulent and civilized. I've been at high-end restaurants before on dates, and it's a different world from my usual fast food treks with my kids.

Brad orders wine and I sip it, though mixed drinks are more to my liking. Wine is more appropriate in this fine restaurant. We linger over salad and the main course and talk or, rather, he talks, and I become more and more enamored. The wine slowly soothes the dancing butterflies in my stomach and the darting self-doubts inhabiting my head.

Brad is witty and clever and ambitious, sharing his plans to become successful in real estate and construction. He mentions going to the theater the night before with his parents. I like that. Family. Culture. Ambition. He's the whole package. How have I fallen into this alternate world of manners and refinement? How can this man be interested in me? A mere commoner.

I'm hardly aware of the surrounding din, of the server checking on us, of my wine glass being refilled. I don't realize until later that he had mostly talked about himself and hadn't asked me much about myself, but I was content to listen to the sound of his voice, to be the recipient of his attention and wit. My life is mundane. I work two part-time jobs and referee two teenagers.

Why is this guy single? I wondered then.

He tells me he's considering running for City

15

Council. That gets us onto the topic of politics, and I discover with chagrin that we're on different ends of the political spectrum. I hadn't thought of our political views as being a deal-breaker. I'm not very political, but I'd like to be able to agree on basic principles.

"No." He shakes his head. "I'm more of a moderate. I bet we're not so different in our views." And he's right about that, and I relax. All is still good.

"You're prettier than your picture," he says, studying me intently. He means it as an observation, not a compliment, which I don't know at the time.

I can feel my face flush. "Thank you." His gaze is disconcerting, and I avert my eyes.

The restaurant is at capacity on this Sunday evening. The low hum of conversations, the clinking of glasses, the tinkling of silverware, and muted laughter linger on the periphery of my awareness. Please don't let that expanding bubble of optimism pop. Don't let the clock strike midnight. Don't let me awaken from this blissful dream. He's concentrating on his plate and grins at me as he dabs his mustache with the white cloth napkin.

Can you fall in love with someone on the first date? A feeling wildly flits through me. Attraction. Longing. I want to skip through this preamble and get to the idyllic life that's beyond, the one I've waited for, the one I've dreamed of, the one I deserve after all my disenchantments.

I reach for my water and my fork clatters to the floor. With embarrassment, I bend to retrieve it. It's somewhere under the table.

"Don't." He stops me by putting his warm hand over mine. Immediately the server responds to his signal.

"The lady needs a clean fork," Brad says.

Within moments, a fork is placed beside my

plate.

"Thank you," I murmur.

This small gesture makes me feel cared for, and it's nice to have someone look after me for a change. He knows how to act, how to move through the world. He's competent and composed. I'm in awe. I have no doubt that he can deal with any situation, that I can sit back in the passenger seat and let him drive me anywhere.

"Thank you," Brad repeats to the server. "We'd like the dessert menu."

"Oh, I'm too full." I balk. The food is rich and filling.

"We're going to share." He smiles. "I like you and want more time with you."

This flattering statement sends a weakness to my knees and causes a twinge of excitement to momentarily surge. I don't know why I've always wasted my time on the wrong men. Maybe deep down I don't think I deserve to be treated well or I don't know what I want, but now I do. I want Brad. And he seems to want me.

Yet I'm out of my element. I don't know how to handle this. Should I feign indifference and play hard to get? Should I be available, or he'll lose interest? I probably would've married him on the spot if he'd asked. He was dynamic. He was self-assured. He was charming and charismatic. His quick smiles send tiny sparks of exhilaration through me.

I'm tired of struggling financially and otherwise. I work two part-time jobs and have insurance through the state. Money is tight with two teenagers who always want something I can't afford. I'm weary of the uphill slog I'm perpetually battling. I need somebody on my side. Somebody who will look out for me. Someone who will take care of me when I'm too worn out to do it myself. Someone who will make my life easier. Someone who will distract me from my perpetual worries and bring me some joy. I need something to look forward to. Something just for me.

I've had many boyfriends over the years. Some sweet and caring with decent jobs. I kick myself for blowing it with them. Why do I always stick it out with the wrong ones? I had the insane idea that I didn't want a serious relationship ever again after I'd gotten screwed over by my ex-husband. Never again, I vowed to myself and passed up some great guys. Or chose the wrong ones. I just can't get it right.

But Brad isn't the wrong one. He's the right one in my eyes. He's the type of man I'd be proud to introduce to people, the type who'd never ask me for money or put his fist through a wall. He isn't the wrong choice.

That evening real promise blossoms. He's the whole package. He doesn't care that I have kids. He doesn't care that I have nothing, that I live in a cheap apartment, that I have low-paying jobs. We enjoy each other's company. We get along. There's an ease to it I marvel at with a side of anticipation. The electricity between us crackles. I can't wait for what is ahead of us.

Chapter 3

To my relief and dismay, Brad calls again and again, making plans with me. He takes me to upscale restaurants, the movies, the theater. His manners are impeccable and old-fashioned. He opens doors for me and pays for everything. He considers me worthy of his time and attention. I've gained entry to a world that I've had little opportunity to encounter.

I hang on his every word as he shares his ambitions. He states that his parents pressured him to continue his education as his older brothers had, but he prefers building his own business. He enjoys the challenge, and I have no doubt that he can accomplish anything he attempts. I hope to be along for the ride and insert supportive comments to show him what a great partner I am.

My head fills with dreams for our future. Together, things will be easier. I could quit my part-time jobs and help him with his business. He could give us a life we'd never have otherwise. Everyone will benefit in my happy fantasy.

Brad meets my kids and they don't scare him away. He doesn't seem very interested in them, but he doesn't run the other way. I tell myself that he'll warm up to them as he gets to know them. They're smart kids and know how to be polite, but it's nerve-racking every time they come in contact. Teenagers can be unpredictable and moody. Yet he takes it all in stride.

He even sends over his plumber when I cry on the phone about my broken toilet and that the apartment manager is unreachable. There are three of us and we have one toilet. I consider this an emergency. Our neighbor lets us use hers until the plumber arrives. Brad saves the day. What would we have done without him?

I'm plagued by pangs of guilt as my kids are left to fend for themselves or eat leftovers while we dine in fine restaurants. My unspoken wish is that they could join us and experience this upscale world, but Brad solves the problem by buying them pizza when we go out. He lets them order as many toppings as they choose. This is a treat for them and helps temper my feelings of guilt.

Brad is a problem solver. He takes care of things. He's practical and easygoing about it. He says every problem has a solution. He makes it sound so simple. He tells me to picture the worst-case scenario, which most likely won't happen, and plan for it. And then you're covered. He wants me to be pragmatic, and I often am, but I tend to panic first and problem solve later. And now I find myself coming to depend on him to fix things.

I tell myself to listen and learn. He's moved around more in the world than I have, and he's absorbed poise and wisdom and knowledge. He's drawn back the curtain for me to view this elite place where opportunities abound and fall across his path. His life seems charmed to me, unlike mine, which draws dark clouds.

I enjoy his company. He's witty and his smile lights my own. He's brimming with energy and enthusiasm and ideas. Things seem possible around him.

And the sex? The best ever. We have explosive chemistry, which is what drew us in the first place. We can't get enough of each other. Our bodies are attuned and in sync. It's like we were made for each other. I'm astounded at how good it is. He tells me he's never had sex this incredible. Points for me. For us. It's all too good to be true.

I spend every Saturday night at Brad's house in his comfortable king-sized bed. I'm wracked with guilt at leaving my kids for the entire night, but I can't drag myself away from him, and my kids don't seem to care. They're always busy with their friends, anyway. I'm torn between my own needs and my kids', but I choose to stay with Brad. He's my lifeline. He's the key to better days ahead for all of us. This is an investment in our future.

And I so need this. I need to have a break to look forward to at the end of the week where I don't have to mediate my kids' arguments or work long hours or worry about how to pay my bills. Brad is my oasis in the turmoil of my life. He's the center of calm.

His house is large, with vaulted ceilings and spacious rooms. He remodeled it with French doors, skylights, a stone fireplace, and a curved patio in the backyard. This is the first house he acquired and remodeled, and he intends to sell it. He's put so much money into it that he's afraid he won't recoup his investment. This is a lesson he's learned. Never put in too much time or too much money. He won't make the same mistake again, he says.

I implore him to keep it, but he says he can't afford to. He borrowed money from his parents to help finance his burgeoning business and wants to repay them, even though they probably don't expect it. He explains he had some money saved and cashed in stocks and bonds his grandparents had placed in a trust when he was born, but he still wouldn't be able to do any of it without financial assistance from his parents. They are his safety net as he is becoming mine.

I wonder how he can afford to spend money so freely and extravagantly when he takes me out. It occurs to me that he grew up with wealth and he takes success for granted. What else is there? You work hard and financial rewards follow. This is what he believes and he'll succeed because he believes he will. I ponder this mindset. Is it foolish or profoundly wise?

I secretly hope no one will buy the house. I see my kids in the bedrooms, all of us eating in the dining room, watching TV in the family room. I see it so clearly that it seems inevitable.

He and his parents can invest in another house to fix up and sell. He'll be thriftier with the remodel and make a bigger profit. He has to live somewhere. Why not just keep this beautiful house, which is in a good location and has wonderful schools? But Brad insists he must stick to his plan to sell it. He'll find his own house later on.

I lie awake at night marveling at my great fortune in meeting Brad. I'd always been drawn to the exhilaration of the rebels, the boys who ignored the rules, the ones who left wakes of mayhem and broken hearts. At the same time, I'd craved stability and dependability and devotion. I know, quite a conundrum.

My ex-husband had been erratic. Sometimes loving and sweet, sometimes angry and resentful. I'd tried to ride the waves with him and navigate his moods, but it was impossible and our marriage grew untenable. He lashed out and blamed me for his unhappiness. He felt trapped, and it was all my fault.

It was a relief when he drove off one day and never came back. I was alarmed at first. I couldn't afford our apartment. I had no car. What was I going to do?

Marcy and Doug stepped in. We lived with them for almost a year. Doug found me a car and his father fixed it. We lived like a big family during that time. I don't know what I would've done without them. They are true friends and I'll always be grateful.

And now here I am with Brad. He's smart, ambitious, easy-going, generous, and polite. He's even good looking and our chemistry sizzles. There's exhilaration but no mayhem. And it's good. Better than good.

What are his flaws? I don't see any. I have a nagging feeling that they lie beneath the surface and one day they will float up into view. But I stifle these thoughts. That's just pessimism. My streak of bad luck can't go on forever.

Marcy thinks his biggest flaw is that he's boring and predictable. But I find him far from boring. I welcome the steadiness of his moods, the assurance of our regular dates, the civility of our conversations, his aversion to rudeness and scenes. And underneath all the good behavior, our attraction pulls at us like two magnets. It's the best of both worlds.

In the meantime, I delight in playing house with Brad as I picture us as a contented family. I sink comfortably into the luxury of domestic daydreams never for a moment envisioning the coming crash that will devastate me in less than a year.

Chapter 4

I remember the moment I truly fell in love with Brad. Up to that point, I was smitten and awestruck. Men like this exist, polite men who watch their language, who know how to treat a woman and speak to servers, who are not intimidated by anyone and can easily handle any situation. At least that's how I see him. He appears invincible. He's good looking and smart and successful or on the way to being successful. He's a born salesman. I would've bought anything from him if I could afford it. His smile lights me up, and his touch makes me shiver with longing.

But the deal is really sealed for me the night we're driving to a movie theater after a delicious dinner. This is what we usually do–dinner and a movie on Saturday night. I know. It's so cliché, but I look forward to it all week. I drive to his house, hop in his car, and he takes care of everything. I leave the restaurant up to him, and he lets me choose the movie most of the time.

First, we have a leisurely dinner with wine. The liquid flows through me like a warm river that washes away my anxieties from the week. He wines and dines me, I realize with satisfaction. Sometimes, we go to a movie first feasting on a large buttered popcorn, which I later bring home to my kids because we never finish it.

I'm in a tranquil state, lounging in the car, thinking about the movie we're on our way to see and wishing I could hold his hand. This is the only quirk in our evenings. I long to hold his hand in the car or the movies. I long for him to greet me with a kiss. I long to touch him affectionately whenever I want, but he's not that sentimental. I've learned that he's not romantic or demonstrative. He's pragmatic and detached. Would it do any good to bring this up, or would he deduce that I'm too needy and too demanding for him? Or would things improve between us? Would it open up a new level of bonding and communication? I'm debating whether I should divulge my concerns and risk this when he interrupts my thoughts.

"What's that?"

"What?"

I haven't noticed anything in the fading light of dusk and don't know what he's observed. I scan the area, trying to determine what's caught his eye. All I see is a brightly lit grocery store with a vast parking lot scattered with parked cars. I glance at the time on the dashboard. There's still plenty of time to make the movie. As it is, we'll be early, which will allow for wait time if there's a line. Sometimes that happens on a Saturday night, but I never mind standing next to Brad in the coolness of evening.

He's already veering off the road into an empty section of the parking lot alongside the store. Light pours out the front, but there are ominous shadows and shapes hugging the side of the building. What's he doing? I want to get to the theater. The wine is going through me, and I'll soon have to use the restroom.

"Why are we stopping?" I ask. "What did you see?"

I peek at the time on the dashboard again as he slows the car. His brow is furrowed in concentration while I'm still perplexed by this minor mystery.

"Something moved by that dumpster." He stops the car and jumps out. "Someone could be hurt."

I swing open my door and peer into the shadows by the dumpster. I still see nothing, but a bit of pride swells up. Brad will save the day. Brad is Superman.

He holds his palm out in front of me. "Don't get out. Let me check it out first."

I stop. I've swung my legs over and sit with my shoes brushing the asphalt. He's protective and is going to save somebody. My Brad is brave. My Brad is a hero.

"Be careful," I call after him.

I have no desire to approach a dangerous situation, but he may soon be in peril with no weapon. Just his wits. What can I do if someone jumps out and attacks him? What if he needs help? My mind is racing. I try to determine if any items in the car could be used as a weapon. There's nothing in the back seat except my jacket. I can only watch and wait.

I squint into the darkness as Brad cautiously steps closer to the corner of the dumpster that's almost out of view. I watch apprehensively, expecting something to jump out at him that he'll wrestle like in some movie. Naturally, he won't need my help. He'll win after a brief battle or he'll save somebody's life, somebody who's been missing for days or weeks. He'll be on the news and get a reward. I'll stand beside him, smiling proudly. Yes, I saw the whole thing.

He's walking back to me. He has not had to fight anyone off. He's safe.

"It's just a dog," he tells me.

"Poor thing," I say. "Is it okay?"

I have a soft spot for animals. When I was growing up, my parents always took in strays, and sometimes we had quite a few dogs and cats coexisting. One cat used to sleep on my bed at night, and I found it calming, especially when I heard a noise in the house's stillness or awoke from a nightmare. I'd pull the cat close to me and her purring would dispel my fears.

"I didn't see a collar." Brad's standing there, staring back at the shadows. "It's scared. I bet it's hungry."

"I wish I could take it. My kids would love a dog, but I can't have any pets..."

"I don't want to leave it," he says, looking at me. "Do you mind if we miss the movie? I could call animal control if you want..."

"No, don't do that. Who knows what will happen to it?" I protest. "Let's take it. We could try to find the owner or find a home for it."

"Oh, man." He grins. "I'm a sucker for animals."

I smile back. "Me too."

He's sentimental, after all. This is encouraging. He can open up to me and let down his defenses. He just needs time.

"Can you keep an eye on it, and I'll run into the store and buy some food for it?"

"Sure," I say. "I want to see it."

"Be careful. It's scared. I don't want it to run off."

"Okay." I step out of the car as Brad jogs over to the entrance to the store. Brad is still a hero. He's going to save this poor lost dog.

I gingerly approach the dumpster. "Hey, little guy," I say gently.

I hear a whine. I hope it's not hurt. I continue to take slow steps until a dark furry face appears. I stop and crouch down, speaking to it softly. "It's going to be okay."

It's a small, dark-brown dog. It wags its tail, whining and whimpering. I can't see it very well as it stays within the shadows. I keep speaking to it in soft tones until my legs ache from crouching. I stand and stretch, looking anxiously toward the store entrance. What's taking so long? I hope they're not calling animal control.

Finally, Brad emerges from the big sliding glass doors pushing a noisy cart. The dog backs further into the shadows.

"You're scaring it," I call. I go to meet him. The cart is brimming. "Let's just take all this stuff over to the car."

"Good idea."

He's bought a case of dog food that he sets in the trunk. I spread the fleece blanket he's purchased on the backseat. He's also bought bowls, a collar and leash, a bag of dry dog food, a rope tug toy, and a box of treats that he opens to entice the dog into the car.

"Looks like you're going to keep it," I observe.

"We'll see." Despite his measured tone, I can tell he's excited about it. This is a side of him I haven't seen, and I like it. He's caring and compassionate.

The dog hungrily gobbles up the treats and hesitantly follows Brad to the car. I sit in the front seat, watching so as not to scare it off. The dog trusts Brad and jumps into the back seat. He sniffs the blanket and settles on it.

"I left my number in the store in case someone is looking for it," Brad tells me as he gets in the car.

"I bet he's thirsty," I say.

"Yeah. I'll give him water at home." He turns to me. "Are you sure you're okay with this?"

"Of course I am. I love animals," I assure him.

"Good." He pats my hand.

After Brad pulls into the garage, he closes the gate and lets the dog out. The little dog runs around the yard, exploring and sniffing.

Brad goes into the house and fills a bowl with filtered water and another with canned dog food, which he places just outside the garage. We stand and watch the dog lap up water and chow down the food.

"I think I'll leave him outside tonight. It's not cold, and he's pretty dirty," Brad says.

"But can't you put him in the laundry room…"

"He'll be happier outside. I'll leave the garage door open a few feet so he can get in," he says. "Let's make him a bed inside the garage."

We fold up the fleece blanket and place it inside the garage. The dog is still exploring the yard. We venture inside and order an on-demand movie but end up checking on the dog every fifteen minutes or so until we both tumble into bed and fall asleep without making love.

When I wake up in the morning, Brad isn't beside me. He's outside playing tug of war with the rope toy he'd bought for the dog. As I stand at the window watching them, a tide of love flows through me. I've just fallen more deeply in love with this man who secretly has a soft spot for animals.

I dress and wander outside. The dog tentatively approaches me, sniffing and swishing his tail. I hold out my hand, and he licks it.

"She's okay," Brad tells the dog, and we both laugh.

"He doesn't look that old," I say. "I wonder if somebody abandoned him or he got lost."

"He's a she."

"Oh. Hmm. Now you have to name her."

"*We* have to name her," he corrects.

This makes me smile. We have a "child" together now. We are a happy little family. This bonds us further, and soon my kids will join us in this big house and have the dog they always wanted, and I'll have the man of my dreams.

Brad stands and places his hand on the small of my back and rubs it. This simple gesture means so much and gives me hope that this dog will change his indifference. Little by little, our lives will entwine and mesh and he'll see how well we fit together.

"We weren't allowed to have pets growing up," he shares.

"Why not?" I grew up with dogs and cats, most of them strays. We always had animals underfoot, lounging on the furniture, barking at passersby, playing in the yard. I've always wanted to give my kids that experience.

"You know, pet hair, the bother of it."

"But you always wanted a dog," I guess.

"I envied my friends who had pets."

Another insight into Brad.

"She has a white chest and white on her paws," he notes.

"And the tips of her ears," I add.

We watch her lap up water from her bowl.

"I should buy her a ball. I bet she'd enjoy chasing a ball."

I hope nobody comes to claim her. Brad finally has the dog he's wanted since he was a kid and probably didn't know he needed.

"How about Coco?" he says suddenly.

"Coco?"

He shrugs. "It's good, right? She's dark like chocolate."

"So, you like dark-haired girls," I tease, tucking my dark hair behind my ears.

He grins. "Apparently."

"Come here, Coco," I call to her.

She runs over, tail wagging.

"I love it," I say to Brad. But what I really want to say is I love him.

Chapter 5

We have our first argument on Valentine's Day. Brad calls them "disagreements." He insists that Valentine's Day is a made-up holiday not worthy of celebration and refuses to take part. I've gotten him a card carefully choosing one that wasn't too effusive, but he derides me for falling prey to marketing.

My heart anticipated this most obvious day of romance expecting to satiate its yearning, at least a little. My wish was that our date on this day would finally give me some emotional gratification, some hint that I hold a special place for him, but he stubbornly withholds the tiniest trace of romantic response, leaving me starved for crumbs. How silly of me to assume Valentine's Day would inspire the affection that's lacking from him, but my heart still insists on some bit of sustenance.

I'm wearing a frilly pink top and black slacks and have pulled my straight dark hair over one shoulder as I sulk in the passenger seat of his car. I put on my sunglasses so he can't see the hurt in my eyes. He has the air conditioner on as usual and I'm chilled. I lean into the heat of the sunlight shining through the passenger window and forlornly gaze out at the posh homes and immaculate lawns zipping by as he takes a shortcut through a neighborhood. Are there blissful couples living in these homes? Are there vases of roses and boxes of chocolates and cards with poetic odes to love?

"I treat you special every time we go out," he points out as he drives. "I don't need some date on a calendar to make me do that."

"I know, but it would've been nice to get flowers or *something*." I pout.

I don't know how to make him comprehend

what's so obvious to everyone else. Why does he have to be so damned stoic? Why can't he ever give me a compliment? Why can't he ever say he's glad to see me, he missed me, he *wants* me? How am I supposed to know his true feelings? Does he have feelings? Does he feel anything? My mind rants on and spirals into a turbulent tempest.

We turn onto a main street and pass flower stands and stationery stores, candy shops and lingerie boutiques. How can I make him see that I need this bit of validation, that I crave a sign that I'm more to him than just a casual thing?

"You're overreacting," he says. "Don't be unreasonable."

His remarks make me see red, and it takes an enormous effort to subdue myself. Overreacting? Unreasonable? How about human? Why doesn't he try being human? Everybody needs love and tenderness. Every normal person craves these things. Am I supposed to shut myself off like him? My anger slowly implodes, shattering inside me and slowly morphing into sadness. I can't do it. I can't shut myself off and I don't want to. I'd rather he opened up.

"I don't like to do something because it's expected," he explains. "If I feel like buying you something, I will. Just expect the unexpected."

"But what about birthdays or Christmas?" I counter.

"That's different."

I groan. I had expected chocolates or flowers all day. At the very least, a card. A gesture. But he's not that guy. He's one of those guys who isn't expressive except during sex. That's how he is. He'll never leave me little notes or write me poetry. He'll never surprise me with little gifts or serenade me. He'll never love me that way I long to be loved, the way I *need* to be loved. He may never love me at all. It's possible he's incapable of experiencing any consuming emotions outside of sex. A thought jolts me. He could be incapable of love.

"You know, you're overly emotional," he pronounces staring ahead at the road. He seems a little peeved.

"I'm not overly emotional," I say evenly. He's underly emotional, if anything.

He doesn't understand me, doesn't know me as I yearn to be known. He's proficient at taking care of practical matters and basic needs, but he can't, won't, fill my emotional needs. He's not even aware I have them.

"Yes, you are." He lets out a derisive laugh. "You cried when your toilet broke."

"You don't know what it's like not to have money for things and to worry about how to pay for everything. You don't know what it's like to be a single mother and work crappy jobs and have no help from the father."

"Well, what good does crying do? Do what you need to do to get it fixed. Crying doesn't help."

I turn back to the window. He just doesn't get it. He doesn't know how spirit-breaking it is to struggle, how soul-sucking it is to agonize about how to pay your bills. How life can beat you down and keep you there.

"No, really." He won't let it go. "You react to things instead of getting whatever it is done. Learn to control yourself."

"It's normal to be emotional," I retort.

"It's *normal* to be practical," he states firmly. "It's more *productive* to be practical."

He makes me want to scream, but I can't give up. I shift in my seat toward him with the impetus to defend myself, to make him comprehend on some level, to get him to view things from my eyes. This is the crux of our differences, and I *need* him to know

33

me, not deride me, not berate me for who I am. I have danced around his indifference and held in what's in my heart for the sake of his comfort level. I've denied my own needs, and, damn it, on this one stupid day, I want him to acknowledge he has feelings, that people have feelings, that it's okay to have feelings, and I think I have a pretty good argument.

"When someone buys a house, what do they say? 'Oh, this is a practical decision'? Or do they say, 'I love it'?"

He doesn't respond. I can tell he's processing what I've said, which gives me a tiny bit of vindication, and I proceed because I sense an opening.

"People make decisions based on emotions. They *buy* things based on emotions. They *love* a car or they *love* the color of a couch."

How can he sell houses without knowing this basic fact of sales? I cross my arms and turn back in my seat. I've made my point, and it's a valid one. I wait for his response while my own emotions churn from anger to sadness to optimism.

"There's an element of truth in that," he admits. "But it still comes down to practicality, if they can afford it and if the schools are good and..."

"But they wouldn't buy the house in the first place if they didn't *love* it," I emphasize. "The emotional part of it comes first."

"True to an extent," he counters. "It also has to be practical."

I want to shriek at him, *Is love practical? Is sex practical?* But I sit silently contemplating. We're so different. How did we ever get together in the first place? What did he see in me? What keeps us together? It can't be all about sex. It's not all about sex. There's something deeper between us. I know it.

I ruminate about this all evening. We never hold

hands or touch each other except in bed. I hadn't allowed myself to dwell on this before because then I'd have to face the reality of our relationship. I've known this on some level from the beginning because I'd suppressed the impulse to run my fingers through his hair or hold his hand at the movies or just touch his arm. I subconsciously knew this was unwelcome, though I've craved contact. I've craved more.

So he's not perfect. I've discovered his big defect. Is that why he's still single? Do other women find this intolerable or has he never felt secure enough to be vulnerable? Will he relax enough with me to allow our passion to lead to affection? If not, can I live without it? This is the big question.

I don't want to live without it, but I also don't want to live without Brad. I can't imagine it. Love is an addiction, and I'm already hooked on him. Is it better to walk away with a broken heart or try to fix his? Sometimes my heart feels so hungry, I have to hold back from devouring his.

When we get back to his house after dinner, I still sense a bit of tension, but I've had a few glasses of wine and don't care as long as he lets me stay. I saunter into the darkness of the house after him and, before he flips on the lights, I succumb to my craving and impulsively pin him against the wall, placing my lips on his beneath the tickle of his mustache. I could never resist kissing him. There's something about his soft, warm lips that draws me like catnip.

I indulge myself by pressing my body against his until I need to take a breath. He never kisses me first, and I usually stifle my ardor to kiss him until we wind up in bed, but the wine has swept aside everything but pure hormonal urges. It's really not so complicated to take what I want, my hazy mind insists.

I muse if kissing is too intimate for him, which is ironic considering the uninhibited sex we engage in, but there's something more intimate about kissing in some odd way. I pause for a moment as my thoughts whir, but he stays still, and I kiss him again until he gently pushes me away laughing.

"Somebody had too much wine. Let me get the lights and put this in the freezer."

He grips a small paper bag that holds a movie we'd rented and a pint of his favorite chocolate chip ice cream we'd picked up on the way home. He heads to the kitchen, and I go into the tiny half bath.

I grip the sink in front of the mirror and draw in a few deep breaths. My face is flushed. I hold a cool washcloth against my forehead, cheeks, and neck. Our chemistry is off the charts. I often lose myself with him in the most intense and satisfying way. This is where he expresses his fervor for me, and I'm free to express all I hold inside the rest of the time. I take a few more deep calming breaths before I wander out into the hall.

The sound of the TV leads me to the family room where I find Brad watching previews on the movie we'd rented with Coco at his feet. He's already dug into the pint of ice cream and holds out a spoon for me.

"I couldn't wait, V." He smiles sheepishly, which I find endearing.

Yes, I still want him despite his stifled emotions. No relationship is ideal. So, I've seen the crack in his smooth façade. The dazzling smile, the politeness, the effortless restraint. There are emotions in there somewhere. He loves Coco. He just doesn't know how to show his love for me. Yet.

I kick off my shoes, put on my glasses, and settle next to him on the large brown sectional. He sits with his bare feet resting on the matching ottoman, and I casually prop my feet beside his, touching. He doesn't pull away.

Brad enjoys comedies. Not *romantic* comedies, just funny movies or action movies. This one is a combination, and we laugh and finish the pint together.

I'm utterly content. Life is good. I was being silly earlier. So what if he doesn't give me a Valentine's Day card or hold my hand or kiss me first? This is better. Much better. This is it.

Chapter 6

Marcy enters my apartment, fanning herself with her hand. A large claw clip gathers up her light brown hair with wisps escaping everywhere. Her face is flushed, and she removes her oversized sunglasses and tosses her car keys on the scratched coffee table.

The blinds are closed to block out the sun, yet narrow slits of light cut across the opposite wall. A large standing fan oscillates slowly distributing a sultry breeze back and forth across the room. The sliding glass door stands open, but the air is hot and stagnant outside. The temperature has crept up into the high 80s.

"Man, it's hot out," Marcy declares, flopping onto my worn couch. "It's not much cooler in here. Where are the kids?"

"At their friends'. Lacie's friend has a pool at her apartment complex. Luke's at the mall, probably at the arcade. Air conditioning."

"Smart kids."

"Where are yours?"

"At my mother's. She's such a glutton for punishment."

"Does she have air conditioning?"

"No. She's taking them to some superhero movie or something. It'll be cool inside the theater."

"Want a popsicle?"

"Hell, yeah."

I pad barefoot into the kitchen in my loose sundress. Even the linoleum doesn't offer much coolness. I've pulled my hair into a ponytail. Earlier I'd pressed a damp washcloth to my face and neck, but I've warmed back up since then. There's not much to do except wait for sunset to bring down the temperature.

"Cherry, orange, or grape?" I stand in front of the open freezer. The chilly air wafts over me and feels good.

"Grape. No, it'll turn my mouth purple. Orange."

"So now you'll have an orange mouth." I grab a cherry one for myself. "I'll get some bowls. These will melt quickly."

"Who thinks of bowls when our lives are at stake? There's something wrong with you," she says, accepting the bowl and popsicle.

"I can't believe it's this hot in February. Usually I can deal with hot weather, but this is crazy."

The sudden heat wave has followed months of cooler weather, and we've had no time to acclimate.

"I know. It should be illegal." Marcy tears the wrapper off her popsicle. "You're right. It's melting already."

"How's Doug?"

"I hate him." Marcy always says this about her husband. "He's going to make me lose my marbles."

"What'd he do now?" I'll be on her side no matter what, though I often think she overreacts or exaggerates innocent situations.

"Do you know what he got me for Valentine's Day?" she demands.

I shake my head. I'm trying to keep up with my dripping popsicle.

"Just a card. That's what."

"What did you get him?" I ask.

"That's what he said." Her eyes go wide with indignation. "That's beside the point. It's their job to worship us. Do you know all the stuff I do for him every day?"

"Okay. Okay."

"Are you really going to go there, Vera? Valentine's Day is the day they get to show us how much they appreciate us for doing things for them every day, like cooking their damn dinner and washing their damn clothes."

I nod and slurp at my popsicle.

"Among other things," she huffs. "Does he ever step foot in the grocery store?"

"Does he?"

"Not as much as I do. That's for sure."

"Uh, huh."

"Sometimes he vacuums, and he takes care of the yard. I hate mowing."

"You each have your chores," I say helpfully

"But I do way more than he does," she asserts.

"You're a great cook."

Marcy waves her popsicle stick. "Exactly. What would that cost at a restaurant? Do you know how much money we save by eating at home every night?"

"Women always do more than men," I say.

"That's my point. Working, housework, shopping, not to mention taking care of the kids." She leans back on the couch as if the thought has exhausted her. "And they have one day to show their gratitude, you know?"

"I hear you."

"A card. How much effort does that take?" She says. "All the romance is gone. That's what happens once you get married."

I finish my popsicle and set the bowl on the coffee table.

"What did Prince Charming get you?" She leans forward with a smile.

I grimace. It's still a sore spot. "He didn't get me anything."

"Nothing?" She raises her eyebrows. "The romance is already gone?"

"He said he doesn't believe in made-up holidays, and it's just a marketing thing to get people to spend money, and he spends money on me all the time because he takes me out every week," I say defensively. She doesn't like him, and I constantly find myself defending him.

"Hmm."

"Well, he spends a lot of money every time we go out," I point out. "And he says he'll buy me things if he feels like it and doesn't like to do what's expected."

"What about your birthday?" she asks.

"That's exactly what I said."

"What did he say?"

"He said that's different."

"Of course he did." She shakes her head. "Did you get him anything?"

"A card."

"Was it romantic?"

"He doesn't like that stuff. He's just not like that."

She sets her bowl containing the popsicle stick on the coffee table. "That cooled me off a little."

"Your mouth is orange." I laugh.

"Yours is red. It probably looks better than mine. I probably look like a clown."

"Where's Doug today?" I'm glad to change the subject.

"Hanging out with his dad. They're doing something manly with tools." She leans back on the couch. "At least I know where he is."

"You can trust him," I assure her.

"How do you know?"

"Doug's a good guy. You wouldn't have married him if he wasn't."

"Yeah, but they're all guys. You can't trust them. It's in their genes."

"I trust Brad." I instantly regret saying that to her.

"I wouldn't. Especially him," she remarks.

"What does that mean? You haven't even met him yet," I object. "Why don't you like him?"

41

"Because you're in love and he's not."

That statement makes me pause, but I don't let myself reflect on it for long. "You don't know how he feels about me."

"Oh, I can read this guy a mile away."

"You haven't even met him!" I repeat emphatically.

"Yeah. And why is that? I bet he doesn't want to meet your friends."

"He never said that, but I don't want you to meet him with your attitude." I sit back on the couch, crossing my arms.

There are a few moments of silence as I stew.

"Okay. I'm sorry. You're right. I haven't met him," she concedes. "I could be wrong about him. I hope I'm wrong."

A slight breeze momentarily drifts through the open sliding glass door toward us. For a few seconds there's respite from the stifling heat, and then the air turns heavy and stagnant again. The heat makes me grumpy and listless.

"I don't want you to get hurt," Marcy says.

"I know, but I'm happy right now. We found that little dog and it's like it's our dog."

"Don't make me throw up."

"Shut up! I'm happy." I shove her shoulder.

"Good. I hope you have lots of puppies together."

We look at each other and burst into laughter. It takes us a few minutes to get it out of our systems. This is the upside of our close friendship. We call it therapy when we laugh till we cry. It's a good stress release, and I consider it crucial to my state of mind.

I turn to her as I wipe my eyes with my fingers. "So really, what's going on with Doug? Is something going on?"

"I don't know." She holds a blue and green throw pillow against her stomach.

"What do you mean? What happened?"

"Nothing. I don't trust men. You know what happened with my mother and father. He had that girlfriend for years. You just can't trust them."

"But that doesn't mean…"

"And my first boyfriend, Lance, in high school. Remember how he lied to me? He broke my heart."

"Lance." I remember Lance. I wave my hand. "That was high school. Everyone's an idiot in high school."

"Especially Lance."

"Especially Lance."

"But not us. Girls don't cheat. Guys do."

"Well, they have to cheat with someone," I reason. "So girls are just as bad."

"But girls don't do that when they're in love."

Brad suddenly intrudes on my thoughts. An image of how he looks in the morning with his hair all mussed in a sexy way pops into my head. The acute way his eyes hone in on me over dinner. The warmth that rushes through me after a glass of wine. The anticipation of the night ahead. That little mischievous smile. His soft lips…

"You are so in love," Marcy interrupts my reverie. "You have this dopey grin on your face."

I feel myself blushing. "So what?"

"Just be prepared for when he dumps you," she cautions.

"What if he doesn't? What if we live happily ever after?" I can't help but hope. Hope fills my daydreams and my night dreams. It fills every pore of my body, and I don't want anybody to take it from me.

"Does he want kids?"

I shrug. "I don't know."

"Well, he's never had kids. That could be a deal breaker for him."

I bite my lip. It could be. I'm older than him and don't intend to have any more kids. What if he wants them? Will it be a deal breaker? I don't want to think about it. He'll fall madly in love with me and it won't matter.

"Does he get along with your kids? If he was serious, he'd spend time with your kids."

"He usually just picks me up."

"Hmm."

"It's still early in our relationship," I remind her. "All that will come later."

"True." She nods, and it makes me feel a little better.

"I don't think you realize how lucky you are." I change the subject back to her. How do we keep talking about Brad? It feels too fragile to pick apart. Why does she have to plant doubts in my mind that grow like weeds?

"Doug loves you. He's a nice guy. You should give him the benefit of the doubt," I say.

She groans. "Whose side are you on?"

"Yours. And I know you really love him, and he really loves you."

"He's okay." She grins at me. "What are you? His PR agent?"

"I just remember your wedding day," I tell her. "You were both so happy."

"Yeah." She frowns. "You know I want things to work out for you, but I'm afraid this one won't be around long. Guys like him marry their own kind."

I scowl. "His kind? What kind is that?"

"You know, someone from a rich, successful family, not a struggling divorced woman with teenagers. Someone highly educated with some big important job."

"He's not highly educated," I argue.

"It doesn't matter. He has wealthy parents who want him to marry up."

"*He* contacted *me*," I remind her. "He answered my ad. The one you made me post."

44

"But that doesn't mean it will turn serious," she says. "His parents aren't going to accept you."

I sigh heavily at her comments. "I just want it to work out."

"I know." She gives me a sympathetic look. "I hope it does."

I don't articulate my own qualms about Brad, though I can sense the depth of his emotions when he touches me. Even if he can't recognize it and won't voice it, I feel the truth deep in my heart. Our souls have touched.

"Vera." Marcy is shaking her head. "I'm telling you he'll never marry you."

Chapter 7

Brad's parents invite me to dinner to meet me. I'm more worked up than when I'd met Brad for the first time. My stomach twists in painful knots as I yank clothing out of my closet. I should dress conservatively, yet comfortably. I don't want to exacerbate my anxiety by being uncomfortable as well. Thanks to Brad, I've gained a few pounds after dining in pricey restaurants for the past few months, and some of my slacks and skirts are now snug. Luckily, I have a pair of black slacks with an elastic waistband. I wear the same cream short-sleeved sweater I'd worn the day I'd met him, hoping it will be lucky. I step into black low-heeled shoes. I've worn flats or low heels since I've met Brad because of his height. It's more comfortable, anyway. Jewelry is easy–small silver hoops in my ears and a simple silver bracelet.

I debate what to do with my hair and play with it for nearly an hour. I want to do something sophisticated with it. Should I sweep it up on one side, twist it into a French braid, or pull it all back? I'm not adept at fixing my hair. I usually wear it loose or in a ponytail when Brad and I go out. I finally leave it loose, so it won't undo itself at some point and make me look disheveled. Such monumental decisions.

I put extra deodorant on and am fanning my underarms when I hear Brad's car pull up. He doesn't like to come in, so I throw on my sweater, grab my purse, and hurry outside to jump in the air-conditioned car.

"You look pretty," he says.

It's a critique because he doesn't give compliments. He's fretting about his parents meeting me. He depends on them financially for his business and strives to please them. I can't help but feel the pressure. This is a significant meeting. It's imperative that they like me. I've never been so overwrought and can't wait for this meeting to be over with.

We drive in silence out to the coast. It's a stunning drive, and I stare out at the rolling surf with the bright reflection of the sun glinting off the water, causing me to don my sunglasses. I envy the seagulls gliding in the breeze and strutting on the sand with not a care in the world.

As we begin the ascent up a long winding road past large affluent homes, my butterflies perk up and begin a more frenzied dance. I feel like an unwelcome intruder breeching this exclusive community. I place my hand on my stomach to halt my mounting dread.

"Are you okay?" Brad glances at me.

"I'm fine."

"Are you sure? We could go back if you don't feel well." Maybe he's looking for an excuse.

"I'm just nervous."

Though I'd prefer to turn around and avoid this meeting meant to judge my worthiness, I'd rather get this unpleasantness over with. If things go well, an approval will be given to our relationship and it can progress. I'm painfully aware of this. But if not? I don't know what will befall us.

The stucco house is perched on a hill along with other million-dollar homes. A variety of drought-resistant plants are aesthetically arranged in the front yard behind the wrought-iron gate, which opens after Brad presses in a code. After we park, he jogs over to the passenger car door to open it, and I step out into the heat. The house looks squat and long, and we approach the arched wooden door. Colorful ceramic pots filled with succulents frame the doorway.

Brad leads me into the cool dimness of the foyer without knocking. I exchange my sunglasses for my regular glasses so I can see clearly inside. I also hope they will make me look studious and serious.

"We're here," he calls out and shrugs at me.

I study the interior of the house. The living room is ahead, sporting a curved gray couch that faces wall to wall windows with an incredible view. To the left is the ocean and to the right miles of flat landscape fan out interspersed with dry rocky hills, clusters of houses, and mountains in the distance.

I start toward the windows, but Brad's mother appears with a welcoming smile. It makes me relax a bit. She's a small woman like me. Her chestnut hair is swept back into a fashionably loose tumble I could never master. Her skin is flawless. She wears light colors—white and cream—that radiate wealth. Diamonds adorn her earlobes, and I try not to gape at the huge diamond on her wedding ring. I could never pull that off.

Brad introduces us. Her name is Beverly, but I address her as Mrs. Fletcher. She holds out her delicate hand and I shake it gently.

She ushers us into the living room, and I'm drawn to the windows, marveling at the view.

"Yes, it's glorious, isn't it?" she says. "When it's clear."

I hope my mouth isn't hanging open.

"Wine?" she asks.

Brad assents for both of us and comes to stand beside me with his hand on the small of my back, quelling my anxiety.

"Don't be nervous," he whispers, which makes me more nervous.

"Thank you, Mrs. Fletcher," I say demurely when I accept the long-stemmed crystal wine glass.

"There you are, Bradley," Brad's father booms entering the room. "Magnificent view, huh?" he says

48

to me.

"It's... fantastic," I say.

Brad introduces us. "Dad, this is Vera. Vera, my father, Winston."

"Nice to meet you, Mr. Fletcher." I smile.

"Everyone calls me Win," he says. "Have a seat." He settles onto the plush curved sofa.

I sink into the cushions while Brad continues to stand, turning his back to the ocean to face us. He's framed in light like a golden god. I feel so fortunate in that moment. He sees potential in me or I wouldn't be sitting here with his father. I hope his parents see it as well.

"Let's get to know you, Vera." Mr. Fletcher waves his hand and ice clinks in the amber liquid filling his tumbler.

I take a gulp of wine.

"You're a single mother, is that right?"

"I have two teenagers."

"Well, now that's got to be tough." He chuckles.

"Do your parents help? And the father?" Mrs. Fletcher asks as she sits in a plush chair.

I shake my head. "They're all back east."

I don't elaborate further. The truth is, I'm not close to my parents. They'd chosen to judge me rather than support me, and my ex chose to move on. I look down at my lap.

"I hope you had a good divorce lawyer." Mrs. Fletcher gives a little snort.

"Mom, that's none of our business," Brad cuts in. "Vera does well on her own."

His rare compliment is followed by a short, awkward silence.

"Now what kind of work do you do? What's your vocation?" Winston asks me.

Vocation? I have two jobs that barely cover the bills. I live paycheck to paycheck. I have no career or prospects for one.

"I work in a call center." I don't even try to make it sound impressive and don't bother to mention my second part-time job.

"Ah, customer service." Winston nods. "The front lines."

"Yes. It has benefits," I add, hoping that counts for something. Despite being part time, one of my jobs provides minimal benefits.

"Why don't I give Vera a tour of the house?" Brad interjects.

He gives me a brief nod and I stand and follow him, thankful for the escape. I hadn't thought about how I would answer their questions. I'd spent all my time and energy fixating on my appearance, and now I have nothing to say. I have to think of something, something that will show I'm worthy of their youngest son.

"The main floor is the living area," Brad intones like a tour guide leading me into the kitchen where a tantalizing aroma greets us.

The cabinets are dark cherry and atop the light gray granite countertops are trays of food covered with tinfoil. Two busy Hispanic women smile at us. There's a wide refrigerator with a frosty glass door. I've never seen a refrigerator that huge. Who knew?

Off the kitchen is an octagonal breakfast nook jutting out the back of the house with a small round table above which is a skylight. Every panel holds a long window expanding on the view. It feels like you're floating in the sky.

I stand and watch the silent waves crashing below. I see myself having breakfast at this table with the morning sun cascading through the windows, bathing the space in golden light. I imagine casually surveying the awakening world below.

Brad has moved through a doorway, and I follow him into the family room with a brown L shaped couch, several recliners, shelves of books, games, and puzzles, and a large TV mounted on the wall.

"This room was for us kids," Brad says. "My parents hardly ever came in here."

Brad's two older brothers live far away. One lives in England and the other lives in New York. They're both married and successful. That's all I know about them. Brad's the one who hasn't finished college, the baby of the family who was indulged.

"This was our boy cave," he says with a smile. "We spent hours in here. My parents always knew where to find us. It was all mine once my brothers moved out."

"That must've been lonely," I say, noticing the board games.

"Nah." He waves his hand. "My friends would come over or I'd go to their houses."

The front of the house hides the lower level that slopes down the back of the property. We descend the stairs to find four bedrooms, each with a view, a queen bed, walk-in closet, and private bathroom. Brad shows me his old room, which is painted a deep blue, but holds few personal items, other than a few books, albums, and trophies. I quickly scan these objects as Brad keeps moving.

We come to the far end of the wide hallway, and I gasp as it opens into the master suite. Windows wrap around the corner of the house, displaying a spectacular view to the west. A thick white comforter looks as though a cloud has draped itself over the enormous bed with white padded headboard. Lacy pastel throw pillows are strategically scattered. A master bath with a skylight contains a huge jetted tub and double shower. There are two walk-in closets that are like small rooms. I can't stop staring out at the waves ebbing and flowing below.

"Check this out," Brad says, and I turn to see him patting a long narrow wooden cabinet whitewashed to match the bedding and dressers.

"What's that?" I can't see what's so special about this skinny enclosure at the foot of the bed.

"There's a TV in there." He grins. "You press a button, and it rises out of the cabinet so you can watch TV in bed. They like to watch the news and stock reports every morning."

"Wow." I'd never seen anything this luxurious. So, this is how the rich live.

"You grew up here?" I trail Brad back down the hall.

"I grew up in a smaller house. They bought this one when we were teenagers. They remodeled it a few years ago. Mom leaves our rooms so we can use them when we visit."

"I can't imagine having to clean this place," I say.

Brad frowns. "My mother doesn't clean."

Of course. They pay someone. It boggles my mind.

"She used to cook, though," he adds. "Sometimes. When she felt like it."

My stomach rudely growls, and I trust Brad hasn't heard it. I hope we're going to eat soon, if I'm able with my agitated stomach.

"Is there a restroom?" I'm a bit lightheaded.

Brad leads me to a half bath off the family room next to the spacious laundry room. Does Beverly do the laundry? Probably not. She has a life of leisure. What does she do all day?

"I'll see you in the living room." Brad turns away.

I want to ask him to wait for me but don't want to appear insecure and watch him head toward the doorway back through the kitchen. I close the bathroom door and look in the mirror. My cheeks are rosy. I pat cold water on my flushed face and fluff my hair with my fingers. My bracelet catches on a strand of hair and yanks as I pull my hand away. *Ouch!* I'm a jittery wreck. I am so out of my element and don't know what to say or do. His parents will never find me suitable. I'll be glad if I don't trip over something and make a total fool of myself. *Not too much wine on an empty stomach,* I admonish myself sternly in the mirror. With a deep breath, I hasten back to the living room.

We seat ourselves at a long dining table of polished dark wood. French doors lead out to a small, shaded patio at the front of the house. Large urns spilling with ferns stand outside the doors. It's like something you'd see in a magazine.

The two Hispanic women silently serve us, and I smile and thank them. It may not be proper, but I do it anyway. It feels like we're in a restaurant as salad with raspberry vinaigrette dressing and warm sourdough rolls are served first, followed by some sort of fish with roasted red potatoes and green beans with slivered almonds. Dessert is thick and creamy. I sip my wine sparingly during the meal and politely decline the coffee or tea offered afterwards, but help myself to an almond cookie that practically melts in my mouth.

During the meal I'm subtly grilled by his parents, but that's to be expected. Brad is unaware or he might be used to their interviewing technique with women he dates. How many women have been subjected to this scrutiny and how much weight does their assessment hold? That's what bothers me. If they deem me unworthy, will I be out or is this his test to see if I can hold my own? Either way, what little composure I'd initially mustered slowly erodes. It's glaringly obvious how incompatible we are. I'm pretty, not beautiful, and that's it. My one asset. I'm certainly not impressing them with my intellect or poise or accomplishments. The brutal truth is that I don't belong in this world, though I wish to be accepted into it, into Brad's life, into his family. I try to envision my kids at this table conversing with his parents. Somehow, I feel they'd make a better impression than me. My kids are smart and well behaved when they choose to be.

Brad's father tells a few jokes as we saunter back to the living room and I laugh. He seems to enjoy an audience, and I'm pleased to provide it. The two Hispanic women are silently clearing the table with a slight clatter and muted voices. I identify more with them.

After a bit more chatting in which, to my great relief, they turn most of their attention to Brad, he rises and says something that gets us moving toward the front door. I thank his parents for the lovely evening and we escape to the car. As soon as Brad pushes my door closed, the tension seeps from my body. I return my sunglasses to my face and let out a exhale of relief.

"Sorry about that, V," Brad says as we pull onto the street.

"About what?" I'm truly baffled why he feels the need to apologize.

"They can be a bit much."

"They were fine."

"They can be snobs." He's concentrating on the winding road.

"You're their son and they want the best for you."

Which isn't me, and we both know it. I turn my face away from him and gaze out the window.

"They don't know what I want," he says and squeezes my knee.

He has said the ideal thing to assuage my anxiety, and I smile toward the horizon. The sun is lazily sinking below the ocean, melting into a pink puddle drenching the sky.

"Look at the sunset."

He catches a glimpse as he drives. "Nice."

He's probably seen sunsets like this a thousand

54

times.

I let out a contented sigh. He's not driving me straight home after discerning how vast our differences are. It doesn't seem to concern him. Therefore, I won't let it concern me. His parents may come to accept me, even like me, because I make their son happy. In the future, I'll know what to expect, be better prepared, and feel more composed. Next time will be easier. Except there is no next time.

Chapter 8

Brad has entered my small apartment because I asked him to come inside instead of waiting in the car for me. It's important that he acknowledge my kids. I've met his parents, and now I want my kids to get used to seeing him. In fact, I've thought about inviting him over for dinner so they can get to know each other better. This is the next step forward in our relationship, yet I can't seem to bring it up. I'm afraid he'll balk, and my kids will act indifferent and sullen.

I try to see my apartment through Brad's eyes as he stands uncomfortably inside the door. After viewing where he grew up with its striking views, heavy, expensive furniture, and immaculate rooms, my apartment looks claustrophobic and the furnishings sadly shabby. Instead of a view of the ocean, we have a view of the parking lot. Instead of polished furniture, we have worn furniture with a thin layer of dust. Lacie was supposed to dust. Instead of carefully placed crystal vases brimming with fresh flowers, the apartment is strewn with the droppings of teenagers. We can see into the kitchen where the counter holds dirty plates and glasses, mismatched at that. Instead of a family room with a large screen TV, we have a small TV on which my son plays video games. He sits cross-legged on the floor leaning against the couch and doesn't look up when Brad enters.

"Luke, say hi to Brad," I instruct.

He briefly turns his head and raises a hand. "Hey." He goes back to his game.

"Looks like you got to a high level on that game," Brad observes.

"Yeah," is Luke's response.

What was I thinking? How can I expose Brad to

my chaotic life and indolent, sometimes hostile, offspring? Am I trying to drive him away? What must he think? But this is my life, and if we're to be serious, he has to accept it. And it hasn't scared him off yet.

"Lacie," I call my daughter.

"I'm on the phone," she yells.

"Come out here a minute," I yell back. "Say hi to Brad before we leave."

I'll get him out of here quickly before he has time to absorb the squalor and desolation of my life. Best to expose him in increments. A home cooked meal will have to wait for now, even though I can impress him with my cooking. I'm a pretty good cook and have a few recipes that will highlight my domestic side. I'm annoyed with my kids because they were supposed to clean up before I got home from work. It always takes several reminders, even occasional threats, to get them to do their chores and pick up after themselves.

Lacie emerges from her bedroom holding the cordless phone.

"Hi, Brad."

"Hi, Lacie," Brad replies.

There's not much more to say, and we all stand awkwardly for a moment. I don't know what I expected, but this isn't it.

"Okay, we're leaving." I grab my purse.

"Bye, Mom." Lacie turns and puts the phone to her ear. "It's my mom's boyfriend."

"Bye." Luke raises his hand again without taking his eyes from the TV screen.

"Remember to do your homework and chores and clean up the kitchen," I call out as I pull the door closed behind us with embarrassment.

I have no illusions that they'll listen, and a tiny shred of guilt tugs at me. How do I balance my responsibilities as a parent with the essential respite from those responsibilities? I remind myself that it's not all selfish. I'm investing in our future, our future as a family.

"I'm sorry," I say. "They can be rude."

I wait for Brad to take off running as we descend the cement steps from the second floor. I wouldn't blame him. I often feel the urge to run away myself. Though I love my kids more than anything in the world, their ungrateful attitudes and the relentless uphill battle of my life often overwhelm me.

"They're not rude. They're teenagers," Brad says.

"I guess that's true."

His comment pacifies me. He doesn't even have kids of his own, and he understands this.

"My parents had to deal with three boys. We were a real handful, awful sometimes," he adds with a grin.

"You were?"

I smile as I try to picture Brad as a little scamp, tagging after his older brothers, causing mayhem in the household, exasperating their parents. I stop on the steps and fumble in my purse for my sunglasses.

"I'll tell you what." He stops on the bottom step and looks up at me. "I can put them to work next weekend. It'll get them out of the house, and they can earn a little money."

"That'd be awesome," I say with delight. "Doing what?"

He shrugs as we walk toward the car across the rough asphalt. A boy sails by us on a skateboard, and my neighbor waves as she drops a bag of garbage in the big dumpster. Someone is barbequing on their balcony, and kids dart past us, shrieking.

Brad holds open the passenger door, and I slide in, arranging myself on the sun-warmed seat, placing my purse by my feet on the floor. He patiently waits until I'm settled before he swings the door shut. He has impeccable manners. My kids could learn from him.

Once we're ensconced in the quiet cocoon of the car, he turns to me to respond. "I have some landscaping at the house. Just some weeding and mowing, and I was thinking of putting in some plants along the front. I could use the help. Do you think they'd be interested?"

"They will if you pay them," I answer enthusiastically.

I'm not quite certain, but it shows his sincere effort to get to know my kids. Another crucial layer in the foundation of our relationship.

"Thanks, Brad."

"No problem. It'll be nice to have the help."

"Maybe we can all go out to dinner after," I casually suggest as he starts the car. I'd like for my kids to experience an upscale restaurant.

"Whoa." Brad laughs. "They might not like me by the end of the day. One step at a time, V." He pats my leg and carefully drives through the long parking lot, avoiding kids riding bikes.

He navigates the busy Saturday traffic to a favorite restaurant close to the movie theater. I'm hungry and can't wait to get a glass of wine to unwind after the stress of the week. I marvel that Brad is still living up to my idealistic image. So far, my kids haven't scared him off, and the unpleasant meeting with his parents hasn't affected our relationship as I'd feared. I have more faith than ever that this will work out long term. My doubts have been wrong. Marcy is wrong. Despite everything, our relationship is strong, and now he's making an effort with my kids. Things are going in the right direction.

I take off my sunglasses and put on my other glasses before we enter the soft lighting and low din of the restaurant. Enticing aromas waft between the tables as we weave our way through the crowded room behind the server. I feel a brief pang of envy at all the families seated together and feel bad about leaving my kids at home. Nevertheless, I'm sure they don't mind the freedom. Besides, they get to eat pizza or fast food, which I don't let them eat any other time.

Brad always selects the wine. I know nothing about wine, but he's noted I prefer the sweeter wines, and he orders them for me. I sip from my glass, though I'd rather have a mixed drink. The wine sends a soothing current through me that is the prelude to an evening that will be filled with sensations. A basket of bread is delivered to our table, and Brad waits while I tear off a piece that I dip in the little white bowl of garlic and olive oil before I take a bite.

He knows this is my favorite restaurant, and I order my usual meal of pasta primavera. The vegetables are tangy fresh and the sauce is rich, and I always have leftovers to bring to work for lunch. I've grown accustomed to the familiar sounds of clinking glasses and muted conversations that envelop us in this world of superb foods and diligent wait staff. I've grown accustomed to the server holding out my chair and draping my cloth napkin over my lap and hovering to refill my wineglass. I enjoy being pampered and spoiled for a change. I enjoy being the one waited on instead of the other way around, but I feel like a visitor to this world when I'd rather be a permanent resident.

After we've ordered, Brad looks at me with a strange expression. I can't read it. He looks ill at ease, as if he's about to deliver bad news. My stomach tightens, ready for the blow.

"I have to tell you something," he states and pauses, looking around the room as if hoping something will interrupt this obligation.

"What is it?"

Anxious thoughts quiver in my head. Is he going

to break up with me? No, why would he offer to put my kids to work if he's going to break up with me? Is he sick? Is he moving away? What could this terrible news be? I begin to tremble.

"I feel really bad about this, V." He leans toward me as if revealing a secret. "You know my birthday is coming up."

"Yes."

I've been wracking my brain about what to get him. He buys himself anything he wants. What could I possibly come up with? It's been driving me nuts.

He takes a sip of wine and looks around the room again. It's not like him to procrastinate.

"Tell me already."

I can't stand the anticipation. I take a gulp of wine. Have his parents demanded he break up with me? I wouldn't be surprised, and I probably wouldn't blame them. Maybe he's come to the rational conclusion that we don't belong together. Why does there always have to be an obstacle to happiness? Whatever it is, I prepare to debate it. If I can just find the right words, the right logical argument, I can persuade him.

"My parents are throwing me a birthday party. You know, mostly their friends and..." He clears his throat. "It's not about me. It's all about what they want, and since I rely on them financially for my business..."

"Why would I be upset about that?" I'm relieved but mystified.

"I'm sorry to tell you this, but..." He shakes his head. "I can't bring you. I have no say in the matter. They've made it clear..." His voice trails off, and he takes a long sip from his wineglass.

"Oh." I lean back in my padded chair. The air has gone out of me like I've been punched. They've thoroughly rejected me.

"I knew they didn't like me," I mumble.

"It's not you, V. They're snobs sometimes." Brad is clearly irritated. "They want me to meet some of their friends' daughters or nieces or something. I don't know what they think..."

"They're going to introduce you to other women at your party?" I ask incredulously. "When they know you have a girlfriend?"

Not only do they not like me, but they actively want to break us up by introducing him to more suitable women. An intervention of sorts.

"Believe me," he says empathetically. "It's not my idea. I don't want my parents setting me up. It puts me in a tough position."

I nod and try not to let tears dampen my eyes. I take a few slugs of wine. His parents want me gone. How disheartening. How discouraging. How disrespectful. How hurtful. Can't they see beyond dollar signs? Don't they see that their son is happy with me? Why can't they let him make up his own mind? Fine. They don't want me at their stupid party, but to introduce him to other women is going too far.

"Let's not let this ruin our evening," Brad says. "I feel bad about it, but it's not up to me, and I wanted to tell you the truth."

"Thank you," I say evenly.

"Don't worry about it, okay? I'm not interested in any of those women. I've met most of them before and they don't interest me."

He's doing his best to reassure me, and I feel a little better.

"Okay," I murmur.

"We'll have our own celebration for my birthday," he says with an encouraging smile.

"Okay." I force myself to smile back.

Brad didn't have to tell me, but insecurities plague me. What if he likes one of these women with whom he'll be set up? His parents may succeed in breaking us up. And there's nothing I can do about it.

Chapter 9

My kids are desperate for money, and they agree to work for Brad for a few hours in his yard. I'm pleased they relented so easily, but Luke wants to buy a new video game and Lacie wants clothes and make-up. I feel bad that I can't buy them the things that they want, but Brad asserts it builds character when you have to earn things.

I drive them over to his house, and their eyes widen at the neighborhood and his large home. Brad is outside in shorts and work boots. His T-shirt is smeared with dirt and he wears work-gloves.

Coco runs up and jumps around Lacie and Luke. She's wiggling around so much she can hardly contain herself. She gives me a cursory lick and leaps around my kids.

"She's so cute." Lacie bends down to pet her and gets licked in the face.

"That's Coco," I say.

"Hey, Coco." Luke picks up the ball at his feet and tosses it. "Go get it."

She takes off like a shot, skidding on the lawn and snagging the ball in her mouth.

"Be careful not to throw it into the plants," Brad cautions.

"Let me." Lacie grabs the ball that Coco returns and tosses it.

Coco again takes off after it.

"Ready to get dirty?" Brad asks my kids.

They mumble at him unenthusiastically. I'm a little worried, unsure how hard he'll work them. Coco is prancing around vying for their attention.

"I'm going to show them where the bathroom is," I tell Brad.

He nods and throws the ball for Coco.

"What does he want us to do?" Lacie asks as we

enter the cool of the house.

"Just some yardwork," I say casually. "Just tell him if you need a break or don't know what to do."

"Wow." Luke looks around as we enter the hallway. "This house is humongous."

I try to see it through their eyes. They've never been in a house like this. The large windows and vaulted ceilings make it feel expansive and bright.

"I didn't know he was rich." Lacie eyes me.

"He's not rich. He fixed up this house and now he's trying to sell it. That's what he does."

"He's rich, all right." Luke starts to wander.

"Luke," I call him back. "This is the bathroom you can use."

He shrugs. They're both trying to peek into the rooms.

"Okay, take a quick look, and then we have to go back outside."

They scamper off, exclaiming at each room.

"Come on, guys," I call and they reappear after a few minutes.

"This house is super fancy," Lacie says.

"He should keep it," Luke adds. "I wouldn't sell it."

"I wish he could," I admit. "But he won't make any money if he does. He wants to sell it and buy another house and keep making money."

"So, this is his job?" Luke furrows his brow.

"Yes. This is what he does for a living."

"But how did he get the money to buy it in the first place?" he asks.

"His parents helped him."

"They must be rich," Lacie declares.

"They have money," I say, and hope more than ever that Brad and I can provide a good life for my kids. I want to give them everything they want and every opportunity to succeed, and I am convinced I can't do that alone. It takes all I have just to keep our heads above water. My kids deserve more, and I want so much to give it to them.

We step out into the brightness of the late morning, and Coco bounds over.

"Okay, we have a lot to do today, so let's get busy," Brad says. "Lacie, how about if you mow the lawn, and, Luke, you can help me put in some ice plants on the slope out front. Then I have some bushes for that area if we get to them."

They look at him blankly for a few moments. Lacie notices the mower inside the garage and heads toward it.

Brad walks over to his work truck in the driveway and lets down the gate to reveal many pots of plants.

"Let's carry these around to the front," he says to Luke.

"I'll see you guys later," I say cheerfully.

"I can drive them home," Brad offers.

I wave and head over to the grocery store. I don't know why it's unsettling leaving them with Brad. It's got to be weird for them to spend almost an entire day with my boyfriend, who they don't really know. This will be good for them, I tell myself. Spending time with a responsible adult male will be good for both of them since their father has chosen not to have a relationship with his kids. It's necessary for Brad to build rapport with them if we're to move closer to being a family someday. This is how it will be, but it's hard for me to let go.

I do the grocery shopping and come home to my quiet apartment, which usually blasts music from competing sources. The silence is nice for a change. I drag the hamper down to the apartment complex laundry room and clean up the kitchen. I straighten up and clean the bathroom.

At the small round dining table, I spread out the bills and get out my checkbook and calculator. It's always a challenge to juggle my limited funds. There have been times when I've sat here in tears, feeling that I'll never catch up. I try to protect my kids from these troubles, but my credit card bills swell every month despite regular payments. I can't dwell on that. I tell myself to just tackle each month, but I can't help projecting when I can pay them off. Too many emergencies have piled onto them, car repairs, odds and ends the kids need, doctor and dental bills. It's always something.

I can't help but daydream. Brad may be the ticket to an easier life. He could be my knight in shining armor. Not that I want to be saved, but when you're drowning, you grab the hand that's there. And I feel like I'm drowning. Naturally, I'd prefer to save myself. I'd applied for a better job at work but hadn't gotten it. That extra money would've made a difference. I just need a break. Some people get to have easier lives. Why not us?

I see myself in Brad's house. I picture my kids in the bedrooms. Coco would enjoy having them around to play with. I'd make home-cooked meals in that spacious sparkling kitchen while Lacie and Luke do their homework. Brad would lean over and patiently help them, and they'd assist him with landscaping and fixing up the homes in which he invests. I can see Brad being a wonderful role model, unlike their deadbeat father and some of the high maintenance guys I've stupidly allowed into our lives. Never again. Things are different now. A better life is around the corner, though it feels so tenuous, so shaky.

I'm absorbed in these optimistic fantasies when my kids barge through the door.

"You're back," I say, standing up. "How was it?"

They're dirty and disheveled, but smiling happily. I glance at the clock. It's been about four and a half hours.

"He gave us $100!" Luke shouts. "Each!"

"Fantastic." I smile. I hadn't expected Brad to be this generous. "Was he... was it okay?"

"I'm wiped out," Lacie groans.

"Where's Brad? Did he leave?"

"He had to park the truck," Luke says.

"I get the shower first!" Lacie runs to her room.

"No fair!" Luke yells and looks at me. "She takes too long."

"You'll get your turn," I promise.

He skulks off to his room.

Brad is chuckling in the front doorway.

"How were they?" I ask. "Did you get everything done?"

"We got most of it done. I worked them pretty hard. They earned their money."

"Thanks for paying them so much," I say.

He shrugs. "It would've cost more to hire landscapers, so I ended up saving money."

I nod. I'm not sure what our plans are that night.

"Hey, I appreciate this," I tell him. "I really do. It was unreasonable of me to ask you to take us all out to dinner too. You just spent a lot of money, and..."

"I think they've had enough of me today," he says with a grin.

"I'm glad it went well," I say with relief.

"Mom!" Luke calls. "Can you take us to the mall tomorrow?"

"Yeah, we can do that," I call back.

"Hey, Luke, remember what I told you," Brad adds. "Don't spend all of it. Save a little."

Bonus. He even talked to them about saving money. This is just what they need. Somebody successful who can guide them to success. Something I can't do.

"I'm going to go home and shower. Give me about an hour and we can go to dinner," Brad tells me. "I'm famished."

"Okay. I'll be over in an hour," I say happily.

He still wants to see me. My kids haven't scared him off. Again, I imagine us as a family. The kids playing with Coco in the yard, Brad and I sipping wine as we make dinner together, a light breeze drifting through the French doors.

"I don't think we can get together next weekend," he says. "My parents have that party for me."

"Okay," I say lightly, but the thought that I'm not good enough for their son is crushing.

Chapter 10

It's been two weeks since we've seen each other because of the party Brad's parents threw for his birthday, the one to which I wasn't invited. I called him the day after hoping to see him for brunch or dinner, but he sounded distracted and said he was too busy. I pressed him for details, but he was vague and finally told me he didn't want to talk about it. I don't know if he's annoyed with me or his parents and fret about it all week. I call him again on Friday, trying to sound upbeat.

"I thought we were going to celebrate your birthday." I can hear the whine creep into my voice. "You said we would and I..."

"Right," he says curtly. "Dinner tomorrow night, okay?"

He sounds impatient. I'm having serious Brad withdrawal and want to get back into our Saturday night routine, but it feels like I've lost all the ground I've gained.

"I can't wait to see you. I miss you."

Damn. That slipped out. I can't help it. I want so much to hear it back, but he tells me what time he'll pick me up and hangs up. He knows precisely how to drive me crazy. It sounds like there's major damage control I must undertake. His parents have created a wedge between us, and I'll have to repair it and get us back to where we were. I'll know how bad it is when I see him.

What do you buy someone who has more money than you? Someone who can buy themselves anything they want? I don't get him a card after the negative reaction to the Valentine's Day card, though I longingly peruse the sappy birthday cards at the stationery store.

I roam the mall for hours with Lacie and Luke

trying to come up with something original to give him. Where can I find the ultimate gift that's practical, yet conveys a subtle sentimental message that will awaken his feelings for me? Impossible. I meander listlessly into a toy store because the stuffed animal display draws me, and Luke wants to check out the video games. I wish Brad would give me a stuffed animal to cuddle when he's not around, but he'd never think to do that.

There's a train chugging along a large circle of tracks around the store that I watch for a bit. Lacie delights in the train and studies the small towns that have been set up at intervals along the tracks. I stand and watch as it passes by and loops endlessly around the store. Slow and steady. Around and around and around. Like the thoughts that constantly whirl round in my head about Brad.

"Mom, look."

Lacie points to a tiny house along the tracks with a For Sale sign stuck in the yard and a miniature black dog standing on the tiny porch.

I lean down to study the minute detail.

"That looks like Coco." She laughs.

"That's brilliant, Lacie," I say. "I'm going to get it for Brad for his birthday."

I impulsively find it on the shelf and buy it. He sells houses and has a dark brown dog. Will he see the whimsy and humor, or will he think it's impractical? Most likely the latter, but I like it and feel compelled to buy it.

I take extra care getting ready on Saturday, hoping he'll realize how much he missed me when he sees me. I pop the small wrapped gift into my purse. I wonder if he'll like it. At the time, I'd thought it was perfect, but now I fear he may find it silly. Will my gift show him how mismatched we are? I could've gotten him something practical like a shirt, but I can't afford the name brand shirts he wears or even know how to pick one out for him. What do rich people buy each other, anyway? I haven't a clue.

Anxiety has settled in the pit of my stomach. I want to know, but dread knowing, what transpired at the party. Had his parents enticed him with a more appropriate female match? Will he break the news to me today that he's met someone else? Is this the last time I'll ever see him?

Money is the big barrier. I'm convinced that if I were more successful, his parents would find me suitable. But my looks may not be helping. I have dark hair and eyes. His parents might favor someone with lighter hair and blue eyes like Brad. That could be another strike against me in their view. I'm curious about the women with whom they set him up. What was it about them they considered preferable? What would make *me* acceptable in their eyes?

Why haven't I managed my life better? Why haven't I made wiser decisions? Brad is an opportunity for me, a way out of the hole in which I find myself. I want to give my kids a better life. They deserve it, and so do I. I'm so tired of constantly struggling.

I've worked myself into quite a state by the time Brad's car pulls into the parking lot. I call goodbye to my kids and run down the stairs. I pull open the car door before he can open it for me and slide onto the seat of the car, slamming the door. I'm not sure what to expect.

"Sorry," he says without looking at me.

"For what?" I'm puzzled by his strange mood.

"Seeing my parents puts me in a foul mood sometimes." He drives slowly across the parking lot. "It's not you." He pats my leg.

Does that mean his parents haven't put doubts in his mind?

"It's okay. I figured."

"I'm stuck because they finance my business right now."

"I know."

"They call the shots." He grimaces. "I have to put up with their interference in my life."

I give him a reassuring smile.

"Thanks for being understanding, V." He pats my leg again.

I'm starved for his touch and long to take his hand but repress the urge.

"I'm just going to hit that Thai place close to my house. Is that okay?"

"Yeah. That sounds good."

I don't care where we go, I'm just happy we're together. The glare of the bright day is making me squint, and I fish around for my sunglasses in my purse. I was overreacting. Things are back to normal. It's Saturday, and all is well.

The Thai restaurant is crowded, and Brad suggests ordering food to bring back to the house. I sit on a chair by the cashier and observe the families, the couples, wedding rings flashing, people guffawing. The décor is sparse and the clattering of dishes and many conversations are loud in this small space. It seems to take forever, and, finally, Brad is handed paper bags containing our food, and we exit the noisy restaurant.

Once at Brad's house, I notice the yard looks neat and manicured with small flowering plants and a freshly mowed lawn. There's the scent of grass in the air. Dog toys are scattered on the patio.

"The yard looks nice," I say.

"Luke and Lacie were a big help."

Brad opens the sliding glass door, and Coco jumps out, wagging her tail.

"Mommy's home," Brad calls out.

That statement immediately eases my tension and puts a smile on my face. He wouldn't say that if he planned on breaking up with me. He thinks of us as a little family.

While I pet Coco, he closes the gate, then leisurely strolls over. Despite his spate of irritability, I marvel at his habitually composed manner as if he never has a care. He's always in control and at ease. It's a demeanor to which I aspire. Is this how people with money feel? All my anxiety seems to stem from not having enough money. Would removing the stress of paying the bills give one a sense of peace?

Brad pours wine for both of us without asking. We arrange our food on the kitchen island and perch upon black wrought iron bar stools with deep green cushions.

As we eat, I pull the little wrapped gift from my purse and set it before him.

"I have a present for you."

"You didn't have to do that."

"It's just a little... It's not much. It's..." I shrug. "I saw it and it made me think of you. Happy birthday."

It suddenly occurs to me that he must've received some exorbitant birthday gifts. My trivial gift will pale in comparison.

He tears off the whimsical wrapping paper and turns the little house over, inspecting it. "What is this?"

"You know. You sell houses and the little dog... it made me think of you," I say.

"Wow. Where did you find this? This is amazing, V."

I perk up. "You really like it?"

"Yes, I do. It even has Coco right there." He chuckles.

I'm beaming. "I'm glad you like it."

And I'm glad he doesn't think it's silly.

"Thanks, V. It's the best present I got."

This gives me a great sense of satisfaction. My

personal little gift means more to him than some big, costly one.

"So how was the party?" I try to sound casual.

"Oh, you know. It was mostly my parents' friends. Lots of food."

He's not telling me what I most want to know, but I don't know how to ask. I deliberate how to phrase the question that may bring an unwelcome response.

We talk a bit about our work weeks, as we usually do. Brad tells me he's taken the house off the market for now. He'll re-list it as a new listing soon, which will entice more buyers to view it. I still harbor hope that he'll decide to keep it and envision us living here. I'm sure the schools are better. My kids would love having a dog, and Coco would love having kids to play with.

"Um," I say while chewing. "So..."

"So?" Brad looks up at me.

"I'm curious."

"About?"

"Did your parents try to set you up with anyone?"

He gives a little laugh, which annoys me, because I don't find it at all amusing.

"Yeah, they did. They encouraged their friends to bring a few single women for me to meet." He shakes his head. "It was awkward."

"And?" I ask casually, as if we're talking about something as benign as the weather.

"And what?"

Geez, do I have to spell it out?

"Did you like any of them?"

"Oh." He laughs again. "They were nice enough. My mother was really pushing one of them."

"Yeah? What was she like?"

"As far as?"

"Well, was she pretty?"

He's making me drag this information out of him and I find it quite annoying.

"I guess so. She was younger than me, probably about five or so years. Your typical California girl. Blonde, blue eyed. They're everywhere around here."

"That's who your mother sees you with," I state. Just as I suspected.

"Maybe." He looks at me with a forkful of food poised before his mouth. "But you're prettier."

I know he's sincere because he doesn't throw out random compliments. This eases my distress and I give him a smile.

"What does she do?" I can't stifle my insecure curiosity.

He thinks. "She's getting some sort of degree. I can't remember. They all run together."

This pacifies me further. I reach down and pet Coco, who is sitting by my feet.

"I'll probably find out at lunch," he says nonchalantly. "My mother wouldn't let up until I agreed to have lunch with her."

The smile disappears from my face.

"You have a date with her?" I ask with disbelief.

"It's not a real date."

"It sounds like a real date."

He shrugs. "My mother thinks it's a date, but we haven't set anything up yet. Besides, she may have been pushed into this as well."

"You think so?" I ask hopefully.

"Most likely."

I hadn't thought of that. This helps to assuage my insecurities, but the date bothers me. They'll find they have things in common and feel attracted to each other because, let's face it, they're both attractive. He'll perceive there are more suitable fish in the sea, fish without teenagers, fish with decent careers, fish that aren't so dependent on him. Oh, my God. What's with the fish? I berate myself. This is totally making me lose my mind.

"For all I know, she has a boyfriend."

"You think so?"

"Who knows? Someone that pretty usually does," he says flippantly.

That does *not* make me feel better.

"That hit the spot." He pushes back from the counter.

"That was yummy. Thanks for buying it."

I'm still wavering between being alarmed and being placated. *Someone that pretty...* But he's mine right now. And he said I'm prettier. I bring our dishes to the sink.

"I'm going to put this on my desk," he says, picking up the miniature house.

And think of me every time he looks at it.

Chapter 11

I'm staring up at the ceiling of Brad's bedroom, trying to rouse myself enough to get out of this comfortable bed and go to the bathroom. Dappled light dances on the white ceiling from the bright light stealing in along the edges of the wood blinds. Brad sleeps silently turned away from me on his side of the king-sized bed. I stare at his bare back and see the familiar freckles on his shoulders that I've come to love and the curl of his hair at the nape of his neck. I long to reach out and touch him or snuggle up to him, but it will wake him, and he doesn't like cuddling.

I think about how he downplayed the events of the birthday party his parents threw him about a month ago. He hasn't said a thing about the date they'd pressured him into since, and I assume it never took place. He could have been right. She already had a boyfriend or wasn't interested in him. Or the date has taken place, and he's kept it from me. Would he lie to me to protect me? To protect himself. He could carry on a relationship with someone else, and how would I know? Except he sees me every Saturday night, "date" night. Wouldn't his other girlfriend question why he wasn't available every Saturday night? I shake off these suspicious thoughts. Paranoid, as usual. I have to stop doing this to myself.

My clothing is draped over the easy chair in the corner, and my shoes are placed neatly side by side before the chair ready for me to sit and slip them on. I should go home before my kids wake up. They usually sleep late on Sundays and, most of the time, I can arrive home before they get up unless Brad and I go to breakfast, which has ceased as guilt has gripped me. I should be home making breakfast for my kids. Yes, I will do that this morning.

I quietly pull aside the comforter and step onto the cool wood floor. I'm wearing one of Brad's T-shirts. He doesn't understand why I like to sleep in his shirts. He stirs and turns onto his back, never opening his eyes. His hair is disheveled and his hand rests on his chest. I stare at him a moment. This is a sight I wouldn't mind seeing every morning. We'd awaken together to begin our day. We'd all go out to breakfast, or I'd make breakfast. Lacie and Luke would play with Coco in the yard and do their chores. I'd do laundry while Brad worked in his office. We'd fix up houses together. Brad would have a team of helpers. My kids would receive real allowances and have spending money. It'd be beneficial for everyone.

Coco lifts her head from the corner where she sleeps on her big oval dog bed. I motion to her and she happily follows me to the family room where I let her out.

I use the bathroom by Brad's office instead of the one off the master bedroom so as not to disturb him. Tiptoeing down the hall, I peek into the orderly office to check the time on the wall clock. 7:50. A gray file cabinet stands like a sentry against the wall. There's a bookcase holding magazines and books on real estate, sales, and marketing. *How to Sell Anything to Anybody* is the title of the one that jumps out at me. I don't know why Brad thinks he has to read a book like that. He has that ability innately. Would it benefit me to read it? I could learn how to "sell" the idea of us to him and remove all doubts. I remember Brad emphasizing that being good at sales is a vital skill. I can see if it's at the library. If nothing else, he'll be impressed that I've taken his advice and read it.

I smile at the miniature house sitting on his uncluttered desk. It had been the right present, after all. Unique and memorable. I hope it makes him think of me with fondness.

I turn to use the bathroom when his answering machine clicks on, startling me and causing my steps to freeze. He keeps the volume high so he can hear it from other rooms in the large house. This landline is his business line with an attached fax machine. I look expectantly at the machine waiting for a fax to print out, hoping this early noise won't abruptly awaken him.

Lately, I've taken to sneaking out in the morning, so he'll find me gone when he wakes. For some reason, I think this will make him miss me more. Plus, he won't be able to talk me into having breakfast with him, which he could easily do, but the machine may disturb him this morning.

"You've reached Brad Fletcher. I'll return your call as soon as possible." Brief. Succinct. So Brad. I smile at that.

But then... a female voice.

"Brad. Are we still on for brunch? I'll drive down and meet you around 11:00ish at the same place. Call if you can't make it. See you there." Click.

I hurry into the small half bath off the hall. My heart is racing and I'm so distracted I hardly know what I'm doing. He has a date. For brunch. She's driving down from somewhere. She didn't say her name or where they're meeting. This means they know each other well, and this is a usual thing. This means he's counting on me leaving. This means there is someone else. Of course there is. Why did I think there wasn't? Obviously, she doesn't know about me. What would she think if she knew he was getting out of bed with someone to meet her?

I tell myself to remain calm. There's an explanation. There has to be, because I can't bear what I'm thinking.

When I step back into the darkened bedroom,

I'm trembling. The light still dances on the ceiling as I fumble with my clothing. Should I stay and see what he does? Would he tell me the truth? What if I said I wanted to go to breakfast? Would he blow her off for me? What should I do? I should go home to my kids, but then he'll go to brunch with her.

"What were you doing in my office?" He's sitting up in bed.

"I wasn't in your office. I was using the bathroom in the hall so I wouldn't wake you up," I answer quickly. "I let Coco out."

We stare at each other for a moment. He must know that I heard the message.

"You're seeing other people?" I ask in a wounded voice.

I don't want to sound so vulnerable, but I can't help it. I hate that I'm so weak. I hate that everything relies on his whims, that I have no power in this situation. He can easily find someone else. I can't.

He gets out of bed and pulls on jeans over his boxers. His ruffled hair looks sexy. I can't lose him. I can't.

"I see people all the time. I have lunch meetings all the time."

"You know what I mean."

I dress reluctantly, placing his shirt on the chair.

He pulls a white Henley shirt over his head and scrunches up the sleeves onto his forearms. He runs his fingers through his hair. White looks good on him. It makes him look clean and rich. I wear a lot of dark colors. Does that reflect my mood, my acceptance of my gloomy lot in life?

"Don't be so dramatic. I spend every Saturday night with you."

This gives me a tiny twinge of optimism. But...

"But you still see other women."

He doesn't answer, and I silently plead with him

81

to give me the words I crave. Please say something so I won't go home and dwell about this all day. Please say what I long to hear.

"Look." He turns to me. "We never said we were exclusive."

"I'm exclusive. I want to be. Don't you want to be exclusive? Things are great between us," I blurt.

I pace, searching for the words to convince him I'm all he needs. At the same time, I'm valiantly fighting the tears threatening to flood my eyes. I aspire to remain relaxed and rational like he is. If only the right words would pop into my head.

"Don't blow this up out of proportion," he cautions. "Don't overreact."

"I'm not overreacting," I say, my voice rising.

I battle to subdue my quavering voice, my trembling lip, my moistening eyes. Doesn't he realize my entire world could crash down with his words?

"Hey," he says gently.

I hate that he's addressing me like a helpless child.

"She's a friend, I swear. We meet maybe twice a year. She drives down from L.A. She's in real estate. We talk business." He shrugs. "No big deal."

Business. That word immediately pacifies me. Yes, it's business. He lives for business. And he spends every Saturday night with me. It's true. Nothing to fret about. No need to feel threatened. She's nothing more than a business acquaintance. How silly of me. I believe him because I need to believe him.

I smile. I don't want to appear clingy or needy or possessive. That will scare him off. Our relationship feels so very fragile, held together by a single thin strand that could easily snap. I don't want to be the one to snap it.

I dawdle hesitating to leave because he'll start getting ready to see another woman, even if it is just a casual business brunch. And it will be another week until I see him again. He always makes time on Saturday nights, but I hate being at the mercy of his schedule and inclination to see me. I hate being always available, waiting for him. It drives me a little crazy. He has all the power, but I don't know how to change the dynamic. I procrastinate helplessly.

"When do you think we'll see each other again?" I ask and inwardly wince.

"Soon. Next Saturday." He grins. "You know I can't go long without my Vera fix."

His comment lifts my spirits, and I give a little laugh.

"Okay. I have to go. I'll miss you."

But he doesn't say it back.

Chapter 12

"I knew it!" Marcy shouts. "The scumbag."

"Shhh."

I just finished pouring my heart out to her, though I don't enjoy giving her ammunition against Brad. She hasn't been on board the Brad train from the beginning, and I hate to tell her anything negative about him, but I desperately need to talk to someone.

We're at a busy fast food place, and I scan the room to see if anyone is staring at us before dipping a French fry in ketchup. I don't like to let my kids eat fast food. It's not healthy, filled with bad fats and salt, but it's a weakness of mine that I indulge with Marcy.

"He said they meet a few times a year for brunch, and it's about business."

It sounds worse when I say it to her.

"That's what they all say." She flips her hair over her shoulder.

"Well, I believe him. He said they talk about real estate and stuff, and you know he's into his business."

"Sure they do."

"If he liked her, why would he be seeing me?" I demand.

Darn. Why had I told her in the first place? But I can't keep anything from Marcy. We've always told each other everything.

"Why do you think?" she says with a smirk. "Look. Guys are different from us. They can see lots of people at the same time and feel no guilt."

"But I know he cares about me, even if he can't say it," I insist.

"He probably does." Marcy takes one of my fries. "Just don't trust him. Take everything he says with a grain of sand."

"Salt. It's a grain of salt."

"Whatever. They're both tiny. You know what I mean."

I take a sip of ice water.

"I don't know why you're not mad," she says. "You should be mad. He'd probably respect you more if you stood up for yourself. Have some balls."

"Wouldn't that be weird?" I say to change the subject.

She bursts out laughing. "Can you imagine? We have enough to deal with. Right?"

I laugh too, but the truth is I don't want to make waves. That's the way to lose him. If he could acknowledge his true feelings for me, everything would be fine. But who knows how long that could take? Why can't he see how ideal we are for each other?

"I'd be mad. No, I'd be furious, and I wouldn't put up with it." She shakes her head and steals another fry.

I wish I could be stronger, like Marcy. She doesn't take any crap, despite being overly distrustful where I would give someone the benefit of the doubt. Somewhere in the middle would be optimal.

I think back to when we met in high school. I'd always admired her guts. She was friends with everyone. She didn't care what clique you were in or how popular or unpopular you were. She was friendly to everyone and even talked to the teachers like they were actual people. Teachers had always intimidated me. She talked to boys too, as friends. Boys! How could she be comfortable talking to boys? She had the self-assurance to be social with everyone.

We had clicked because we had the same silly sense of humor. She also trusted me not to go after her boyfriend. Doug was popular and completely smitten with her, though other girls often flirted with him. But he only had eyes for Marcy. She hadn't seemed interested at first, and I'd been surprised when she'd confirmed her mutual affection for him.

There's a group of boisterous teenage boys a few tables away. They're talking loudly and cursing every other word. It's male posturing and hope my son doesn't act like that in public. When do they grow out of that behavior?

A cluster of teenage girls is gathered at another table. How different they are. No cursing, no belligerence, quiet, polite in public. They steal glimpses of the boys as they whisper and giggle. How on earth do these two opposites ever get together?

I sigh and return to my fries. Life gets truly complicated the older you get, especially if you make stupid mistakes as I have that radiate out and affect all that comes after. Was I still making them? Would I keep on making mistakes over and over like a skipping record?

"Remember when we used to take our kids to the park together?" I ask wistfully.

"Yeah. When they were little and would listen to us," Marcy says ruefully.

"I miss holding my kids on my lap. They were so soft and cuddly."

"I know. Babies smell good."

"Yeah. That baby scent."

"But we had to drag them everywhere, and it was always a pain trying to get a sitter."

"It was a relief when we didn't need sitters anymore," I agree.

"Remember, you had that one who drank all the alcohol in your apartment?"

"I remember that! She was a nightmare." I shake my head. "How could I have left my kids with her?"

"You didn't know until later."

"What a nightmare." I'm still shaking my head. My poor kids.

"And we could never have an uninterrupted conversation," Marcy reminds me. "That was so frustrating. I used to lose my marbles every day with those kids."

"I miss sitting and watching Sesame Street with them. I loved that show," I say.

"Me too, and it kept them riveted for an hour. I could get stuff done in the house."

"I miss when my kids were little. Life was simple. You said something, and they listened."

"Then they turn into the teenagers from hell." Marcy laughs.

I smile. "And make us feel old."

"Don't you go there, Vera," she warns. "Time flies when you have kids."

"Why do things have to be so hard?" I grumble. "I'm tired of things being hard. Every month, I stress about bills. Every day, my kids argue with me about something. They can't just do their chores or their homework. They have to argue about every little thing with me and each other. And Brad can't just go out with me and be happy. He has to be indifferent and seeing other people. I'm so tired of everything."

There. I had to get that out.

Marcy holds a fry suspended before her mouth.

"I just want things to be easy for a change," I conclude.

Marcy eats the fry and chews thoughtfully. "I think we should run away."

"I like that idea."

"We could change our names and move to Canada. Didn't you take French in high school?"

"They speak English too."

"Whatever." She waves her hand. "Seriously, what are you going to do about Brad? You can't just let this go."

"What choice do I have? He said it's business. As far as I know, he hasn't seen anyone else since we started dating. We're together every Saturday night," I point out.

"Yes, but there are six other days in the week. What does he do on those other nights?" She dangles a fry at me.

"Quit eating my fries." I grab it out of her hand. "If you wanted fries, why didn't you order them yourself?"

"Because I don't want to get fat."

"And my fries aren't fattening?"

"I won't eat as many if we share, and neither will you. You should thank me," she huffs.

"Thanks," I say sarcastically and hand her the fry back.

"You know Doug would never cheat on me," she says. "He's too scared of me. Besides, he knows I'd flip out or kill him. *Or* flip out *and* kill him."

"Uh, huh."

"In the worst way I can think of."

I look at my watch. I should be home. I have a mountain of laundry to do. How does the laundry accumulate so fast? It seems like I just did it. I'd already thrown potatoes and veggies into the crock pot, so it'll be percolating away making dinner for later and will fill the apartment with an enticing aroma. The kids will get home from visiting their friends soon. I have to remember to ask them if they did their homework. They always wait till the last minute. I also have to remind Lacie to return her library book or I can drop it off on my way home from work tomorrow.

"But I'm beginning to have my suspicions."

"What?" I suddenly return to what Marcy has said.

The boys next to us are leaving and one of them

bumps my chair. It will be quieter with them gone. The girls giggle and watch them. They probably have crushes on these rude boys. Why don't we have common sense when we're younger? Or older.

"Huh?"

Marcy said something that I missed. She shoots me an annoyed look.

"Am I boring you?"

"No. I was thinking about what I should do when I get home." I look at my watch again. "Anyway, Doug would never cheat on you. He adores you. You know that. And you just said he's too scared of you."

"He's been *working late* a lot." She puts air quotes around "working late."

"So what? He's working late. You can trust him. If he says he's working late, then he's working late."

"You're too trusting."

"You're too suspicious," I respond.

"He's a man," she answers.

"I'm sure he's really working late."

"But how do I *know* for sure?"

I shrug. "You know you can trust him, Marcy."

"Unless..." She raises her eyebrows.

"Unless what?" I ask slowly.

"Do you want to cement the bonds of our friendship?"

"Our bonds are pretty cemented. I've been letting you eat all my fries. Unless what?"

"Unless you sit outside his office and see if he goes somewhere after work."

"Are you crazy? I'm not doing that."

"You owe me."

"What do I owe you for?"

"Probably something."

"Why don't *you* do it?"

"Because he knows my car, and I can't risk him seeing me. Besides, he'll think I don't trust him."

"You don't!" I cry.

Marcy leans toward me and lowers her voice as if we're discussing a covert mission. "You work close to him and get off before he does. I could never make it over there in time. You could run over there after work and follow him to see where he goes when he leaves."

"I'm not doing that. No way." I shake my head adamantly.

"I *have* to know for sure," she insists.

"Oh, my God." I lean back in my chair and eat the last of my fries. "And after I shared my fries with you."

"Thanks, Vera." She smiles. "I owe you."

"I told you I'm not doing it." I cross my arms.

Chapter 13

What was I thinking? Why do I let Marcy talk me into these things? I'm angry at myself as I sit in my parked car in a strip mall parking lot across the street facing Doug's office building. It's a red brick building and there's a glare bouncing off a window right into my eyes. How am I supposed to see him come out? And what if he already left work? There are many flaws in this plan. I'm afraid to take my eyes off the entrance for a second, as that would most likely be the moment he exits.

It's hot and stuffy in my car. I opened my window and now there's a fly buzzing around the interior along the dashboard. I try to swat it out the window, but it evades me. I just want to go home. I deliberate it. I don't have to be here. I can tell Marcy I won't be a party to this. I can tell her to do it herself. I can tell her...

I sit up straight as the door of the building opens and two women step out talking and laughing. One holds the door open for a man behind her. I squint. Is that Doug? I watch for a moment. No. Not Doug. Unsuspecting Doug. I feel awful for spying on him.

I pull out my flip phone and look at the time. How long would be realistic to wait before I can tell Marcy I did my best? This is ridiculous. Why do I let her talk me into things? There was the time we followed a girl home from school when Marcy thought she was seeing Doug. We kept jumping into bushes and even attempted hiding behind a telephone pole when she turned around.

"I see you," she'd called out to us.

I felt like such an idiot. Doug hadn't been seeing anyone but Marcy. It was just her foolish fears.

There was also the time we'd followed her father, who actually had been cheating on her mother. That

91

was where all this mistrust had begun. I was shocked at the time that Marcy had been right. What a disaster that had been.

I hear a car door open beside me. A woman is ushering her child into the back seat where she fastens him into his car seat. After she straightens up and shuts the door, she turns my way. I give her a weak smile and pretend to look at my phone.

The fly sails past me out the window, and I look up to see Doug crossing the street. Has he seen me? My heart pounds as I duck down. The woman next to me gives me a strange look as she starts her car and backs up. I must look like a lunatic.

I peek my head up and look straight at Doug as he sees me. My eyes widen and he looks a bit startled but jogs over to my window.

Doug has red hair, freckles, and a trim beard and mustache. His skin reddens easily if he spends too much time in the sun. That's why Marcy and I would take the kids to the beach without him. She would obsess about what he was doing while she was gone, but I always defended him. He never had an ulterior motive. He just didn't want to get sunburned.

I study his face as he draws closer. He isn't a great-looking guy, but there's something appealing about him. It must be his eyes. He has kind eyes, trusting eyes. I immediately feel regret. I'm going to kill Marcy for making me do this.

"Vera, what are you doing here?" He leans down, resting his hand on the top of my car.

It hadn't even occurred to me to have an alibi ready in case he saw me. Some detective I am. I get spotted and have no alibi.

"Uh..." I hope my face isn't getting red like it does when I can't lie. "I was..."

Damn. Why hadn't I looked at the stores so I could say I was shopping? I am *never* letting Marcy talk me into spying on anyone ever again. She can do her own snooping from now on.

"Yeah." He looks around squinting in the sun. "I hope Marcy didn't talk you into following me." He chuckles.

"Oh. Funny." I force a laugh.

"She's so paranoid."

His wedding ring flashes in the sun. Some guys don't even wear rings. He wears his proudly.

"Want to have a drink?" He nods his head toward a tavern at the end of the strip mall.

"I should..."

"Come on. It's hot. It's been a long day. You just got off work, right?"

"All right."

I can't think why not, so I grab my purse and close my window. He opens my car door and I step out. I'm wearing dress slacks and a thin blouse that's sticking to me.

The tavern is dark and busy and air-conditioned. The cool air feels good after the suffocating heat of my car. I follow Doug to a table, and he asks me what I want. I want to go home but tell him a Pina Colada.

"Ah, going tropical. Excellent choice." He grins. "I'll be right back."

I watch him wend his way to the bar as I fret about my pending report to Marcy. I scan the work crowd and plan what to tell her. She's going to be upset that he spotted me. I try to come up with excuses. The sun was in my eyes. It's true. There was a glare off the windows of the building. The lady with the kid distracted me. There was a fly in the car. She hates flies. She might be sympathetic to that one.

I suddenly think I see Brad and my heart jumps. What would he think if he saw me having a drink with another man? Would he feel jealous? Would it make him realize he prefers being exclusive rather than risk losing me? But no, it's not him. He'd never come to a place like this. I think I see Brad all the time. It must be wishful thinking.

A server places a basket of chips and a small bowl of salsa on the table. "Can I get you something?"

"No, thanks. My friend…"

Doug appears with a tall Pina Colada and a beer. "We're good," he tells the server.

Doug is a beer kind of guy. I can't see him drinking wine like Brad. He seats himself and unbuttons the top two buttons of his dress shirt. He tilts the bottle and takes a long slug. "Ahhh."

I smile and take a long sip through the straw jutting out of my frothy drink. "Mmm." I take another sip.

"Can I try that?" he asks. "I can't remember the last time I had one of those."

I push it toward him and he lifts it to his lips. Then he makes a face and shakes his head.

"Too sweet."

He slides it back to me, leaving a wet trail along the tabletop. I notice how cute he is. Marcy doesn't know how lucky she is. How would she handle Brad? Oh, that would never work. My mind returns to frantically trying to come up with an alibi for Doug. He'll want to know what I was doing sitting in my car across the street from his building.

"How are the kids?" he asks.

"Well, they're teenagers."

"I hear you." He's leaning back in his chair and tilts forward to scoop up salsa with a chip.

"I've never been in this place. Do you come here a lot?"

He frowns at me. He knows I'm fishing for information. I contritely look down and sip my drink. The alcohol sends lazy tendrils into all the tight places within me, and I relax.

"How's that guy you've been seeing?" Doug asks. "What's his name? How's that going?"

"Brad. Okay... I don't know." I grimace. It's hard to explain it.

"Marcy doesn't like him."

"She hasn't even met him."

He nods. "Where is he tonight?"

"Probably working. We only see each other on Saturday night and..."

"Why?"

I'm stumped by the question. "He works a lot. We both work. I have kids."

"Do you see other people then?"

"*I* don't but..." My voice trails off and I sip my drink.

He leans his elbows on the table. At some point, he must've rolled up his sleeves. I study the light hair on his arms. I can get a man's opinion here, an *honest* opinion.

I lean forward as well, deciding to confide in him. "I don't know what to think, Doug. I mean, I can tell he really likes me. We have incredible chemistry, but his parents don't think I'm right for him. They have money. But when we're together..."

"Yeah." He nods thoughtfully. "Some guys are jerks."

His comment surprises me.

"He's not a jerk. He treats me really well when we're together."

"Does he call you during the week? Do you talk on the phone every day?"

"He's not a big talker. He's one of those guys that's not real sentimental, you know?"

"Uh, huh." He's crunching a chip.

"How can I deal with a guy like that? How can I make him see how right we are for each other?" I'm hoping Doug will have the magic answer.

95

He leans back. "Maybe you're not."

That's not what I want to hear. I lean back too. "I think we are. He just holds himself in. How can I make him see that it's right?"

"Well, then tell me this." He leans forward again. "How can I make my wife trust me?"

Marcy is a fool. Doug is a devoted husband. He always has been. I wish Brad were so devoted.

"She's just cynical," I say.

"Why?"

"Her father cheated on her mother, and it's hard for her to trust. You know that."

"Yeah, but I'm not him." He brushes his hands together, and grains of salt and bits of chips bounce on the table. He has a small piece of chip stuck in his beard. I reach over and brush it away.

"Thanks. I'm a mess, huh?"

"You're fine." I sip on my straw. "Okay. So, why isn't Marcy here having a drink with you? Why do you come here alone?"

"You make it sound like I come here every day. What does she tell you?"

"Nothing." I shrug.

"You'd have to ask Marcy why she doesn't want to meet me for a drink. She probably thinks I drink too much beer." He stares at his beer bottle for a moment. "I don't know. She thinks I'm going to flirt with other women or something. She doesn't trust me. I only come here once or twice a week to unwind after work. Do you think that's wrong?" He suddenly looks up and his light eyes meet mine.

"No." I shake my head.

"Okay." He taps his bottle on the table.

My drink is almost finished. It was ambrosial. The tension has seeped from all the constricted places in my body. I can see why people have a drink after work before heading home. I'll have to deal with my kids. Have they done their homework? Will they be fighting over something trivial that I'll have to resolve? What will I make for dinner? I don't feel like cooking. I could pick up a pizza on my way home. It's okay to splurge now and then.

Doug taps his beer bottle against my glass. "What are you going to do about your guy?"

"What do you think I should do?"

"Dump him if he doesn't appreciate you."

I don't know what to say for a few seconds. "It's complicated."

"It always is. One person is always saner than the other."

I let out a snort-laugh.

"That was attractive," he teases.

"What are you going to do about Marcy?" I ask.

"Well, what's your report going to be? Was I a good boy? Did you catch me with another woman?"

"Yeah," I say deadpan. "Me."

We both laugh.

Chapter 14

I walk in the door with a pizza. Money is tight and I don't do this often, usually when Brad and I go out. Luke is doing his homework at the small dining table. He looks exasperated.

"I hate Algebra!" he exclaims and throws his pen.

I pick up the pen and place the pizza on the kitchen counter. I'm not proficient at math, but Lacie excels at it.

"What's your sister doing?" I can hear music blasting from her room.

"She won't help me," he grumbles. "And I'm not asking her."

Call me! Marcy texts.

Tomorrow, I text back. She knows I have limited texting, so I hope she leaves me alone the rest of the evening.

"Lace." I approach her closed door. "Lacie." I knock.

"What?" She flings open her door with that petulant look that teenagers give their parents.

"What are you doing?" Why did I ask her that? It will make her defensive.

"Nothing. Listening to music. Why?" She narrows her eyes.

"What is it? I like it," I say to diffuse her mood.

She shows me the CD cover of an obscure band.

"Hmm." I pretend more interest than I feel. "Oh, hey, can you help your brother with Algebra? He's stuck."

"Mo-om," she moans.

"Please, Lace. Real quick so we can get his books off the table. Then we can have pizza."

"Pizza?" Her face lights up. She heads toward the kitchen without lowering her music. I discreetly shut her door and follow her.

"Don't just give him the answers," I call after her.

What happened??? Another text from Marcy.

I change into sweatpants and a T-shirt and find my kids in the kitchen eating pizza while working on Luke's homework. So much for eating together, but this is good. They're not yelling and killing each other.

"You got the right answer. See?" Lacie says patiently. "They just want you to show how you got it."

"I don't know how I got it," Luke groans.

I duck back into my bedroom to call Marcy before she texts me again. She's relentless. Obviously, Doug hasn't said anything to her and is letting her wallow in her overactive imagination. She probably deserves it. I still don't know what to say to her, but there's no way I'm doing anything like this again. That's for sure. Though it was nice unwinding with Doug.

"It's about time." She answers the phone this way. "I'm losing my marbles over here."

"Sorry I have a life. And kids," I say sarcastically.

"Did you see him?"

"Is he home? Did he say anything to you?"

"He's watching the news on TV. Why? What happened? Did he see you?"

I'm debating whether to let her suffer longer. She's clearly creating a problem where there is none. I think about how lackadaisical Doug was about it, how he puts up with her mistrust, how lucky she is to have someone who wants to be with her and have a beer with her. Someone who doesn't subject her to his disapproving parents and "friend" dates. Someone who gets the significance of Valentine's Day cards and bunches of flowers and compliments and lets her choose what to drink and...

"What? What is it?" she demands urgently in a

hushed voice. "What did you see? Who is she? Do I need a lawyer? Shit!"

"He went to that tavern in that little strip mall across from his work and had a beer."

"I knew I could smell it on him."

"He's entitled to have a beer after work, Marcy. He just had one. It was really hot and he..."

"Was he alone?"

"Um. No. He wasn't sitting alone."

"Who was he with? Work buddies or a woman? Why are you making me drag this out of you?"

"Well, he was actually with a woman..." I'm enjoying this.

"I knew it! What did she look like? Did you take a picture?"

"No, I didn't take a picture." I laugh. "I'm not a real detective. In fact..."

"Was she pretty? Please don't tell me she was pretty. Is she younger than us?"

"She's our age. You could say she's pretty."

Marcy told me I was pretty when we were teenagers. She said she envied my looks because I could twist boys around my finger, but I never knew how to do that. I was too honest to be manipulative. Maybe I'd had a certain power all along, and if I learned how to use it, I'd be much better off in life. But who wants to be liked just for their looks?

"I'm going to kill him."

"Marcy." I laugh as I come back to the conversation.

"Why are you laughing?" she demands. "This isn't funny."

"Marcy, calm down," I say. "It was me. Okay? He saw me in my car and invited me to have a drink with him."

"Oh, my God! Why didn't you just tell me that in the first place? You gave me a heart attack. I was ready to hire a lawyer."

"Sorry." But I really wasn't.

"Anyway, how could you let him see you?"

"Oh, well, there was this glare on the building..."

"The building is brick."

"On the windows. The glare was in my eyes..."

"Really, Vera?"

"There was a fly in my car and then this woman with a kid..."

"You're not very good at this."

"That's exactly why I didn't want to do it," I assert.

"Mom!" It's Luke.

"Be right there," I call.

"And wait a minute. Why were *you* having a drink with *my* husband? Whose side are you on?"

I groan. "It's unbelievable how paranoid you are. Now you don't trust *me*?"

"I trust you, but why would you cozy up to my husband and have a drink..."

"Marcy! I wasn't *cozying* up to him. You're crazy. I don't know how Doug puts up with it."

"Okay. I didn't mean that. You know I didn't mean that."

"I know, but how do you think it makes him feel knowing you don't trust him?" I reason. "He saw me and I'm sure he figured out right away that you had me spying on him. Just like that time in high school when we followed that girl, and you were wrong then too."

She doesn't respond.

"How would it make you feel if you knew he didn't trust you?" I argue. "Especially when you haven't done anything, and there's no reason..."

"Okay. Okay," she says. "I get it."

"Good. I'm going to go eat dinner with my kids if there's any left."

"Yeah. Talk tomorrow."

"Be nice to Doug," I advise. "He's a good one." I

hope she listens.

I stand a moment, trying to pick up the thread of a thought from a few moments before. Brad didn't just like me for my looks, did he? My looks had probably initially enticed him. That was to be expected, but we went to dinner and movies, had conversations and adopted a dog together, sort of. If he was only interested in the way I looked, he wouldn't take me anywhere, unless he wanted to show me off. But he wasn't like that, and I wasn't the type of beautiful woman a man would flaunt. Then a comforting thought occurs to me. He made an effort with my kids by putting them to work at his house. He surely wouldn't have done that if he was only interested in me superficially.

But a question still nags at me. One that Doug brought up. Why doesn't he call me during the week? I think about him all week long. Doesn't he think of me? Doesn't he want to hear my voice or connect with me in some way? Doesn't he *miss* me?

Lacie and Luke are on the couch watching TV. Bits of pizza crust are on plates on the coffee table.

"Was the pizza good?" I ask, picking up the plates.

They both mumble a response.

"Luke, did you finish your homework?"

"Yeah." His eyes remain on the TV.

"Thanks for helping him, Lacie." I turn toward the kitchen.

"Thanks for the pizza, Mom," she says.

"Yeah, thanks," Luke echoes.

Unprompted thanks. How nice is that? I place one plate on the counter by the sink and snag a slice for myself that I put on the other plate.

I join my kids on the couch, but my thoughts are elsewhere. I miss Brad. I wish he were here sitting with us having a family evening. I envision what it would be like. He probably would've helped Luke with his homework while I had prepared dinner. We would've sat around the table sharing our days, laughing and teasing each other. Coco would wag her tail, begging for scraps. My kids would enjoy having a dog. We'd be living in a house instead of an apartment. It would be quieter. Noise from the neighbors wouldn't seep through the walls.

Brad would like the feeling of family, comfortable and casual, not formal and uptight like his. He's really taken to Coco, and deep down he cares for me. Why can't he see how good it can be? I just have to hang in there and be patient.

Chapter 15

It was inevitable, though I wasn't looking forward to it, and felt almost as jittery as when I'd met Brad's parents. Marcy asked when she was going to meet "this jerk." I cautioned her to be civil and had prepared myself for Brad's polite decline to meet my best friend when I tentatively broached the subject, but he surprised me and suggested the four of us have brunch together one Sunday.

"Okay, let me meet this crazy friend of yours." He relents more easily than I expected. "Let's get it over with."

Apparently, he doesn't know what he's in for. Marcy will be in protective mode, and there's no telling what she'll say to him. What terrible things had I told each about the other? This is worrisome because I'm converging my two worlds, two worlds that were most likely never meant to mingle. More like a collision, I fear. They're both outspoken and opinionated. What if they hate each other? What if they like each other? Would that be a dangerous alliance? I honestly don't know what to hope for. Only that they get along and not judge me for the other.

Both my kids had spent the night at their friends' while I had spent the night at Brad's. We arrange to meet Marcy and Doug at a place that featured a build-your-own-omelet buffet. It was Brad's favorite brunch place. The food was delicious and probably pricey. I'd never looked at the prices, but I thought it would be a good place to take my kids sometime. I vowed to splurge one Sunday and bring them there.

Marcy and Doug pull into the parking lot at the same time as we do. I wave to Marcy while Doug parks his car. They get out and walk over to where we're standing by Brad's car. They're dressed nicely. Marcy is even wearing a skirt. She and I embrace, and I introduce everyone. The guys shake hands.

I glance at Marcy, and she slightly raises her eyebrows that I decipher to mean she thinks Brad is good looking. I give her a brief nod. I hope we don't dissolve into a laughing fit, which frequently possesses us without warning when we get together. I already feel a bit giddy.

Brad holds open the door for everyone, and we're quickly seated in a booth despite the place appearing busy. I wonder if it's a coincidence or because of Brad's frequent patronage.

"I made a reservation," he says as we settle in the booth, answering my silent question.

It wouldn't have occurred to me to do that. I have so much to learn. We all order orange juice, and I recall the time Marcy made me laugh so hard that orange juice came out of my nose. Or was it some other beverage? I decide not to share this memory with everyone, though it would tickle her.

It's a little noisy but, as it's late morning, people have started to clear out. We get in line for the omelet buffet and return to the table with our plates laden with all things brunch related.

"This looks good. I'm hungry," Doug says. I'm grateful he's broken the awkward silence.

"I hear you have kids," Brad says.

Marcy launches into a diatribe about their kids, which Doug tries to temper with humor. One of their sons isn't getting good grades, and the other mercilessly teases the other.

"You're lucky you don't have kids," Marcy says to Brad. "They're evil spawn."

I laugh because I get Marcy's humor, but I'm sure Brad doesn't know what to think. We should get onto another subject, but I can't think of anything quickly enough.

"So, Doug, what do you do?" Brad asks.

Thank you, Brad! I shoot Marcy a look and she shrugs.

Doug talks about his job, and soon Brad is describing what he does. I'm glad the guys are getting along. I zone out a bit when they discuss construction and concentrate on my food. I try not to meet Marcy's eyes, so we won't spontaneously start giggling for no reason.

"We hardly ever go out for brunch," Doug declares. "I think I'll have a drink. Do they have a bar here? A Mimosa sounds good. What's in a Mimosa, anyway?"

"They have a bar. It's orange juice and champagne," Brad says and summons the server. "Can you make these orange juices into Mimosas for us?"

"Absolutely," she says with a bright smile.

"Unless you want something else." He turns to me.

"You had a Pina Colada that time at the bar," Doug reminds me.

"I'll have a Mimosa," I tell the server.

"For everyone?" She looks around the table and everyone assents.

"You had a Pina Colada that night?" Marcy asks me as if it's a betrayal.

"What night?" Brad asks.

"The night my husband and your girlfriend had a date," Marcy says wryly.

"Doug and I had drinks after work one day," I clarify, waving my hand flippantly.

"The time my wife asked Vera to follow me to make sure I wasn't meeting some other woman after work." Doug isn't embarrassed to share this tidbit of information. Why have they opened this can of worms?

Brad raises his eyebrows. "You don't trust your

husband?" he asks Marcy.

"Oh, I trust him." She smiles sweetly at Doug. "I just had to be sure."

"As you do," Brad mutters.

Thankfully, the drinks arrive at that moment, and we each take a long essential sip.

"Orange juice and champagne," I say to redirect the subject. "Yum."

"I like it," Doug announces.

We talk about drinks for a while, and everyone shares their favorite drinks or an unusual drink they've had. Then Brad delves into expensive wines, and I catch Marcy rolling her eyes. I hope Brad doesn't notice. I try to kick her but can't find her leg under the table and don't want to kick Doug accidentally.

"That's too rich for us," Doug says. "We're simple folk. I'm more of a beer guy."

"How long have you two been together?" Brad points his drink at them.

"Long enough to have two kids and lose track," Marcy says.

"Let's see." Doug furrows his brow, and I discern how mellow he is and how much I like him. He balances out Marcy perfectly. Again, I think how lucky Marcy is. "Sixteen years. Yeah, it's been sixteen years and going strong."

Marcy leans forward and I don't like the look on her face. I should've known better than to let her have alcohol during this initial meeting. Her glass holds only a few more sips by now. Did she drink that fast or am I drinking slow?

"So, Brad." She has a funny little smile on her face, like she expects to catch him in a lie. "What about you and Vera? Do you have honorable intentions?"

Doug is a little buzzed, and he laughs. "Honorable," he repeats.

This time I do kick Marcy under the table.

"Ow." Doug grabs his shin.

"Sorry, Doug. I was crossing my legs," I blurt.

Darn. Where is her leg under there?

"Well, Brad?" Marcy presses.

I shoot her a warning look, but she ignores me. At the same time, I'm curious to hear his response.

"Who knows what the future holds?" Brad downs the rest of his drink, unflustered by her question. Cool as a cucumber as usual.

"Vera is my best friend in the world, and she deserves the best," Marcy intones.

"Yes, she does," Brad agrees. "No argument."

"No argument," Doug repeats with a lackadaisical grin.

Marcy glares at Brad. How can she argue with someone who agrees with her?

She turns to me. "Didn't you tell me he's conservative? What's up with that?"

"I lean conservative, but I'd really call myself a centrist," Brad answers unprovoked. "I'm sure we lean more in the same direction than you think."

"Lean?" she says.

I shake my head at her. "Let's not get into politics."

"Doug." She elbows him. "Say something."

"Marcy, let's go to the restroom," I suggest.

Brad lets me out of the booth, and Marcy stalks after me. I contain my anger as we weave around tables, patrons, and staff. I smile cordially until I push open the door to the restroom.

"Are you out of your mind?" I demand as soon as we're safely behind closed doors. "Why are you picking fights with him?"

"What?" She puts up her hands defensively.

"Can't you behave yourself for one meal?"

I go into a stall, and I hear her do the same.

"I so want you to like each other," I say as I wash

my hands. "Can't you see how important this is to me?"

"All right. I'm sorry. Whatever."

"You're so hard on everyone."

"I'm just direct." Then she smiles. "He's cute, though."

"Right?" I brighten. "He really is amazing. Give him a chance. Please?"

"Fine."

"I can't take you anywhere," I say.

"I know. I'm so inappropriate. Can you tell I don't get out much?"

We return to the table, and I plaster on a pleasant smile as I take a long sip of my remaining Mimosa.

"So, how come you had a birthday party and didn't invite Vera?" Marcy demands.

"Marcy!" I admonish.

"Marcy." Doug shakes his head at her, and I give him an exasperated look.

"I wasn't in charge of the guest list," Brad says, unperturbed by her barrage of attacks. "It was mostly my parents' friends."

"We had our own celebration," I add.

"Vera gave me the best present."

"I bet she did," Marcy murmurs.

I ignore her remark and vow to kill her later. "You remember. I told you about that little house I found when I was at the mall with the kids. Brad has it on his desk," I say.

"It was perfect." Brad smiles at me.

"What house?" Doug asks, and I describe it for him as he nods.

"Okay. Okay." Marcy holds up her hands. "You guys are kind of cute together. I give you my approval."

"I approve, too." Doug holds up his glass and sees it's empty.

"More drinks?" the server stops by and asks.

"No," Brad and I say together.

"Okay, then. When you're ready." She places the bill on the table.

Brad picks it up and takes out his wallet.

"Hey, let me give you something for that." Doug extracts his wallet from his back pocket.

"No. I got this." Brad waves his money away. "I just sold a house."

"You did?" It was news to me. I knew he'd been working on two other houses, but he hardly ever talked about them, and I hadn't been good about asking. I make a mental note to take more interest in his work.

"Appreciate it, Brad. We'll get it next time," Doug says.

"Thank you," I say sincerely. Money is tight for Marcy and Doug.

"Yeah, thanks," Marcy echoes.

Out in the sunshine, Marcy and I embrace again and Brad shakes Doug's hand. We say our goodbyes and get into our separate cars. I'm thinking of fifty different ways to kill Marcy.

"Whoo. Your friend is a lunatic." Brad laughs as he backs up.

"Sorry about that."

What can I say? He's gone above and beyond and didn't allow Marcy to get to him. I'm more impressed than ever with his social aplomb. Either things slide off his back or he keeps them in. Perhaps things don't affect him emotionally and only us lesser beings get caught up in the turmoil of our moods.

"I like Doug, though. Nice guy."

"Yeah. He is." Who doesn't like Doug?

"How does he put up with her?"

"He knows she's not that bad. She means well. Her bark is worse than her bite."

"Why put up with a bark or a bite?" he asks, turning onto the main road.

"I don't know. It works for them. He balances her out."

"Right. She's a little uptight and intense."

"Sorry. I didn't know she was going to interrogate you like that."

"Well, I guess we're even now. You had to put up with meeting my parents. Now we've both been through the fire."

I laugh and appreciate his understanding and making light of it.

"I can see that she cares about you as a friend. She's looking out for you," he says.

"Yes, that's for sure."

My anger is abating. Marcy was doing it for me. She's protective, a true friend. Okay, maybe I won't kill her.

"You want somebody like that on your side."

"Yeah," I agree

"But, V?"

"What?"

"Never ask me to do that again."

Chapter 16

"I should, but I won't kill you for your rude behavior toward my boyfriend," I say to Marcy that evening on the phone.

By now I've mellowed and am feeling much better about the day. I made a hearty lentil and veggie stew for dinner and feel like I've met my maternal responsibilities by feeding my kids a healthy meal, though they'd begged for fast food. I'd recently discovered that bulk beans were more cost efficient than meat and probably healthier. It was always good to save money while eating better. Way to stretch a dollar!

"I never knew you had such a penchant for violence," Marcy responds drolly.

"Well, you said you were going to kill your husband recently," I remind her.

"Hmm. Sounds like we're both psycho killers."

"You're lucky I don't believe in violence."

"Just threats," she says.

"Guess I didn't scare you."

I peek into the kitchen. I'd asked Lacie to do the dishes because Luke hadn't done his homework yet and it was due tomorrow. Lacie had finished hers. I didn't want to punish her for this, so I told her I'd make sure Luke cleaned up next time. We rotated their chores to be fair, and both my kids had learned to clean thoroughly by now. Lacie was at the sink with the water running and Luke was at the table. I duck back into the hallway to continue my conversation with Marcy.

"Seriously, he seems like a decent guy," she was saying. "It was really nice of him to pay."

"I know. I've been telling you."

"But I don't get it."

"Get what?"

"No offense, but he's out of your league. His family has money, and he's more... I don't know, refined than us."

"That's what I thought, too."

"He's good looking, and you said his parents are trying to set him up with other women."

Doubts scatter through my thoughts again. Darn her for deflating my happiness with reality.

"His parents will never let him marry you, you know."

"Will you stop saying that to me?" I ask impatiently.

"I don't think you should get your hopes up."

This isn't what I want to hear. I want her to tell me how wonderful he is. How lucky I am. How I've finally hit the relationship jackpot. All the losers I've dated are a thing of the past. There are no more dark clouds hanging over me. The sun has come out and will shine brightly on me and my kids from now on.

"I just need this to work," I say softly. "We could move into his beautiful house and have nice things and not stress about money ever again. I don't want to worry if I can afford to buy food or pay my rent or pay my bills."

"I know," Marcy says sympathetically.

"I want to be happy. I want my kids to be happy. I want Brad to be happy. With us. With his dog, Coco. We could be a family. Why can't he see that?"

"Maybe he does," she says. "It could all work out. What do I know?"

My eyes fill with tears. The extent of my desperation sometimes brims over. I can't keep it tamped down for long. It engulfs me, and it's exhausting. I wipe my eyes with my fingers before my kids see me. I try not to let them see me cry. I don't want to burden them with the troubles I carry around daily.

"He's short," I say.

"I noticed."

"I mean, that might be why he's available. I don't think women like being taller than men."

"That's true," she says. "A lot of women like tall men."

"Right. So, he probably finds my height appealing."

"You're the right height for him," she comments.

"Exactly."

"Okay. Big bonus points for you. I didn't think of that."

"I hope this works out."

"Me too. I double really do, Vera. If anybody deserves it, you do. I hate that asshole ex-husband of yours. I still think you should go after him for support."

"I don't even know where he is. He probably has nothing anyway."

"Yeah, well..."

"What about you? Are you being nice to Doug? He's a good guy."

"Yeah. But I have to keep him on his toes," she says. "I'm trying to trust him."

"You should."

"But I checked his texts when he was in the shower."

"Marcy!"

"And his emails."

"Oh, my God, Marcy."

"Aren't you going to ask me if I found anything?"

"Did you?"

"Nothing."

"Then you should trust him now."

"I will."

"Okay."

"For now."

I groan and she laughs.

"You know, if you think about it, things are sort

of good for both of us right now," she points out.

"Things are easier for a change," I say. "It's like Brad is there for me. He got that plumber over here when my toilet didn't work. I don't know what I would've done."

"Did the apartment manager get the owner to pay for it?"

"They won't," I tell her. "They said they have their own plumber, and we shouldn't have paid for one."

"You could take them to small claims court."

"Brad paid for it. He said not to worry about it."

Marcy is quiet for a moment. "If a guy pays to have your toilet fixed, he really cares about you," she pronounces.

I laugh. "So that's the criteria now?"

"Yes," she says emphatically. "Any guy you date, you have to break your toilet and see if he pays to fix it."

"What if I date a plumber?"

"That's cheating!" she cries.

We both laugh.

"This has something to do with names," she says slowly.

"What are you talking about?"

"Good-looking guys have certain names. You know, like Brad, while guys named Doug are average looking."

"I think Doug is cute."

"Shut up. That's my husband, but really, Brad guys are good looking."

I ponder this. "What about women?"

"That's an interesting question. Obviously, Veras are pretty and Marcys are average."

I laugh again. Marcy always makes me laugh. She comes up with the oddest theories and observations.

"That's not true! Marcys are crazier than the

average population, though."

"Hey!"

We dissolve into laughter once again.

"What?" I hear Marcy call out to someone. "I'm on the phone with Vera."

I wait.

"Doug says hi," she tells me.

"Say hi back," I say. "Oh, what did he think of Brad?"

"He didn't say much."

"I just want to get a guy's opinion..."

I hear the phone fumble around.

"Hi, Vera," Doug says.

"Hi, Doug."

"That was cool of Brad to treat us this morning. He didn't have to do that. I could've paid for us."

"I know," I assure him. "Brad's like that. He's generous."

"Well, we'll pay next time."

It's sweet that Doug assumes there will be a next time.

"Okay. I'll tell him," I say. "I wanted to ask you what you thought, you know, of Brad. I want to get a guy's take on him."

"He seems like an okay guy. He put up with Marcy's questioning pretty well. He's a good sport."

"Right, but I was more interested in what you thought of... us. Together. Could you get a sense of how serious he is or..."

"Yeah, that's tough... Uh..."

"Doug, please be honest. Did you get any sense of how he feels about me?" I persist.

"Uh... I don't know. He paid attention to how you were doing. You know, if your meal was okay and did you want another drink. He... I don't know. You looked like a couple to me."

"We did?" I like the sound of that.

"Well, yeah."

116

"We still only see each other on weekends," I tell him.

"He sounds kind of busy. He was telling me about the work he does on those houses," he says. "He has some long days."

"Yeah," I say thoughtfully. "Thanks, Doug."

"Sure. Here's Marcy back."

"Did he break the Brad code?" Marcy asks.

"I wish." But Doug's assessment is encouraging.

Chapter 17

The house is quiet except for the thumping of Coco's tail on the floor. She'd lifted her head when I woke up. I always woke before Brad and liked to watch him in slumber, steadily breathing deep into his mysterious dreams, the closeness of his body warming me. Does he ever have sweet dreams of me? What does he dream?

Coco is looking at me expectantly. I slip silently out of bed to let her out. We pad down the hallway together, and I open the sliding glass door off the family room. She darts out and sniffs around until she finds a good place to squat. I shut the door. She won't mind being out for a while.

I stop at the bathroom and return to the quiet bedroom and quickly dress to go home. Lacie and Luke will still be asleep for a few more hours, and I can make pancakes for breakfast when they get up.

Brad yawns as I put on my shoes.

"Are you going home?"

"Yeah."

"Okay."

He turns over and goes back to sleep. Oh, well, that's the way he is. I'm used to it by now. I go outside and pet Coco for a few minutes before letting her back into the house so I can open the gate and drive out. I stand looking at the window of Brad's bedroom. I wish I didn't have to leave and we could spend the day together. He told me he had to go to one of his houses today and finish painting. I long to go with him and paint beside him. He'd probably welcome the company. I can see us working side by side, talking and laughing.

With a resigned sigh, I dig in my purse to find my keys and pull open the car door. The interior is cold, but it will heat up once I start driving. I stick

118

the key in the ignition and turn. Nothing. I try again and again. It won't start. Oh, my God. What now? I can't afford car repairs, and now I'm stuck at Brad's house and he's asleep. I don't want to wake him with one of my stupid problems. What would Brad do? If I let the car sit, it might start. It could be flooded or something.

I exit the cold car and go sit in one of the wooden deck chairs on the small patio in the early morning sunlight. It's peaceful, if a bit chilly.

I try not to dwell on car repairs and costs. I can't get to work without my car, and I can't afford repairs, especially if I can't get to work. I tell myself to be stoic like Brad. It might be nothing and it will start up in a few minutes or it could be something easy that Brad can tweak and it'll start and I'll be on my way. There could be loose wires on the battery. I should probably lift the hood and take a look. If it doesn't start in a few minutes, I'll do that. At least when Brad gets up, it'll look like I'm doing something besides freaking out like I usually do. Eventually he's going to tire of rescuing me.

I put my head in my hands. *Don't cry*, I tell myself firmly. The last thing I need is for Brad to find me crying on his patio. Why does something always have to go wrong? Why can't things ever be easy?

Brad slides open the door and steps out. He's still in his boxers and T-shirt. "What's wrong?"

Coco runs over to me, whipping her tail furiously. At least she's glad I'm still here.

"You're up," I say, forcing a smile.

"Coco started licking my hand and woke me up." He looks at my car. "Your car?"

I grimace. "Won't start."

"Give me the keys." He holds out his hand, and I place the keys in it.

He walks over barefoot and gets in. I hope it will start and hold my breath. Nope. He gets out and

119

looks underneath it.

"There's water."

"There is?"

"Has it overheated lately?"

"No."

"It might be your water pump."

My mind races. How much will that cost? How will I get it to a garage? How long will it take? How will I get to work?

"Don't panic, V." He walks over and pats my shoulder. "I have AAA. They can tow it over to my mechanic."

One problem solved but...

"How about this?" He squints down at me. "I'll loan you my car until yours is fixed."

"But what will you drive?"

"I have my work truck."

"Really?"

My spirits rise at the thought of driving Brad's newer car for a day or two. He trusts me with his car.

"I'll call my mechanic tomorrow and see when he can fit it in," he says. "He should be able to get it done this week."

I hope not for a few days at least so I can drive Brad's car. I look over at the garage door. His silver Camry sits unsuspecting inside.

"I filled the gas tank yesterday so you shouldn't have to buy gas. You won't put too many miles on it just driving to work."

He walks over and enters the code to open the garage. The door jolts and slowly rolls upward. Coco trots into the garage to sniff around and comes galloping back.

"Brad, thank you so much," I gush.

"I'll get the keys. I know you have to go." He waves his hand at Coco. "Inside, Coco."

I see I've left the gate open. Brad returns wearing

jeans but still barefoot. He backs the car out for me and faces it toward the street.

"The brakes are really sensitive," he cautions. "I'll get your car towed and let you know what my mechanic says. Okay?"

"You're a lifesaver," I say gratefully.

I long to grab him into a hug but restrain myself. Instead, I grab my purse from my car and get into Brad's. I adjust the seat and mirrors and peruse the dashboard. Brad leans in and points.

"Here are your lights and here are the wipers, but it shouldn't rain this week." He straightens. "I'll call you when I know something. Don't worry, okay?"

Easy for him to say.

"Should I be here for the tow truck?" I squint up at him.

"No, it's fine. I've got the keys. Is there anything you need in the car?"

"No."

"Okay."

He shuts the car door and steps back. I return his wave and put the car in gear. It drives so much more smoothly than mine. I can't wait until it warms up so I can open the sunroof. Momentarily, I forget about my troublesome car. Driving this car changes the way I feel. I feel lighter, luckier, less like mere baggage in the world and more like I belong. It sounds silly, but it's funny how your perception of yourself and your feeling of worth hinge on your net worth and material things. Buoyant optimism replaces the dark cloud that usually hovers over me. Brad wouldn't lend me his car if he didn't trust me, if he didn't think of me as someone special in his life.

I make pancakes for breakfast, and the kids awaken sleepily drawn into the kitchen.

"What happened?" Lacie perceives my upbeat mood.

"Look outside in the parking lot," I respond.

121

She stands in front of the window, peering out.

"I don't see anything."

"Do you see our car?"

"No. Where is it?"

"Did the car break down again?" Luke asks, joining her at the window.

"Yes," I answer. "I'm driving Brad's car until ours is fixed."

They stare out the window for a moment, letting this news soak in.

"Can we go to the mall?" Luke blurts.

"Okay." I laugh.

I welcome excuses to drive the car. I enjoy it. I like to pretend it's mine. This will also give me an excuse to drop by Marcy's because she lives on the way to the mall. Her birthday is in a few days, and I've already sent her a card, but I could also pick up something at the mall for her. What's a few more charges on the credit card?

The kids rush through breakfast, and I clean up the kitchen while they get ready to go. A newer Camry isn't a luxury car to most people, but to me it is, and it'll be fun to show it off. Marcy will also get the significance of Brad letting me drive his car. I text her quickly to make sure she'll be home. She texts back that Doug is over at his friend's where they'll drink beer and Doug will pretend to help him tune up his car. Doug knows nothing about cars.

"Open the sunroof," Lacie demands once in the car.

I oblige and let the brightness of the day spill into the interior along with a refreshing breeze. I slowly pull out of the parking lot, hoping some of my neighbors will see us and upgrade their opinions of me. I always feel like I come off as a poverty-stricken single mother, which I am, but I want people to see I'm more than that. This makes sense to me at the time, as my ego is so fragile and beaten down.

"I wish we could have a car like this," Lacie laments.

Me too. Her statement gives me a little twinge of despair that I can't provide things like a decent car that doesn't break down all the time for my kids, but today we're driving in style, and it feeds my dreams for the future.

At the mall, Lacie and Luke scatter in different directions, and we agree to meet up in an hour. I'm going to buy a birthday present for Marcy and head over to the gourmet candy store because she loves peanut brittle. I buy her a pound, which doesn't look like much, but it should be enough to give her a few well-worth-it cavities. I sneak a little piece for myself. It's addictive, but I allow myself no more and vow to return on my own birthday and buy some for myself. Maybe some fudge too. I'm practically salivating on the counter as I pay. To be able to indulge in every little whim is something I can't conceive.

Lacie meets me as agreed and has purchased a pretty T-shirt edged with lace with some of the money she'd earned from Brad. She eagerly shows me the discounted item she found on a sale rack. Finding deals always excites us.

We track Luke down in a toy store, studying the video games. He's trying to decide which one to buy, and as I wait for him, a box holding net bags of marbles grabs my attention. I laugh suddenly and impulsively grab one along with two mini Rubik's cubes and pay for my three items. Luke makes his purchase, and we exit the mall.

I hand the kids the Rubik's cubes in the car, and they immediately challenge each other to see who can solve the puzzle first.

"I'm hungry," Luke announces.

"We're going to stop at Marcy's for a little while and then we'll go home."

I've learned not to question Luke's hunger. I still feel stuffed, but he's a growing teenager.

"Can you drop us off at home first?" Lacie asks.

"Marcy's is on the way home," I say. "I promise we won't stay long."

I navigate the residential roads to her house and park in front.

"I'll be right back," I tell Lacie and Luke.

"I got your card," Marcy says with a smile when she opens the door. "Thanks."

"You're welcome." I smile back and step aside to give her a view of the curb.

She gasps. "What are you driving? Is that his car? Why are you driving his car? Where's your car?"

"Mine broke down at his house, and he's having it towed to his mechanic's."

"He gave you his car to drive?" She steps outside in her flip flops and we approach the car. "Guys, go inside," she says to my kids. "The boys are watching cartoons. There are bagels on the counter."

Luke runs into the house while Lacie saunters up the walk, still working on the Rubik's cube. "I'm going to beat you," she yells to Luke.

"Isn't it nice? It has a sunroof." I'm beaming at the car.

Marcy looks at me and nods. She recognizes the magnitude of Brad trusting me with his car. We're a real couple. This is serious.

"He's driving his truck this week, so I can have the car," I continue.

"I'm impressed."

She walks over and opens the door and nods again. She squints up at the open sunroof. "Cool."

"What are you doing for your birthday tomorrow? Is Doug taking you out?"

She sighs. "He hasn't said anything yet. He better or I'll lose my marbles, I swear."

"Why do you always say that? That you're going

to lose your marbles," I ask.

It was an odd choice of words, an expression you don't hear much nowadays. And then I remember. "Your mother used to say that."

"Yeah, it must've rubbed off on me. Just one of her many quirks that I inherited." She shrugs.

"Then it's a good thing I got you some for your birthday."

"Some what?" She gives me a bemused look as I reach into the car and pull out a small brown shopping bag. I pause dramatically before extracting the net bag of marbles with a big grin.

"Ta-da! I bought you some marbles so you'll have extra in case you lose any."

I can no longer hold in my laughter and she joins me. We let it all out, all the stress and exasperation. My eyes start to tear and Marcy is doubled over. The neighbors must think we're nuts.

"That's awesome," she gasps.

I wait until we've regained our composure before I hand her the box of peanut brittle.

"Happy birthday," I say.

"Oooh," Marcy squeals. "My favorite. Thanks, Vera. I can always count on you."

Chapter 18

My car is fixed by Wednesday and Brad wants me to come over to his house to exchange cars. He doesn't mention dinner or hanging out, so I try to convince him to let me keep the car until we see each on Saturday night.

"I need my car back, V," he says.

"I don't get paid till Friday," I tell him. "I can't give you any money for the repairs until then."

I haven't queried what was wrong with my car or how much it cost. It doesn't matter because I can't afford whatever it is. I could bring my checkbook and postdate a check, I suppose. This will really hit my budget. Back to dark clouds and reality.

"Don't worry about it for now. I just need my car back." He sounds tired.

"Okay. I'll be over as soon as I can."

I heat leftovers for the kids and remind them to do their homework. I don't take the time to eat and don't feel hungry. I drive Brad's car for the last time over to his house and pull through the open gate parking next to my poor sad little car. It's early evening and dusk is shifting the light. I stand in the quiet of the landscaped yard and look up into the darkening sky to see a brightly twinkling star.

Star light, star bright,
First star I see tonight.
Wish I may, wish I might,
Have the wish I wish tonight.

I close my eyes for a few seconds and wish with all my being that very soon my kids and I will be living in this lovely home with Brad and Coco and that everything will work out. He'll recognize what a great addition to his life we are. His parents will

126

come around and bond with my kids as true grandparents who spoil them. We'll have family holidays and...

Coco is suddenly nuzzling my hand.

"What are you doing?" Brad stands at the open door. "Close the gate so Coco doesn't run out."

I jog over and swing the black wrought-iron gate shut. Coco ignores her opportunity for freedom and runs along with me. I walk solemnly back to Brad, matching his mood. He holds open the door for me. This is encouraging. I step inside and hand him his keys back. He gives me mine.

"I was just looking at the stars. It's a nice night. Is something wrong?" I ask.

He rubs his eyes. "Just work stuff."

If this is how he is during the week, it's probably better to only see each other on Saturdays. I follow him inside, not sure if he wants me to stay.

"What's going on with work? Is there a problem at one of the houses?"

"I thought one of them sold, but the buyers backed out because the inspection turned up a plumbing issue," he tells me wearily.

"That doesn't sound too bad," I venture. "Can't you just fix it?"

"It's major. I have to re-pipe the entire house," he explains.

"That sounds expensive," I say sympathetically. "I can give you a post-dated check for the car. How much was it?" I fish in my purse for my checkbook.

He gives me a thin smile. "Don't worry about it."

"I have my checkbook right here." I show it to him. "Have you eaten? Why don't we go get something to eat? I'll treat."

Brad smiles and pats my arm, which makes me long to touch him. I've missed him. I miss him every week and count the days till Saturday.

"I picked some food up on the way home. Want

some?"

"Sure."

I follow him into the kitchen. Coco has been vying for my attention, and I squat down and pet her for a few minutes. My mind is scrambling to find something to say or do to lift Brad's mood.

"You know, I've been meaning to bring this up," I say. "Me and my kids could help you do stuff at your houses. Like paint. On the weekends. Whatever you need. You don't have to pay us. It'll be fun."

"Thanks." He gives me another slight smile.

"I like to paint," I say, though I don't recall ever painting a room in my life, but how hard can it be?

"Right now, I need plumbing help, but I'll keep it in mind," he says, and I get the feeling he's saying it to appease me when I'm trying to do something for him for a change.

He gets out plates and silverware and we sit at the island in the kitchen as we've done many times before. Coco sits staring at him expectantly, and I wonder if he throws her scraps of food.

"Do you want me to feed her?"

"She's already eaten."

"I can give you a check, Brad," I offer again. "I can afford it. Just tell me how much..."

He shakes his head. "Let's just consider this your birthday present."

My birthday is about three weeks away. For a moment, I don't know what to say. I'm disappointed that I won't find out what special gift he would've picked out for me, but immensely relieved not to have to fret about a pricey car repair.

"Okay. That's really generous. You don't have to..."

"Happy early birthday." He gives me a genuine smile.

"Thank you," I say effusively. "That really helps me out. That doesn't leave you short for the repairs at the house, does it?"

He waves his hand. "I have money set aside for things like this. I was just hoping the inspector wouldn't find it because that cuts into my profit."

I take a bite of a spring roll before his remark sets in. What? Did he just disclose that he knew about the problem? I must've heard him wrong.

"You knew about the plumbing issue?" I ask.

"We found it when we tore apart the bathroom, but I wasn't about to fix it. It's costly."

"But..." I'm bewildered. "But you shouldn't... It's wrong to stick someone else with an expensive repair when you could've..."

"It's business, Vera," he interrupts impatiently. "Everybody expects to have to repair *something* when they buy an older house."

But that's not right, I object silently. A slight crack has appeared in my smooth image of Brad. It's barely perceptible, a hairline. I could never lie, cheat, steal or swindle. No, he hasn't swindled anyone. It's the way the real estate market works. I'm just not getting it. I definitely don't have a mind for business. That's why I have a low paying hourly job and probably always will.

"So, you're fixing it now?" I confirm.

"I have to. I didn't expect them to find it. It's an extra expense I didn't plan on." He frowns.

"You won't make a profit on this house?"

He looks at me like I'm an idiot.

"I'll make money on it, just not as much as I wanted. That gives me less money to turn around and invest in another property. It just sets me back."

"Right," I blurt. "Frustrating, huh?"

I smile and push all negative thoughts aside. I must've misunderstood what he meant. Brad's a good man. He's generous and thoughtful. He saved a dog. He'd never do anything dishonest. Would he?

I take the dishes to the sink and wash them

absentmindedly, trying to wrap my head around this.

"You can't let personal feelings get in the way of making money," Brad states. "You need a certain mindset to be successful."

Well, then I'll never be successful, I think ruefully. I turn and smile and nod at Brad. Is this how his parents raised him, to be detached, to only think of his own gain? Is this how rich people get rich?

"I have to go in my office and crunch some numbers." Brad indicates the hallway that leads to his office.

"I have work tomorrow," I say.

"See you Saturday, V."

"Thanks so much for paying for my car." I grab my keys. "You help me out so much, and I appreciate it. I truly do. I wish I could do something for you."

What would I do without him? He's been so good to me, it's hard to reconcile with this new tidbit of information about his character. I'm not wrong about him. Maybe this type of issue has only come up with this one house. Yes, that's it. He's under a lot of pressure from his parents, and he feels desperate to make a sale. This is a onetime occurrence. Brad is a good person. He wouldn't routinely cheat people.

I'm deep in these musings as I drive home through the pale-yellow puddles of light cast onto the road by intermittent streetlights. Brad's home bathed in solar lights recedes in my rearview mirror. An almost full moon peers at me through the windshield, and dim stars are scattered in the night sky, hardly visible. The stars of my childhood were much brighter.

Chapter 19

By the time Saturday rolls around, I've mostly dismissed Brad's inadvertent admission chalking it up to a misunderstanding. I don't have a head for business. What do I know about construction? He knows what he's doing, and I trust him. He paid to repair my car, and I'm thankful because I don't want to keep running up my credit card. I'd made a dent in it and want to keep chipping away at my debt. But I miss driving his car.

We've been seeing each other for almost a year, and I'm sure he has deep feelings for me whether he acknowledges them or not. Driving his car has emboldened me and triggered impatience. Our relationship needs to move forward. It's hard to continue keeping my anxiety at bay. I can't stand my relentless insecurity but have never felt empowered enough to bring up a commitment to him. Now I feel compelled and vow to do so.

I drive slowly to his house, going over and over in my mind what I'll say and try to anticipate his response. I expect him to mull it over briefly and conclude that making our relationship official makes sense. All I require is a pledge to be exclusive, though I assume he has been, and for him to inform his parents that he isn't interested in dating anyone else. I want to feel legitimate, if only in his word.

My nervousness increases as I draw closer to the house. This might not be a good idea. Pressuring him could have the opposite effect. *Don't chicken out,* I tell myself. I had this conversation with Marcy, and she's all for confronting him. Easy for her to say.

Brad is out on the patio with Coco, who trots over wagging her tail. I wish Brad had the same enthusiasm when he sees me. It's still sunny out, and I sit in another wooden deck chair beside him.

If I felt more sanguine about our relationship, I would've kissed him hello. I long to do things like that, hold his hand, touch him more, express my affection. I've been playing by his rules long enough.

"Is the car running okay?" he asks.

"Yeah, it's fine, but I miss driving your car," I say with an exaggerated pout.

"I know you covet my car." He grins and hands me a section of the newspaper. "Here. Check if there are any movies you want to see."

I stare at the paper without seeing trying to get my nerve up. What am I so afraid of? I berate myself.

"Brad," I say, not sure how to begin.

"V," he answers teasingly.

"Um..." I gaze out at the flowers bobbing in the light breeze. "I... we need to talk about our relationship."

"What about it?" His tone is neutral.

"It's been almost a year..."

"Has it?"

"Yeah. We met about eleven months ago."

"Wow. Times flies when you're having fun, right?"

"Yes. I..." I turn toward him. "Things are good between us. They couldn't be better as far as I'm concerned."

I pause, waiting for him to agree, but he says nothing. He's staring out at the yard.

"Is that a bald spot in the lawn?" he asks. "I hadn't noticed that. I'll have to throw down some grass seed."

Is he even listening?

"Brad."

He looks at me. "What were you saying?"

I clear my throat. "How are things going with the house?"

"We're just finishing up. I should be able to get it back on the market next week."

"That's good news."

I pet Coco, who has dropped her ball by my feet. I toss it and touch Brad's forearm. He looks at me.

"I wanted to talk to you about our relationship."

"Okay," he says slowly.

"Everything is amazing, as I said. At least, for me. I'm going through a rough time being a single mother and not making much money right now, but things will change. I applied for a promotion at work..."

"That's great, V," he says with enthusiasm. "You just need a break."

"Exactly. My life won't be a mess forever."

Maybe he does get it, and he does see my potential. This raises my hopes.

"Anyway, we've been seeing each other for a while and things are great. So, I think it's time that we... that we should make more of a commitment, you know, like agreeing not to see other people. Not that I have. I don't want to date anyone else, and I just want to, you know, agree that we don't need to see other people. That's all."

I ramble a bit, but I'm sure he'll see the practicality. I'm not asking for much, just for validation for what I assume we already have. I'm relieved I've gotten it out. Why hadn't I done this sooner? We'd be past all this uncertainty by now.

"After all, I am Coco's mommy," I say, petting her as she tries to lick my face.

Brad lets out a little laugh and then rubs his eyes. He pats Coco. He scratches his chin and smooths his mustache.

"I don't know, V," he says, and my heart drops.

"I don't want to see anyone else. I'm sick of dating," I say decisively.

"You were married before, and you've dated a lot more than me. I haven't had time. I've been focused on my business and haven't had many

133

relationships. I went out a little in high school and with a few women my parents pushed on me, but I haven't had the chance to get out there much."

"You're saying you want to see other people?" I ask, dreading the answer.

"I don't know. Probably." He pats my hand. "Things are good with us, I agree, but I don't really know what else is out there yet."

Yet. I catch his use of that word. It's not a good sign.

"I can tell you that our kind of chemistry doesn't come along very often," I say. "I don't think you'll find it with anyone else."

"That may be true, but there's more to a relationship than chemistry."

"Yeah." My mind is spinning. "But I think we have the whole package. You're not seeing me at my best right now."

Why did I open this can of worms? It's backfiring on me. I assumed this would go well. Now I may have screwed myself over. I can't bear the thought of losing him. I have the urge to blurt out the L word, but that will make things worse. Yet that's how I feel about him. I love him. Why can't I say it?

"Look. Let's not talk about this now, Vera," he says. "Let's go to a movie and enjoy the evening. We don't have to decide now. Let me think about it."

I fight back tears. I can't let him see me cry, but it feels like my entire world is crashing down. The future I'd pictured together is slipping from my grasp.

"Okay," I assent softly.

I don't have to panic just yet, I tell myself. Nothing's changed for now. Nevertheless, I feel an impending sense of doom. What have I done? Why hadn't I kept my mouth shut? He would've eventually settled into the idea, and everything would've organically evolved. Yes, that was the way to handle it. What is wrong with me? Why do I screw things up?

We go to dinner and I'm encouraged that things appear normal between us. Everything might be okay. I bring the paper and study it while we wait for our food. I gratefully sip the wine Brad orders, welcoming the soothing relaxation it brings.

"Let's rent a movie and go back to the house," I suggest putting down the paper.

"Sounds fine to me." Brad shrugs.

I figure it will be less expensive for him. He spends a good chunk of money every Saturday when we go out. He never bats an eye, but the expense might be giving him pause. I'll invite him to my place for dinner next week. I can make something impressive like lasagna, which I don't make often. It will be a treat for the kids too. Yes, that's a fantastic idea. He'll relish a home cooked meal, something he never has that I can provide.

Brad lets Coco out into the yard when we arrive back at his house. Before he can even reach for the light switch, I am on him. I impulsively grab him, reacting to a surge of overwhelming desire, and kiss him fervently. I suddenly feel insatiable. He drops the movie and ice cream on the coffee table and almost falls backward. I push him down onto the couch and tear at his clothing. Mine is quickly shed, and I submit to the anxious yearning I usually keep suppressed, always responding to his signals and ignoring my own.

I run my fingers through his hair and grip it in tight handfuls before raking my nails down his back. Both of us are panting, almost gasping. It's fierce and frantic. I can't get enough of him and, if I lose this, I'll go out of my mind.

He reciprocates more passionately than ever. It's raw and primal. A floodgate has been opened, and we're drowning in a torrent of emotions. This is the true expression of our feelings for each other. It'll never be this potent, this all-consuming, this satisfying with anyone else. I want him to know that I'm the only one that can make him feel this way.

We're gasping and drenched in a mixture of our sweat. We peel our sticky bodies apart. His hair is matted to his forehead. He's sprawled on the couch, and I fall next to him, half on the ottoman. I'm completely drained. The doubts and insecurities have emptied from my mind. Neither of us speaks as we pant to catch our breaths.

I finally get up the energy to rise to my feet. Snatching the ice cream from the coffee table, I walk naked into the kitchen and place it in the freezer before heading to the bathroom.

When I come out, only our piles of clothing remain in the family room. I wander down the hallway to the bedroom where he's laying naked on the bed. I crawl up beside him and gently curl against him.

"Vera," he whispers.

We turn to each other once again and, this time, make love slowly. Yes, it feels like love this time.

Chapter 20

I play music as I make the lasagna and sing or hum along if I don't know the words. I'm in a fabulous mood. Last Saturday night had cleared the air. We hadn't spoken at all after the second time we'd made love. We'd simply fallen asleep with our bodies touching, and I'd gotten up as usual and gone home. But I still feel under the spell of it and am sure he does too. Brad had never reacted so ardently before, and this has changed everything. Our lovemaking has sped up the progression of our relationship. I'm sure of it.

I text him mid-week and invite him to dinner and he accepts. Now he'll see what a good cook I am and begin to crave my home cooking. He'll be drawn to the cozy domesticity and perceive there's more depth to our bond, more substance, more I can give him rather than him always giving to me. A sense of family will mesh with his fervor, and soon his heart and soul will long for me as mine do for him. Finally, it will be mutual. Why haven't I invited him to dinner before?

I told Marcy what had transpired between us. How I'd totally lost control of myself but that he had responded with matching zeal.

"Maybe you broke down his walls," she said.

She'd put it into words precisely. I'd broken through his protective walls and allowed him to access what was in his heart.

"I love lasagna." Lacie comes into the kitchen.

"Who doesn't?" I answer.

"Can I have dinner at Kerry's?"

"You just said you love lasagna." I raise my eyebrows.

"I know, but I want to go to Kerry's..." Her voice trails off.

"No. Brad is coming over for dinner. You can go to her house after dinner."

"Brad," she mutters walking away.

I sprinkle parmesan over the last layer of mozzarella. My Italian mother had taught me to make lasagna. I'd bought a large French baguette planning to make garlic butter while the lasagna bakes. I'd considered throwing together a salad as well, but I don't want Brad to fill up on salad and not fully savor the lasagna. It's a heavy but satiating meal. There's nothing better than tomato sauce and garlic and bread with which to sop it up.

I am in love. I feel joyful and light. I'm blissfully floating in a sea of optimism. The sky is bluer. The grass is greener. The sun is brighter. The dark clouds have lifted and scurried away. Brad's love protects me from doom and gloom. I'm certain he feels it too. I wholly *believe* that things have shifted for us. The earth moved and adjusted its course, and everything is different now. All the little pieces will fall into place.

The baking lasagna and garlic bread release luscious whiffs into the apartment. I set four places at my little round dining table in a nook tucked at one end of the kitchen. I straighten up the apartment. My furniture is old and the cushions on the couch are stained and sag. The coffee table is scratched and chipped. The easy chair is worn through on the arms. I've never bought new furniture. Everything is used and shows it, but we've always had a roof over our heads and food to eat. Though I struggle to pay the bills every month, I can still pay them. We're more fortunate than many, and I never forget that.

And now I have a great man in my life who loves me and who will complete our family. Brad will be a wonderful stepfather. He'll be a good provider and stabilizing influence. Luke needs a male role model.

Lacie does too.

I'll invite Brad to dinner every few weeks or so. It will help him bond with the kids, and I'm sure he'll look forward to having a home cooked meal every time he sits at this table.

I always feel hot when I'm cooking, so I put on a light sundress and pull my hair back into a loose ponytail to get it off my sweaty neck. Marcy had always coveted my dark eyelashes and eyebrows. I never wear make-up, but I'd always been envious of the light hair on her arms.

Brad arrives, and though I long to greet him with a kiss, I resist. He had suggested bringing a bottle of wine, but I'd asked him not to because of the kids. I don't like to drink in front of them, not that it's a bad thing for them to see me have a glass of wine, but I prefer to be alcohol free at home. I try to set a good example.

"It smells good," he says as soon as he steps inside.

"Thanks. There's something about garlic, isn't there?" I say. "Dinner's almost done."

He's never spent much time in my apartment and looks around. I try to see things through his eyes.

"I need new furniture," I say, slightly embarrassed by the sheer shabbiness.

"I hear you can't have nice stuff when you have kids," he says.

"I guess that's true," I say reluctantly. We stand awkwardly for a moment. "Lacie! Luke! Come say hi to Brad," I call.

"Hey, Brad." Luke charges into the room. "Want to see my new video game?"

"Sure." Brad settles on the couch while Luke loads the game.

Luke swivels around from his position on the floor. "Want to play? This is the one I told you about."

"Okay. I haven't played video games in a while."

Brad removes his shoes and sits next to Luke on the floor. I smile at the sight of them side by side and go into the kitchen to check on the lasagna and slice the bread.

"Hi, Brad." I hear Lacie's voice as she heads toward the kitchen. "Mom, when are we eating? I'm sooo hungry."

"Soon. Here." I hand her a basket and kitchen towel. "Put the towel in the basket and then place the bread on top and cover it with the ends of the towel."

"Why?" She makes a face.

"This is what they do in restaurants to keep the bread warm. Just do it."

I pull the bubbling lasagna from the oven. I hear the sounds of the video game and Luke and Brad laughing and exclaiming.

"Lacie, can you bring me the plates from the table?"

"Why?"

I groan. "I have to put lasagna on them."

"Can't we help ourselves?"

"It's too messy. Get me the plates, please."

"Fine."

She sets the basket of bread on the table and retrieves the plates.

"Lacie," I say in a low voice when she stands next to me. "Please be nice, okay? I really like Brad, and I want everything to go well."

"Okay. Can I go to Kerry's after dinner?"

"Yes. I already said yes." I take out the spatula. "Do you like Brad?" I venture.

"Yeah. He's okay."

"Maybe he'll let you work for him again."

"He made us work really hard."

"But he paid you a lot of money."

"I know."

"Can you let Luke and Brad know that dinner's ready and they can come to the table?"

"Mom said to come to the table," she yells.

I groan again. "I meant for you to go get them. I could've yelled to them." I shake my head.

Lacie shrugs and sits at the table.

"We just have to finish this game, Mom," Luke yells back.

"Okay," I call.

I step into the living room and watch them play. I know enough not to speak and break their concentration. Brad looks like he's having fun, and Luke enjoys having another player.

"Ha! I beat you again," Luke says.

"That looked too violent," I remark.

"It's just a game," Brad says getting up.

"Yeah. It's just a game," Luke echoes.

Brad will have to learn to back me up. I follow them into the kitchen, and everyone seats themselves. I place their steaming plates before them.

"Be careful. It's hot," I caution.

"This looks delicious," Brad says.

"There's garlic bread in the basket," I say.

"Like a restaurant," Lacie adds.

"I found a Rubik's cube in my car," Brad says. "Did one of you guys lose a Rubik's cube?"

"I was looking for that," Lacie cries.

"It looks like you solved it," Brad says, clearly impressed.

She shrugs like it's nothing.

"I couldn't do that," I say.

"I couldn't either," Brad admits.

"I did mine too," Luke offers, taking a big bite of bread.

"You took longer to do yours," Lacie taunts.

"Only because you were distracting me," he

retorts.

"Was not!"

"Was too!"

"But you both did them," I interject. "That's very good."

"How are your grades in school?" Brad asks.

"Okay." Lacie focuses on her plate.

Lacie gets better grades, though Luke's just as intelligent.

"Luke is more creative," I say.

"What are your favorite subjects?" Brad queries.

"Math," Lacie answers. "It's easy."

"I like art. I like to draw," is Luke's answer. "I want to be an animator."

"Well, between the two of them, you have all the necessary stuff covered," Brad says to me.

I beam.

After dinner, I let Lacie go to Kerry's, which is within walking distance. Luke and Brad help me clean up the kitchen. I promise Luke it will be Lacie's turn to clean up next time, and then we drive him to his friend's house.

I'm happy with how this evening has gone. My kids are well fed and occupied, and Brad has bonded with them more. They didn't argue too much and were generally well behaved. We had a casual conversation over dinner, and Brad liked the food. He even had seconds. I'm already planning my next menu in my head. I might make manicotti.

"I'm stuffed," Brad had said, pushing away from the table. "It was really good. Better than restaurant food."

It was exactly how I wanted him to react, but the bonus was how impressed he was with Lacie and Luke.

"Your kids are smart," Brad says to me in the car as we head to his house. "I didn't realize."

"Yeah. It's hard to tell with their teenage

attitudes." I laugh.

"Lacie's good at math. That's significant. It's a sign of her pragmatism, her analytical mind."

I can see why he admires this ability. I'm glad he has a high opinion of my kids, and I hope his parents will eventually share that opinion. Lacie and Luke are the best of me.

Chapter 21

I'm feeling more confident than ever. I've broken through Brad's resistance, and he has a favorable impression of my kids, which was unexpected. I hadn't envisioned that things would turn out this well.

I've had a setback, though. I hadn't gotten the promotion at work because I wasn't bilingual and continued part-time in the call center. If I'd gotten the position, I would've been able to quit my other part-time job and make more money with regular full-time hours. Everything else has gone so well that I'd actually assumed I'd be promoted. I'm getting burned out working at the call center. We're expected to turn over calls quickly, and our time is closely monitored, even when we go to the restroom. It's demeaning. On top of that, if customers are angry with the company, they take it out on us. I'm paying my dues, I tell myself. Of course, I've always been paying my dues, but things could finally turn around.

We go to a new restaurant that Brad wants to try. It's a soup and salad place. It's more casual and smells delectable when we walk in. There are no booths, only small square tables covered with forest green tablecloths. There's a large salad bar and soup station with numerous choices and breads.

There are so many bins of salad fixings to pile onto our plates that I end up with more than I can eat. At both ends of the station are large stainless-steel containers of dressings and ladles.

"This is so healthy," I enthuse once back at our table.

It would be nice to bring the kids here. They need to eat more nutritionally. Part of that is my fault. I let them eat fast food and convenience foods more and more as I try to stretch my time and money in all directions. It will be nice when the four of us can go to places like this together and be like the families sitting at other tables.

I'm torn between cream of broccoli, minestrone, and corn chowder when we scrutinize the soups. I place my hand casually on Brad's shoulder while we wait in line. I've made it a point to touch him more, hoping to get him used to it. He seems unperturbed, and I feel a sense of minor victory.

"Take a little of each," Brad advises.

"I can't. I'm so full already," I object.

He helps himself to a large serving of tomato lentil soup and heads back to the table. I stand indecisively, holding up the line behind me until I ladle corn chowder into my white bowl. I snatch a spoon from the bin and follow him.

"This is the best corn chowder I've ever tasted," I say after my first bite. "They must make everything from scratch here. How's yours?"

"Delicious," he answers.

He's been quieter than usual. It must be work worries. I should be more tuned into him.

"How are things going at the house?" I ask. "Did you do the open house yet?"

I try to remember what he'd told me about it. I really must pay more attention when he talks about his business. My mind is incessantly juggling so much that I forget to ask Brad about his work. I'll have to do a better job of being supportive.

"It's next weekend," he says.

"Right. Well, let me know how it..."

"Actually, we need to talk about something," he says, putting his spoon down.

My first thought is that I shouldn't have touched his shoulder. I'm encroaching into his comfort zone, and I'll have to pull back a bit. I can do that.

"Okay." I smile and reach over and touch his

hand. Darn! I pull my hand away quickly.

"We've been seeing each other for a while now, and everything is great between us," he begins.

"Yes, it is," I agree.

Maybe he's about to tell me he's ready to go to the next level. He could ask me to move in with him. This is what I've been waiting for. My hopes rise like a hot-air balloon drifting through a cloudless sky. This is it!

"I wasn't looking for a relationship," he continues somberly.

"Me neither." I tell a white lie.

He leans forward. "It's crazy how intense it is between us. We have incredible chemistry. Off the charts."

"I know." My face gets hot.

"I can talk to you. I trust you. I feel comfortable with you."

"Me too."

My heart quickens. Wait till I tell Marcy. Wait till I tell the kids. They'll love living in that beautiful house. I'll tell them they'll have to do chores and help in the yard. We'll donate the furniture except for the kids' beds and pack up the rest.

"We've discussed this before, more in theory, but we need to get this straight between us."

I'm not sure what he's saying. What have we discussed before in theory? What do we need to get straight? His statements sound ominous. And then the words I've feared most drop between us and detonate.

"I think we should see other people."

He picks his spoon back up and slurps his soup. I am stunned into silence. A shock wave runs through me, dragging a chill in its wake. I can't move.

He looks up at me. "We've talked about this before."

"But things have changed between us. We're closer. We... things are different now. I thought..."

"It's fine, Vera."

I can't stand the slow torture of his words. I steel myself. What does this mean?

"Are you breaking up with me?"

"No. No." He shakes his head. "I still want to see you. I..." He sets his spoon down again. "I just want to see other people too."

"You mean you want to *sleep* with other people," I clarify.

He shrugs. "That's not what I'm saying, but it's a possibility."

A possibility? Like rain? Like catching a cold? Like running into a friend?

"Brad." I lean forward and lower my voice. "You're not going to find anybody that's... that you feel the same way about. We're amazing together. You won't find that with anybody else."

"You might be right, but I have to find that out for myself."

I wrack my brain for the right words to convince him that we belong together, that I'm all he needs, that he won't find anyone else out there who will love him as I do. And I can't find them.

"How long?"

He looks up. "How long what?"

"How long do you need to date other women before you decide what you want?" I demand coldly.

He furrows his brow. "I don't know. I guess I'll know when I know."

I vacillate between distress and anger. Why does he insist on putting more obstacles between us? I can't stand the thought of him sleeping with someone else. It makes me absolutely crazy. Have his parents pressured him to date other women again? I'll have to face it. He may have already. He probably has. We have briefly discussed this before, but I'd always dismissed it as a fleeting whim. It would go away if I ignored it. But now this is really happening. He might have been seeing other women all along.

"Have you slept with anyone else?"

"We never said we were exclusive." He sets down his spoon again. "I want to be honest with you. Don't blow this up out of proportion. Nothing needs to change between us. I don't want to break up with you. I want to keep seeing you just like we've been doing. I just don't want to lie to you."

I stare into his blue-blue eyes that always melt me a little. His hair is sticking out behind his ear and his neat beard hugs his jaw. He's gained weight since I've known him and has a bit of a paunch. Some women won't like that or the fact that he's short, except that he's so dynamic, so charismatic, so charming.

"I don't want to date other people," I say resolutely. I cross my arms.

"Well, I do."

As far as I'm concerned, everything has just changed. My hopes have been dashed. Dark clouds have settled back over my head. Bad luck has gleefully returned to plague me once again. The tides have turned. The sun shines elsewhere. Brad doesn't love me.

And he never answered my question.

We return to his house and my mind is whirling. He can't just expect things to be the same, can he? He takes my hand and slowly draws me toward the bedroom with a mischievous grin. He never takes my hand like this.

"Do you have a condom?" I pull my hand from his.

He looks surprised and lets out a laugh which infuriates me.

"We've never used one before."

148

"Well, I didn't know you were sleeping around before," I retort, glaring at him.

Please deny it, I beg silently. Please give me a reason to feel better about this. Please reassure me.

"Sleeping around," he repeats. "How do I know who you've been with?"

"Really? I work two jobs and have kids, Brad. When would I have time to see someone else?"

"Don't be like this, V," he cajoles softening me. "Nothing's changed between us."

He's speaking to me as if I'm an irrational child. Am I being irrational? My thoughts ricochet back and forth. Walk away, I tell myself. Have some dignity. Let him miss me. Let him know I mean business. But I can't resist him. I hate myself, but I can't.

I cling to him in bed. I can't help myself. I never want to let him go. I never want to let my dreams of us go. He falls right asleep afterward, as usual as if nothing is different. I lie awake for a long time, staring into the darkness of the ceiling. Am I being a fool?

Chapter 22

"Brad," I say from the chair in the bedroom where I've just put on my shoes. I'd spent a sleepless night beside him, staring at the slivers of light from the full moon on the wall as I'd sunk deeper into a murky well of despair.

How many other women have sat in this very chair putting on their shoes? I will not cry. I blink as Coco thumps her tail. I go let her out and meander through the silent house with just the ticking of the wall clock in the kitchen. I pause in the doorway of his office and see the little house I'd bought him for his birthday sitting beside the landline. I never leave anything at his house, not even a toothbrush, so there's nothing to gather. I return to the bedroom before I lose my resolve.

"Brad," I say sharply.

"Huh?" He lifts his head.

"I wanted to say goodbye."

"Okay." He turns over.

"Brad!"

"What?" he asks with irritation. He sits up and rubs his eyes. "What's wrong?"

What's wrong? I want to scream at him.

"I... I'm going home."

"Okay." He yawns.

"I... I don't think we should see each other anymore... I can't..."

"What are you saying, V?" He jumps out of bed and approaches me in his boxers.

I back up and hit the doorjamb. "I can't do this, Brad..." I shake my head.

"Don't say that, Vera. Don't say that."

He suddenly grabs me and kisses me hard and then wraps his arms around me in a bear hug. I'm startled and stagger backwards through the

150

doorway into the hall while he clutches me tightly. He's never shown such spontaneous emotions with me, except for that one intense evening weeks ago. The thought of losing me must've set something off in him.

"Don't go like this, V," he murmurs in my ear. "Please. Don't leave like this. You know how I feel about you."

I think I do know. I think I know better than he does. Why can't he say it? His parents did this to him. They raised him to be stoic, to be detached, to stuff his feelings way down where they were no longer accessible. I'm sure that's why he can't express himself. It's not his fault.

He releases me from his tight embrace and puts his hands on my shoulders. "Be rational," he says softly, gazing into my eyes.

"Brad, you should know this," I say with a shaky voice. "I love you and I can't do this anymore."

I pull away and push around him to grab my purse.

"Don't be hasty, Vera," he admonishes blocking my exit. "I'll call you during the week, and we'll talk about this more. Okay?"

"Don't call me, Brad, unless you only want to see me." I brush past him.

I let Coco back in so I can open the gate. I glance over my shoulder to see if Brad has followed me. He hasn't.

Once I've driven down the street, I pull over. I'd been holding in my tears for so long, I expect a deluge, but I'm numb and no tears come. I slowly drive home in a daze. Part of me refuses to accept that it's over. His reaction has truly mystified me. Perhaps all is not lost, but no, I can't allow myself to harbor hope. It will only devastate me even further later on. It's over. It's over. It's over, I repeat to myself. I never thought I'd be the one to break it off, but he'd pushed me too far. He'd been so sure I'd accept anything to keep seeing him. The insult of not being invited to his parent's party, the woman's voice on his answering machine, only seeing him once a week. Doug had thought that was strange. That was a clue I may have overlooked. Had Brad been seeing other women during the week? Have I been a trusting idiot?

I need to talk to Marcy. It's early, but I drive straight to her house and knock on the door. Her older son answers, looking perplexed.

"Mom's sleeping," he says.

"Can you please tell her I'm here?" I ask. "I need to talk to her. I'll be out here."

I pace on the sidewalk by my car until Marcy comes out in her bathrobe.

"What happened?" Her face is filled with concern.

"I just broke up with Brad. Get in the car. It's warmer."

"Oh, my God," she says, opening the car door. "Was he cheating on you? I knew it."

"No. Maybe. I don't know." I close the door, cocooning us in my car as I relay the events the best I can recall in the turmoil of my thoughts.

She sits silently for a few minutes and that's when I begin to cry.

"Vera, I'm proud of you. You did the right thing. I knew he'd never marry you. I hate to say I told you so, but I did. I never trusted him." Her voice is filled with venom.

I ignore her words. "It was so perfect, Marcy. It was," I sob. I dig for tissues in my purse and then search my glove compartment where I find napkins. "Why can't he see that? Why can't anything ever go right? Nothing ever works out. I'm so tired of this."

"I know." She pats my shoulder. "Do you want to go to breakfast? I can get dressed real quick and

152

let Doug know. I'll pay."

"Doug's a great guy." I blow my nose.

"Yes, he is."

"I should get home to the kids."

"Okay, but I'm here for you. Call me anytime."

I don't tell Marcy, but I still cling to a shred of hope. Brad's reaction certainly sparked it, and I can't help but think this may have jolted his heart.

I won't let my kids see me cry. I cry in the shower or in my car or at night in bed. I don't tell them anything. I'll wait until Saturday to tell them. Maybe by then things will change somehow.

On Wednesday evening I arrive home to an enormous bouquet of red and yellow roses interspersed with the tiny white flowers of baby's breath in a green glass vase.

"Brad sent you flowers," Lacie announces when I walk in the door.

"Did you read the card?" I ask.

"No, but who else would send you flowers?"

I breathe in the lovely rose scent before I snatch the little envelope. It's still sealed. Hope explodes in me as I tear it open and read the card.

See you Saturday? Not *I miss you. I need you. I love you. I don't want anybody else.* Just see you Saturday for our weekly sex. That's what he thinks. My last shred of hope is decimated. He truly doesn't get it, and he never will.

My insides shrivel up, and I wake up every morning shaking. I can't bear this feeling. I can't bear to never see him again. I go about my life in a daze.

He texts on Thursday asking if I got the flowers. I respond with *Yes.* That's it. He texts on Friday and asks about Saturday. *No,* I text. I will not give in. He texts again on Saturday. I don't reply.

On Saturday, I tell my kids Brad and I broke up.

They look at each other.

"Why?" Luke asks.

I've been going over my response to this question in my mind all week. How do I answer this? How do I explain something that makes no sense to me? And how can I keep from tainting their view of relationships? I want them to view life with optimism. I want them to find love and happiness.

"We want different things," I respond vaguely.

"Like what?" Luke persists. "I like him."

This breaks my heart even more. Luke needs a male role model in his life and I can't give him that.

"I like him too, but he doesn't want a serious relationship right now," I answer honestly. "I really thought this was going to work out, but it just didn't."

Don't cry, I tell myself.

"He's not good enough for you, Mom," Lacie states.

God, I love my kids.

The Present

Chapter 23

It's Saturday and I've slept late. I had a dream about Brad that I can't recall. It sits on the edge of my memory, teasing me, tantalizing me. I can think about him now without an unbearable ache in my heart. I have become immune, such as after a virus. I'm wearing green sweatpants and a faded T-shirt as I pace in and out of the shafts of sunlight splaying across the living room in my house while I eat a bagel. Laundry awaits. This thought flits through my mind as I sink into a patch of sunlight and lean my back against the ottoman.

I hold Brad's business card in my hand and run my thumb over the raised letters of his name. I can think of nothing else since I'd seen him at the airport yesterday like a sudden apparition from the past haunting me, breaking open the past, threatening to pull me into the undertow of long suppressed memories.

It's been almost fifteen years since he'd broken my heart. The last time I'd seen him was the morning I fled his house, hoping he'd pursue me and persuade me that he couldn't live without me. But that wasn't Brad. He'd displayed a burst of desperation when I said I was leaving. At least I knew then that he had genuine feelings for me, but he must've been seeing other women because, apparently, he'd married not long after that.

My kids have grown up and moved out years ago. My nights are now free, and I do nothing but watch TV or read after work. Ironic now that I have the freedom to come and go, the impetus is gone. There's no exciting boyfriend to look forward to seeing in the evenings or on weekends. It's been years since anybody has kissed me or touched me. How many? Six? Seven?

I remember all the times Brad and I had lounged on his couch or in bed. Sometimes eating. Sometimes watching a movie. Sometimes making love. But had it been love? Had we ever loved each other? I still feel a tingle at the thought of him. But it had really been lust, hadn't it? For both of us. We had an insatiable desire for each other, but not much else. Not anything that would've sustained a long relationship. How foolish I'd been to mistake sex for love.

I'd been consumed with envy and admiration for his drive and ambition, his ability to achieve, his self-assurance, his poise, perhaps hoping some of it would rub off on me. There had been much to praise, but had I even *liked* him? Sometimes I didn't like who he was. When I saw him exploit a client to close a sale, when he confided fabricating contributions to charity on his taxes, when he twisted the truth to benefit himself, his imperfections appeared. How can you respect that? How can you trust someone like that?

I'm curious about his wife. Is she like him, pragmatic and apathetic? No romance. No tenderness. Does he lie to her? Does he remember their anniversary? Does she? Are they happy or do they not think in those terms? Is it a practical arrangement?

I'm tempted to call him. Besides curiosity, I want him to see that I'm not such a disaster anymore, despite my attire at the airport. I'd raised my kids, and they were doing well. I finally had a good job and owned a house. I had done it all without anyone's help. I could afford to go to an expensive restaurant if I wanted. I could afford a mechanic for my car or a plumber for my toilet. I didn't need to be rescued anymore. I was no longer overwrought and overwhelmed. I wanted him to know I no longer needed anybody. I no longer needed him.

I can't blame him for backing away from me those years ago. I can see now that he had done the right thing for both of us. I never would've found my own strength leaning on him. We'd probably be bitterly divorced by now. Maybe I'd been saved from years of upheaval. Infidelity. Indifference. Insincerity.

I can't find any remnants of love for him remaining in the hidden corners of my heart. How strange. I'd been so convinced I was madly in love with him, but it was the same with my ex. Maybe I'd never been in love at all, or maybe it had died after being dragged through the fire.

My eyes are open now. I've seen Brad's shortcomings, and I'm a stronger person now. He can't get to me anymore. He can't capture my heart again. What remains isn't love. But I do feel drawn. I do feel an attraction, a tiny surge of lust. It has been a long time, after all. I also feel traces of affection for him. We spent many intimate days and nights together, and he was a wonderful boyfriend in many ways.

He should've been able to discern my potential. Through our many conversations and debates, he'd learned I was intelligent, though not educated, and had my own mind. Sure, I'd lacked confidence and let him manipulate me, but I had ultimately stood up for myself.

Why hadn't he defended me to his parents? Why hadn't he stood up to them? That had truly hurt me, but he hadn't and that revealed his weakness. Was he still under their thumb?

Suddenly it occurs to me he could've used his parents as an excuse. It was true they hadn't been thrilled with me, but maybe they hadn't threatened to withdraw their financial interests in his fledging business. He could've easily lied to me. That was what he did. He did whatever was necessary to get what he wanted and he wanted to hold me at arm's length, keep me around but have his freedom.

That thought makes me even more determined to show him how capable I am, how he and his parents had been wrong about me. I will call him. I set my glasses on the coffee table and pick up my cell phone.

I've hesitated to talk to Marcy about Brad. Marcy still lives in Southern California. We moved away after my daughter got into college in Northern California. It was the ideal excuse to get out from under the gloom that had begun with the breakup. I'd also gotten laid off from my job and was having trouble finding another. I'd felt totally beaten down and defeated. A fresh start was what I'd needed, but Marcy has always blamed Brad for my move.

I still consider her my closest friend. We've known each other for decades and seen each other through too much to let that go, but we disagree at times. Marcy and I could always see each other's lives with crystal clarity, while our own remained murky as mud. So, we had our disagreements and tiffs over the decades.

She never liked Brad, even though he was nice to her when they met. He didn't like her either, which didn't help matters. He called her an "airhead." Not to her face, but to me whenever I mentioned her, so I stopped mentioning her. And our friendship had suffered as I'd spent more time with him and he became my priority.

"Hello?" Marcy's familiar voice comes on the phone. "Why didn't you call me last night? You know, after seeing asshole at the airport."

"I was tired," I say.

But the truth is, I'd wanted to be alone with my thoughts and memories. I'd wanted to explore my feelings before tainting them with someone else's opinion. And I knew Marcy's opinion of Brad.

"I wish you still lived down here," she moans. "The thing I hate most about him is he chased you away."

"You know that's not how it was. We didn't move until I lost my job, and Lacie wanted to go to college up here."

"He had a lot to do with it. There were too many reminders here."

"Yeah, well..."

"So how did he look?"

"The same, just a little older. A little heavier..."

"He got fat!" she says gleefully.

"No. Only a little heavier," I say. "He's still good looking."

"He was a cute guy."

"He still is." I debate continuing, but I do. "He was great, except he might've been seeing his wife at the same time as me."

"He was great except for that little cheating thing," she says sarcastically.

"She could be the one who called that one morning. Remember, I heard a woman on his answering machine?"

"Probably was. That cheating jerk."

"I know you never liked him," I acknowledge. "Remember what a hard time you gave him when we had brunch with you and Doug?" I giggle at the memory.

She giggles with me. "He deserved it."

"He was really good to me," I say. "Do you realize how many dinners he bought me? In pricey restaurants. Plus, he fixed my car and my toilet."

"How could he afford all that? He wasn't making much money then."

"That's a good question. He was making some, but he never worried about money. He just did what he wanted. That's how the rich live, I guess."

"Must be nice when Mommy and Daddy can bail

160

you out."

"He was a good boyfriend, though," I insist.

"He treated you like shit."

"He took me out all the time," I protest. "He even gave my kids money to work for him. Remember that?"

"That was cool of him, but you were a wreck when you were together."

"Things were great between us most of the time. We rescued that dog together. What was her name? She was so sweet. Coco, that's it."

"Yeah. Yeah. Everything was great until he dumped you."

"He didn't dump me. Technically, I broke up with him."

"You did? I don't remember that. I remember you coming over to my house and getting me out of bed and crying in your car. I thought you were going to have a nervous breakdown."

"Yeah," I mumble. "I broke up with him because he said he wanted to see other women. I just couldn't... I reached the end of my rope."

"You sure did," she says. "Hey, I should've bought you some rope. Remember when you gave me those marbles?" She laughs. "In case I lost mine?"

I laugh with her. "That was funny."

"I probably should've given you some of mine that day."

"I know. I was a mess." I clear my throat. "He gave me his business card. He seems pretty successful. He wants to talk on the phone and catch up."

"Oh, my God! He's married. He's unbelievable."

"Well, I'm a little curious."

"About what?"

"About his wife and kids. About his life now. If he has any regrets," I say.

"A guy like that doesn't have a conscience. He won't have any regrets."

"He's not as bad as you think," I say. "I was so high maintenance then. I couldn't even pay my bills or keep a job."

"You've come a long way, baby."

"I have. I wonder how things would've turned out if I'd been more together."

"Like now?"

"Yeah. I'm kind of curious," I say. "It's like we're more on the same level now. It'd be interesting to talk to him."

"Don't you dare call him, Vera," Marcy warns.

Chapter 24

I find my thoughts once again fixated on Brad. But in a different way. I no longer feel desperate to see him or eager for his attention. How obsessed I'd been. It's a relief to be free of that. I idly think of him as I load the washing machine. How different things would've been if we'd met at another time in my life.

It had been a shock to run into him again. I could definitely see his appeal through an objective lens. He always dressed nicely and was well groomed, even when he was casual, and had an engaging, teasing smile. Did it come naturally or was it calculated? It was clear to me we still had chemistry. When he'd grabbed my arm to pull me out of the way at the airport, I'd felt a little twinge of excitement. He could still do that to me.

That smile. That hint of mischief. That promise of exhilaration. Did other women react to him as I did, or was it something special between us? Is it like that with his wife? I can't help wondering.

I want to hear his version of things, his perspective on our relationship. We can talk honestly now. No one will get hurt. I'd never been able to get into his head before, and I'd spent so much of my time trying to fathom what he was thinking, what he wanted, what I should say to get what I wanted. Now is my opportunity to find all this out.

Suddenly my dream comes back to me. We were in a parking lot and I had turned away from him. He grips my arm and I look into his eyes. I see straight into him. I see his racing blood, his pounding heart, the words tumbling from his mouth in tiny letters hurtling toward me.

"You could always see right through me." His voice reverberates. "You always knew how I felt."

And yes, I think I had. He had always had strong feelings for me. That's why he treated me well, paid my kids to work for him, and had dinner with us in my shabby apartment. That's why he'd reacted as he had when I'd said goodbye. His response had taken both of us by surprise, erupting in a rush of raw emotions. It could've been the moment that things turned around for us if he had only accepted what was in his heart. His heart knew he didn't want to let me go.

Marcy doesn't understand. How can she? She doesn't know what was between us, the depth of our passion, the draw like two magnets. It was difficult to let that go, but he'd chosen to explore his options and ultimately marry someone else. And I had chosen to move away.

Getting back to being objective, the cold hard facts were that we were mismatched on every other level. Our personalities, our politics, our temperaments, none of it meshed, so it was just as well. It never would've worked. Would it?

I should vacuum, but I don't feel like it. I flop onto the couch. I could read, but I won't be able to concentrate. I want to dwell on my memories. I want to sink into the past, remember the thrill, the anticipation I used to feel before I saw him, the wine at dinner releasing all the tension of the work week and unpaid bills, the smooth wood floors in his house, his plush king-sized bed, his soft T-shirt that I used to sleep in. I wish I still had it.

Brad. Brad. Brad. Why have our paths crossed again? I pick up his business card from the coffee table and enter his number in my phone's address book. My stomach twists with nervousness and, before I can change my mind, I press the call button. I haven't rehearsed what to say, and relief floods through me when his voicemail answers.

"You've reached Brad Fletcher of Fletcher

Construction and Renovation. Leave me a brief message and I'll get right back to you." *Beep!*

"Uh, hi. It's Vera. I..." What if his wife listens to his messages? "We ran into each other at the airport and... well, give me a call back if you get a chance. Okay, bye."

Ugh! How awkward. Why hadn't I thought through what to say? A thousand things have jumbled my mind, but now I sound just as insecure as I'd been back then. Whatever. It doesn't matter.

The phone startles me when it vibrates in my hand. I answer it.

"V! I'm glad you called. I have to meet with clients, but I have some time to talk."

"Okay." I'm unsure how to begin. "Sounds like your business is doing well. That's awesome."

I trace a flower in the pattern on my couch with my fingertip as I ponder what to say. I have so many questions, but I don't want to blurt them out. I want to sound casual, even disinterested.

"Thanks. You remember how hard it was in the beginning," he says.

Yeah, relying on your parents' money.

"But how you're doing?"

"I'm doing fantastic," I finally get the chance to say. "I have a good job and I bought a house."

"That's great. What kind of house?"

Naturally, he'd ask about the house rather than my job or my kids.

"It's just a small house with a tiny yard. Three bedrooms and two bathrooms. It worked for me and the kids."

"Right. What's the square footage?"

"Under 1200."

"Must've been expensive up there. Where are you? By San Francisco?"

"We're further north and inland a bit. It's more affordable," I tell him. "It's just me now. The kids are off on their own."

"Has that much time passed?" He chuckles. "I remember when you used to feel bad about spending the night and leaving them alone."

I feel a pang of remorse. Why had I put him before my kids?

"Yeah. Those were tough times."

"But you got through it. I knew you would," he says. "It wasn't easy, but you did."

"Thanks." I don't know what else to say. My mind has gone blank.

"Are you down here often?" he asks.

"Not much. I had to go to a training seminar for work," I say. "Anyway, congratulations on your marriage and your kids. That's what you wanted."

"Yes. Everything worked out for both of us."

"Yeah. What does your wife do?" My curiosity is bursting. Had he known her when we were together? Was she the woman his parents had pushed on him? Is she beautiful and brilliant?

"Julia was in marketing, but she got her realtor license so we could work together renovating houses."

Julia. Her name is Julia. What she looks like? She must be rich and pragmatic like him.

"You're flipping houses?" I enjoy watching the house flipping shows on HGTV, and they give me good ideas. I'm envious that they get to do these fun things together.

"We're renovating and selling..."

"Flipping," I repeat.

"I wouldn't call it that."

He doesn't seem to like that term.

"You're sort of at the mercy of the housing market," I say.

A ray of sunlight has moved into my eyes, and I shift on the couch, leaning against a pink throw pillow. He'd probably hate my floral theme. His

166

house had been dark colors, mostly browns, very masculine. Somewhat stark and bland now that I think about it. What would *their* house look like? Are there feminine touches? Pinks and purples.

"Not totally. You can always make money in any market. Sometimes we do new construction, or we find houses to renovate or do projects for homeowners. There's always housing you can find that can be fixed up and turned around. Worse-case scenario is you rent until the market picks up and you can sell."

"Does that happen a lot?"

"Only once so far, but we sold it to the renters. It worked out."

"Good."

"Just about broke even on that one."

Why are we talking about his work? It's the last thing I'm interested in.

"Hey," I break in because of the many questions bouncing around in my head like ping-pong balls, but this is the one that presses on me the most. "Was your wife the one who called that morning? Remember, she left a message on your answering machine about breakfast or brunch or something?"

I need to know. Was she the reason he wanted to see other people out of the blue? And keep me on the side. How cold and selfish.

"I don't remember that," he says flatly.

I should've known he'd say that.

"Don't you remember? We had an argument about it," I persist.

"We had a few disagreements. I don't remember every one of them." He gives a little laugh.

"Okay." I furrow my brow and rephrase. "Did you see her while you were still seeing me? And don't avoid the question. I just want to know. It's no big deal."

"Honestly, V, I don't remember. You may have

167

overlapped."

"Braaaad..." I say in a mock warning tone.

He laughs. "I have to admit..." He lowers his voice. "I've been thinking about you since the airport."

"I was a mess at the airport. I just wanted to be comfortable on the plane."

"Who cares about that?" he says dismissively. "I've seen you in all kinds of clothing and non-clothing, but what I mean is, we could always talk. I always felt completely at ease with you."

"Don't you feel that way with your wife?" I can't resist a little jibe.

"It's not the same," he answers unperturbed. "She expects..." He sighs. "I don't want to talk about her. It's funny, but I miss you in some ways."

"What do you mean?" I prod.

"Well, like what I said about being able to really talk. I've told you things I've never told anyone before because I trust you," he reveals.

"Really?" I'm astonished to hear this. Does he not confide in his wife of over a decade?

"Sure. I've told you things I'm not proud of. I don't know why I felt I could tell you these things. Probably because you never judged me and you always..." He pauses and I wait breathlessly for his next words. "You just seemed to respect me no matter what I did."

"I did," I profess.

"It was like I could do no wrong in your eyes."

"I thought you were perfect," I confess, because I did. Almost. I did notice some of his faults, though I chose not to focus on them.

"There! That's it."

"I was good for your fragile male ego," I tease.

"Not to mention the amazing physical connection we had."

"Not to mention," I repeat, smiling to myself.

"You know, you sound different, more confident. I can hear it in your voice. I like it."

I *am* feeling more confident. Talking about his wife hasn't bothered me, especially since it doesn't sound like they have the closest relationship. I'd probably dodged a bullet because here he is flirting with me. I sense it even through the phone. Is he incapable of fidelity? Does he always do whatever he wants?

"If you still lived down here, we could meet for dinner. I'd like to talk in person."

"I don't think your wife would appreciate that." I can't help reminding him about her, about the limitations of his marriage while I remain unencumbered.

"I have business dinners with women all the time," he responds.

Hadn't he said the same thing to me at one time?

"But not ex-girlfriends," I say.

"No, not ex-girlfriends," he concedes.

"And this isn't business."

"No, most definitely not," he says.

I may be good for his ego, but he's also good for mine. Nobody has ever made me feel as desirable. And here I am flirting with a married man, and it feels good. Why does he have to be married? A second time around might've worked for us.

"This has nothing to do with her," he breaks into my thoughts. "I want to stay in touch. As friends. Can we do that?"

"Okay." There's no harm in a few phone calls, I tell myself, and I still have many questions I'd like answered. Distance ensures that we'll remain chaste. This is safe.

"I wish we could talk longer, but I have to go meet some clients. Let's talk again soon."

"All right."

He no longer thinks of me as a lost cause. I don't

know why his opinion is still so important to me. The past is over and gone. I guess I don't want anyone to remember me at my lowest, and his parents certainly wouldn't be overjoyed to know we're in contact again. That gives me a little buzz of satisfaction.

I'm glad I called Brad. There was an ease to our conversation. Our connection runs deep, like a natural current that relentlessly flows beneath the surface. I look forward to our next phone call. More than I should.

Chapter 25

Again, I dream of Brad. This time I wake with the memory of it and stay in bed, savoring the sheer lucidity of it. His physical presence, his acute blue-blue eyes, the sound of the waves on a windswept beach at sunset. I don't think we were ever on a beach at sunset or any other time. No, wait. Early on, we had a picnic on the beach one sultry day. I'd gotten badly sunburned and so had he, but I remember the salty taste of his lips when I'd leaned over to kiss him and the roar of the waves and the lightheaded way I'd felt. We were alongside a dune affording privacy and he wanted to have sex right there, but I'd resisted. The slickness of the oil we'd smoothed onto each other's bare skin, the scantiness of our swimwear, the newness of him, the way he'd looked at me. I don't know how I summoned the willpower.

But this is a dream, and I endeavor to recover the words we'd spoken to each other. I sense they're significant words with a veiled message as dreams so often contain.

Brad says something indecipherable to me.

"But we don't love each other," I say.

"Nobody does," is his reply.

I contemplate this brief exchange in my dream. What message is my subconscious trying to convey? That we never loved each other? That love doesn't exist? That we're incapable of love? Or does it mean something else altogether? Whatever it means, it bothers me. It bothers me a lot.

The morning rain has given the crisp air a fresh smell as I take a walk around the neighborhood. Bark and rock are strewn around plants in some front yards, and others sprout neat rectangles of grass. My yard is a mixture. I'm not skilled at landscaping. I view the sparse bushes in my yard when I round the corner back to my house and debate how to improve their appearance. Perhaps I need to trim them. Rummaging in the garage doesn't produce the clippers. Where could I have put them?

My phone rings as I step back into the warmth of the house. I pull off my sneakers and head to the kitchen for a glass of water.

"Hello?" I already know who it is because of the caller ID.

"You sound out of breath," Brad says.

"I just got back from a walk."

"Oh. It's too hot here."

I fill a glass with filtered water and thirstily gulp it down. I enjoy our casual and slightly flirtatious conversations. There's no longer the pressure of a relationship or the constant fear of losing him. I wonder where his wife is during these calls, but I don't ask.

"How's your job?" he always begins by asking.

"Well," I say. "Remember I told you about my boss resigning?"

"Right. Did you talk to the department head like I said?"

"Yes," I continue. "But I found out why he resigned."

"Why?"

"He had an affair with one of the receptionists," I reveal. "It was a big deal. I heard his wife is divorcing him, but I don't know if the receptionist was fired. Someone said she was sent to work at another location."

"Shake up at the office," he remarks. "But what did the department head say when you talked to him?"

That's what he's most interested in. Not the human foibles, but the business end of it. My career advancement. The bottom line for him.

"Actually, I talked to my friend in HR. She told me to apply for the position once they post it, but she knows I'm interested."

"Good. Make sure you get in there. I still think you should talk to the department head. Be assertive," he advises. "You've been there a long time and you're qualified. Make them see it, too. Get there before somebody else does."

"Okay."

But what I don't tell Brad is that I don't really want to advance to that position. I'm not competitive and eschew the responsibility. Besides, I'm probably not qualified with my lack of education. I'm content to sit in my little cubicle and collect my paycheck. I like my job, but business doesn't really interest me. Some thrive on it. I see the jockeying and betrayal around me and want no part of it. While Brad admires ambition and power and wealth, that's not me, but he doesn't comprehend that not everyone cares about these things. Some of us are happy to go to work and make enough to pay our bills and be a little extravagant now and then.

"How are your parents?" I ask to change the subject as I settle onto the floral couch and rest my feet on the edge of the coffee table.

"They're in Europe."

"I told Marcy that we've been talking on the phone," I tell him.

"Marcy?"

"Remember my friend you met years ago? You never liked each other."

"You're still friends with her? Doesn't she live down here?"

"Yes. We kept in touch."

"What did she have to say?"

"She doesn't think I should give you the time of day."

"Aww. It wasn't so bad, was it, V?" I can hear the

smile in his voice.

"No. It was actually pretty incredible," I acknowledge. "But it never would've worked out for us."

"You don't think so?" There's surprise in his voice.

"No. I was too needy, and, besides, you wanted kids," I answer. "We would've ended up divorced."

This I'm sure of. Our differences would've imploded our relationship at some point.

"Maybe not," he says.

"Your parents didn't like me," I remind him.

"I should've stood up to them. I always felt bad about that," he confesses. "It wasn't fair to you."

I sit up on the couch. I can't believe my ears. We're actually having an honest conversation about the past. It feels as fragile as a glass-blown ornament that will shatter if we handle it carelessly.

"You had no choice. You depended on them for financial..."

"I should've learned to stand on my own two feet. It would've been good for me. I would've survived."

I astonished by the words coming through the phone. I only wish he'd said them then. Would things have turned out differently?

"We both should've been stronger," I say.

"Can't change the past, right?"

"Right."

I stand and pace. A breeze rustles my plants in front of the window and draws my distracted attention. There are kids running along the sidewalk, shouting at each other. There's the faint smell of a barbeque somewhere. A lawnmower in the distance. A dog barking.

"You know I had feelings for you, V."

How I'd longed to hear these sentiments years ago. How I'd hungered for them with the desperation of a starving person. His love had been my sustenance, and he'd only scattered crumbs while his heart had remained impenetrable. At times, I'd questioned if he had one, but then I'd seen glimpses with Coco and had hoped his heart would open for me as well.

"Sometimes I wonder if it was just sex," I broach.

"Well, it wasn't," he answers.

I don't even know what to say. What is he telling me? What opportunity was lost? I'd craved the sound of these elusive and precious words now softening my memories of our shared time and soothing the pain and guilt that lingers.

"Brad..."

"Sorry, V. I have to go." He says it gently and hangs up.

Does he feel he's said too much? I sit with the phone in my hand. Though I feel a great fondness for him, I still don't think I love him any longer. Or maybe I never had. No, I don't love him. I don't. It was hope and lust that had tricked my heart, swirling within me, taking over my sensibilities, and obscuring the truth.

The truth was, I had ignored my maternal responsibilities to pursue a phantom that I had mistaken for something else, for something real, for an escape into a better future. But Brad had never offered it or intended to. He had simply given me a temporary reprieve, a break from the stress, a brief bit of pampering. Not to diminish that. It was essential to my sanity. I just wish I'd seen it for what it was. My dire situation had clouded my judgement.

But what would've or could've been possible if he'd recognized his burgeoning feelings for me? If I'd had it more together? If we'd been more mature? Like we are now. I have become more practical, more realistic, more stoic. Brad has become more open. I see his flaws more clearly than ever. He was never the ideal man I'd believed him to be, but he liked seeing that reflection of himself in my eyes.

I shake my head and contemplate why he's opening up to me now. Perhaps the distance gives him a certain sense of safety. Does he have unresolved feelings from the past, or does he just need someone to talk to? Where is his wife during our phone calls? Are things not as rosy as I think?

Chapter 26

At work, I debate talking to my supervisor about the promotion. Brad has put it in my head, but I feel uncomfortable bringing it up with him. I tell myself I deserve a promotion and a raise. More money would be welcome, but I don't want more responsibility and the pressure that goes with it. Then again, it would look good on a resume if I ever had to look for another job. Brad's right. It's a smart move.

Still, I can't make myself enter my supervisor's office as I lurk in the hall trying to get up the nerve. Talking to the department head is even more intimidating. With resignation, I accept that I'm a coward and flee to my cubicle. Maybe I'll have the courage tomorrow.

I sit there berating myself. Brad's right. I should be more ambitious. I should push myself out of my comfort zone and go after things. I should promote myself and be unafraid of rejection. I should jump over every obstacle. If I've learned anything from him, this should be my lesson. Brad doesn't have an education, yet he didn't let it stop him. He achieved through sheer persistence and a belief that he deserves it. I deserve it too.

Why do I let insecurity dictate my life? I consider this as I saunter to the break room to fill my water bottle. The room is empty, and I stand before the window staring out at the hazy glare of the sun glinting off car hoods in the employee parking lot. A few people stand outside the back door in the building's shade, smoking. I envy their camaraderie.

I take a sip of cool water and turn to go. A book on one of the small round tables catches my eye. Someone attached a sticky note on the cover. *Free.*

A long section of the counter is empty by the

window. I place the book there and head back to my cubicle with an idea. I open a Word document and type a notice in large font:

Donate books to the lending library
Read and return

I also type up an email announcing the idea that I send it to everyone in my department. I get a few immediate responses praising it. Some people still like to read physical books. I have shelves of books at home. This is an opportunity to clean them out.

The next day I bring in seven books and find another five sitting there on the counter. I feel a sense of gratification from contributing to this little library at the office.

Over the weeks, this spontaneous idea spreads through the building, and books accumulate in the break room. Our library grows until someone brings in a small bookcase and neatly arranges the messy stacks of books on it. People sit and read while eating lunch, and eventually, magazines are added to the shelves.

This gives me a wonderful feeling of accomplishment, though I still can't bring myself to enter my supervisor's office to pitch myself for the vacant position. Instead, I pay heed to the anxiety that prevents me from applying, even when the job is posted on our intranet. Once someone is hired, I feel a sense of relief. I'm more comfortable being a little worker bee. I'm not meant to be a leader. And that's okay.

I fail to mention Brad when I talk to my kids. I'm not sure how they remember him, probably as another one of my failed relationships. I have no reason to bring him up other than he's often on my mind, but there are more exciting things going on with Lacie. She's married and about to have her first child. I'm going to be a grandmother. I can't wrap my head around it, and I'll also be fifty this year. That number scares me. I don't want to grow old alone. I never envisioned I would, but here I am.

"I've been fixing up the baby's room, but it's hard to decorate not knowing what it's going to be," Lacie says.

She and her husband, Brandon, have chosen not to know the sex beforehand. I like that idea.

"Choose colors like yellow or green," I advise. "Or you could do a room that's blue and pink."

I'm standing before my living room window gazing out at the morning mist. The sparse grass is dripping with dew, though the sun will soon burn it off and dry it to a motley brown.

I should get outside and do some yardwork before it gets hot, but I can't get motivated. And I can't stop thinking about Brad. It's only because I haven't had much male attention in the past few years, I tell myself. I do get a little tingle when we talk. I've always found his attention intoxicating and arousing. Even the sound of his voice can excite me.

"I'll have to think about that." Lacie breaks into my meandering musings. "Will you help me paint the room? Brandon is working all the time."

He's an IT manager and there are always fires to put out.

"Sure. It'll be fun." I shake off my thoughts to focus on babies and colors. "When do you want to do it?"

"Can we go to the paint store today?" she asks. "I just have to take a shower."

"Sure. I'll get ready and come over."

"Okay. We can pick out colors. I'm going to get low VOC paint. You know, the low toxicity stuff."

"That sounds like a good idea," I say.

The yard will have to wait, which is okay with

me. I throw on some jeans and an old T-shirt that I can get paint on just in case we start today. All the while, Brad sits in a corner of my mind, refusing to leave. It annoys me and I try to toss him out, but he comes right back like a boomerang.

I call my son before I drive over to Lacie's house. I'm so proud of both my kids. They've grown up and gotten jobs and found compatible partners for themselves, so much more than I accomplished at their ages. I'm glad my dysfunctional relationship history hasn't affected their choices.

I'd told my kids that I didn't want them to feel pressured to marry and have kids. I wanted them to do what made them happy. For Lacie, having a career and getting married and having a baby made her happy. So much for her being the first woman president or scientist who saves the world from climate change or researcher who discovers a cure for cancer. She enjoys working as a project manager, and I'm immensely proud of her. She's sensible and kind and smart and strong beyond my capacity. She's all I wished I had been.

Luke has also found a career he excels at as a CAD drafter and a partner, Serena, who is his equal. They live together in a house he purchased a few years back. He's grown into a good man. He isn't threatened by a strong woman and does his own laundry. He can cook and clean and shop for food. He doesn't expect his girlfriend to take care of him. No, my kids won't change the world, but they're good honest people, and I'm so proud of how they turned out.

Lacie and I spend a long time at the paint store studying colors. Who knew there were so many shades of each color? We feel more confused than ever, and she finally grabs little sample cards of the colors we're able to narrow it down to so she can show Brandon. We spend some time with the clerk choosing supplies such as brushes, tarps, trays, spackle, and tape.

"I'm glad I'm only painting one room," she says.

She has long dark hair as I had in my twenties, but she braids it or puts it up most of the time. Today she has it pulled back into a ponytail.

"I can help you," I say, peeking at my phone. Brad has called.

I toss him from my mind and go back to Lacie's to prep the room with her. We spackle holes in the wall and line the edge of the ceiling, window, and door with painter's tape. The room is devoid of furniture. Lacie has purchased a crib, and it's in a box in the garage ready to be assembled once the room is painted.

I place my hand on her rounded tummy. I can't help doing this every time I see her, but there's no stirring today.

"The baby must be sleeping," I whisper.

Lacie laughs. "I don't think you'll wake him or her up."

"I can't wait to meet you," I say to her belly.

"Can you help me paint next weekend?" she asks. "Brandon and I will decide on the color, and I'll pick up the paint during the week."

"Okay."

"I can't wait to get the crib put together." She sighs and rubs her belly in that protective, absentminded way pregnant women do. "Mom, I wanted to ask you something."

"What?"

I trail behind her as she wanders into the kitchen. She gets two glasses out of the cabinet and fills them with filtered water. We've built up a thirst and drain our glasses.

"I was talking to my doctor, and she asked me who I wanted in the delivery room." She furrows her brow. "I think Brandon will do fine, but who knows?

He can be squeamish about things."

"I'll be there," I say instantly.

She smiles. "Good. I want you there too. You know, to hold my hand."

"Of course I'll be there," I promise, giving her a reassuring hug.

I almost wish she were little again so I could hug her tight and never let go. I miss when my kids would let me hold them on my lap, and their wispy dark hair would tickle my face. Sometimes they'd fall asleep, and I wouldn't want to move until my arm went numb. It was the most peaceful feeling, listening to their steady breathing and imagining what they were dreaming. Now I'll get to do that with Lacie's baby. It makes my heart dance to think about it.

Chapter 27

I pace as I wait for Marcy to answer the phone. I stand in front of my living room window, as I often do while on the phone, and watch kids riding their bikes in the cul-de-sac. A dog runs after them, barking and wagging his tail joyfully.

I had put off this phone call. Every time I talked to Marcy on the phone, I felt dishonest. I've avoided telling her that Brad and I have been communicating because I'm sure of her reaction. She'll list all the reasons I shouldn't speak to him, as any good friend would, and then I'll defend my actions. She won't understand how much I need to hear his voice, how good it makes me feel to know that someone cares, that Brad cares. I look forward to our calls, maybe a little too much.

"Hello?"

"Hi, Marcy. What are you doing?"

"I'm home by myself wondering where the heck my husband is."

I roll my eyes. "Why? Where is Doug supposed to be?"

"Oh, never mind. He just pulled up. I'll deal with him later."

"Give him a break, Marcy. You can trust him." I shake my head at her lunacy.

"I know. I don't know why my mind always goes there."

"It's all the stuff from your childhood. Doug is not your father. You have to trust him," I say for the zillionth time. "He's proven that you can by now."

"You're right." I hear her greet him and then she's back. "How're things with you?"

"Well, actually..." I say slowly gathering the courage to face her ire.

"You met someone!" she exclaims.

"No, but I have to tell you something, and I don't want you to judge me."

"Why would I judge you? What did you do?"

"Well..."

"Spit it out, Vera. How bad can it be? What did you do? Rob a 7-11 and flee to Mexico? Oh, wait. You're closer to Canada now, aren't you? Are you hiding out in Canada?" She laughs at her own joke.

"I... So..."

"You're secretly an international jewel thief?"

"I..."

"You're a cyber security hacker? I knew it. You only pretend to hate computers."

"I don't hate computers."

"So, you admit it?"

"What are you talking about?"

"You're with the CIA?"

"I've been talking to Brad on the phone," I cut in and wince, waiting for her reaction.

"Brad? Wait a minute. Brad? Tell me you're not serious. Didn't you learn the last time? Oh, my God, Vera! He's married!" she cries.

"We're just talking. I mean, we can't do anything over the phone. Not that I would, but..."

"I can't believe you're giving him the time of day after what he put you through."

"I didn't expect you to understand." I groan.

The kids on their bikes are further down the street, and there's an adult attaching a leash to the dog's collar. I suddenly think of Coco. She'd be long gone by now. Sweet Coco.

"Then why don't you explain it to me?" Marcy demands.

"You have Doug," I say. "You don't know what it's like to be alone. Most of the time I like it, but I'm turning fifty this year, and the thought of growing old by myself scares me."

"I get it," she says with a little more sympathy.

"Where did the decades go?"

"I'm not trying to break up his marriage," I maintain. "It's just nice to have someone care about me and pay attention to me."

"I'd pay more attention to you if you lived closer."

"I miss you too."

"You should go online to meet someone. Doug has a coworker who met his wife that way."

That's how I'd met Brad. Marcy had convinced me to place an ad years ago. Have I come full circle?

"I don't know." I sink onto the couch. "You know what's weird? I don't think I'm in love with him anymore. Maybe I never was. Maybe it was just lust."

"Really?" Her voice is laced with doubt.

"Yeah. It's been healing being able to talk about the past."

"So, what did he say about it?" she asks. "Was he seeing someone else like you thought?"

"He says he doesn't remember."

"Yeah, right."

"I'm pretty sure he met his wife before we broke up. It sounds like he got married right after."

"I'm not surprised."

"I know you didn't like him, but things were good, and I was a mess back then. It might've worked out if I'd had it more together."

"I never trusted him."

"You don't trust anybody." I laugh.

"That's true." She laughs too. "Hey, he's like a virus. You caught him once and now you're immune."

"Ha! That's right."

"Okay, so I'm going to sign you up on a singles site, and you're going to meet some incredible guy, and I'll fly up there for your wedding," she says.

I give a sarcastic laugh. "That's how I met Brad."

"That was my fault, wasn't it? But this time you'll meet someone better."

"Better than Brad? I doubt that."

"Seriously, it's like shopping online. You'll get the upgraded model."

"I don't want to deal with relationships anymore. It's nice to be off that rollercoaster. My life is peaceful and drama free."

"You just told me you're lonely."

"Well, yeah, sometimes, but once the baby comes, I'll be pretty busy. I'll be helping Lacie and babysitting. I can't wait."

I can't picture Lacie's little baby. It seems surreal that my baby is having a baby. I haven't held one in decades. I can't wait to see that little thing.

"Wow. I can't believe you're going to be a grandmother. That sounds so old."

"You're the same age as me," I remind her.

"I am three months younger," she protests indignantly.

"You'll be a grandmother someday."

"Don't you dare say that to me."

"Anyway, I'm glad I could finally tell you about talking to Brad. I felt so bad keeping something from you."

"Well, I still don't like it. Tell him if he wants to talk, to go talk to his wife," she says.

I nod to myself. She's right.

"Do you know what she looks like?"

"No, but I bet she's pretty."

"I'm sure she is," she says. "You shouldn't be talking to him after everything. You don't need him."

"I don't need him." I agree.

And, with a sense of satisfaction, I realize that's true. I don't need anybody. I can take care of myself now. I raised my kids alone, and they turned out just fine. I have a good job and a roof over my head that I own. I have my little house and my little yard and my tranquil little life.

Brad made his choice long ago. He married

someone who is his partner in business. They have two precious children together. His parents adore their daughter-in-law and spoil their grandchildren. Brad and Julia probably had a huge wedding and went to Europe on their long romantic honeymoon. They moved into a big spacious house with overpriced furniture and a gorgeous view of the ocean. They make love every night and sleep snuggled in their king-sized bed. They count their money together and buy each other exorbitant gifts. They toast each other with glasses of wine in the restaurant we used to frequent. They played with Coco in the yard when their children were little. I was Coco's mommy. It should've been me.

I don't love him. I hate him.

"Hey, are you there?" Marcy asks.

"Yeah." I rub my face. "Life isn't fair."

I stand and stretch my legs. I look out the window and down the street. The kids are gone, and the ground looks wet. I'm suddenly tired, even though I've only been up a few hours. Every day is the same, an endless string of days looping into infinity. Soon we'll have the joy of a new baby in the family. Lacie and Brandon will have that challenge ahead of them, and I'll be there whenever they need me, but then what is there? Life has worn me out. I'm getting older and something is missing.

"I'm serious. I'm signing you up on that singles site that Doug's coworker used as soon as I find out which one it is," Marcy vows.

"No. I don't want to do that."

"Why not? The four of us will take vacations together. Don't you want to go to Egypt and see the pyramids?"

"Where do you come up with this stuff?" I can't help smiling. God, I miss Marcy. Everyone should have a crazy friend like her.

"We'll go to Bora Bora and sit under a tree and

think about nothing all day."

"I'd like to think about nothing all day."

"Wouldn't that be amazing?" she enthuses. "Imagine not worrying about anything and living in the moment."

"We're supposed to take cruises or drive around in an RV when we get older," I say.

"We can do that," she says. "I'll go anywhere as long as I don't have to cook and clean."

"That's your criteria?"

"That's it."

"We better start saving our money for all these things."

"Oh, man, and there's the catch," she says.

"There's always a catch," I respond.

"What a bummer. If I win the lottery, I'll pay for everything."

"I think I hate Brad now," I pronounce.

"You do?" Marcy asks.

"Yeah, Brad with his beautiful wife and his big house and his rich parents and his exciting life and always getting what he wants."

Why did I have to run into him at the airport? Why did he have to ask me to call him? Why did he still have to look so good? Why does his voice still make me warm all over? Why can't he leave the past alone? Why can't I?

Brad. Here I am again, obsessed with him, though now I hate him. I resent his ability to manipulate me. I didn't want to talk to him in the first place but, somehow, he always gets his way. I'm jealous of his utopian life. He has it all.

Then why does he want to converse with me on the phone? Does he enjoy the flirtatious banter or dispensing advice or the ease of manipulating me? Does he enjoy the decadence of having his cake and eating it too? Why can't he let me go? No. I'm not in love with him anymore. I'm not. But why can't I let *him* go?

My mind wrestles with these questions. I thought I'd find closure, but hearing his voice pries the past open further. His voice is like a soothing wave that draws me into a riptide. How does he do this to me? How does he have this effect on me?

Marcy's right. I shouldn't give him the time of day. This can only lead to a dead end. There is no future for us, and I don't want one with him, anyway. I don't want to put myself through the disapproval of his snobby parents. I don't want to wonder every time the phone rings if it's another woman.

I feel a twinge of sympathy for his wife. She doesn't know he engages in flirtatious phone calls with an old girlfriend. Does she know the character of the man she married, or is she just like him? Maybe they deserve each other.

Chapter 28

Lacie and I paint the baby's room a soft pastel green. The open window allows a lazy breeze to drift in. I'm astonished at the transformation a little paint creates. It's a calming color and I think about painting some of my rooms, especially the bedroom. A relaxing sanctuary like this would be nice.

Brad calls and I send him a quick text. *Busy.*

I can never call him. I always have to wait for him to call me. Everything is always on his terms. I'm sick of it, and I don't have to put up with it any longer. I need to learn to stand up for myself. This has always been one of my problems. I can't let anyone take advantage of me or treat me badly anymore.

Indignant thoughts swirl around in my head while I roll on the color and Lacie paints around the edges. It's a small room and we get it done quickly. Lacie debates whether to paint the same color inside the small closet but decides against it.

We clean up and eat leftover soup she made in the crock pot the day before. The baby is moving a lot today, and I place my hand on Lacie's tummy. A little hand or foot bumps my palm a few times and then slides across her stomach. We look at each other and laugh.

"Can you help me put the crib together?" she asks.

"Today?"

"I want to get the room done. We can do it another day if you want."

"It might take a few hours. Let's do it when we have more time," I suggest.

"You're probably right. Let's just move the rocking chair in there."

We carry the rocking chair into the room and

place it in the corner. I visualize Lacie rocking a baby in her arms with the muted glow of moonlight or early morning.

She sits in the chair and looks toward the window, rocking slowly. "I'm tired."

"That's normal," I say. "I should get home and let you rest. We can put together the crib next weekend if you and Brandon don't get a chance."

"That sounds good. Thanks, Mom."

"Anytime, Lace."

I lean down and give her a quick hug.

"Why don't you go lie down?"

"Okay."

But I can hear the creak of the rocker as I make my way through the house and out to my car. I'm glad we don't live too far from each other. I've resisted the impulse to go to the store and clean out the baby department. I'll save that trip for after her shower, and then we can go together and pick out cute baby clothes and other necessities before the baby arrives. That will be fun.

~ ~ ~

My house is heavy with warm air, and I open the windows and the sliding glass door. A couple pushes a stroller down the sidewalk. I should buy Lacie a stroller for that little grandbaby. The smell of cut grass is in the air, and I sit out in the sun and read a bit before it sinks lower in the clear blue sky.

I've just stretched out my legs on the lounge chair when my phone rings again. Brad. My anger has dissipated with the lazy warmth of the sunlight, and his voice mollifies my mood further.

"I've been thinking about you," are his first words.

"What have you been thinking?" My tone is coy. I can't help it.

191

I bask in his words as I bask in the sun. He has been my sun as my thoughts incessantly twirl around him. What else do I have to occupy my mind? Other than Lacie and my future grandchild, that is. But Brad's attention, of which I'd many times been starved, feels satiating. He's finally giving me what I've always wanted from him, though too little, too late. Still, I bask in it.

"I've been thinking how luscious you looked at the airport," he says.

"Well, you had your chance," I remind him.

"We always had something..."

"We had a strong attraction."

"Yes. The best."

"Better than with your wife?"

"Don't go there, V."

I've been reprimanded, but it had to be said.

"It's never been like that with anyone," he reveals, confirming the answer to my question despite his protest.

"But it wasn't enough for you," I say, smarting from the ache of old wounds.

This conversation is different. I don't know why the tone has changed, but it's more personal, more intimate. I must remember that I'm talking to a married man. He made his choice years ago, and it wasn't me. I can't let his words soften me into clay that he shapes to his will. How ironic that now I have too much attention from Brad. Why is our timing always off?

"We've been over this," he says, but his tone is gentle. "I felt overwhelmed by your dependence, but I get it. You were a struggling single mother."

"You met me at a low point."

"Exactly. But you always knew how I felt about you."

"We had amazing sex," I say. "That was our relationship."

"Come on, V. It was more than that."

"Was it?" I muse. "If there was more to it, things would've turned out differently between us."

"You know I cared about you."

"I know you did," I concede. "You were good to me, but when you come right down to it..."

"You're wrong."

"It's okay, Brad," I assure him. "You don't have to spare my feelings. Let's be honest. It was really all about sex, and that's okay. We had a good time together. I'm not going to make it into anything more than it was."

"You're wrong, V," he repeats.

"You don't have to say that," I insist. "I'm not scarred for life or anything."

"You sound so different," he says. "You're much more rational."

"Thanks," I answer. "Everything turned out as it should. You wanted kids and now you have a family."

"Yes, I do."

"Oh, I idolized you when we were together. I thought you could do anything. You were Superman to me. Like when you saved Coco."

"She was a great dog."

"Yeah," I agree. "But that's a lot of pressure to put on someone when you expect them to be perfect all the time."

"You made me feel like I could do anything. You had more faith in me than anyone else. More than my parents," he says.

"Yeah, well, they were wrong about both of us."

"Yes, they were," he states. "You're much stronger than I gave you credit for. I should've seen your potential. I should've..."

"We did what we did," I cut him off.

Why wallow in the past? There's nothing to be done about it, though I appreciate his encouraging words. He no longer sees me as a disaster. This gives me a sense of satisfaction and momentarily makes me feel better about myself. At the same time, memories have broken loose and are churning up from the depths.

"I was devastated when you told me you wanted to see other people." I recall the deep cut of his words. "I know it was the right decision then. It never would've worked between us, but it was..."

"I was unfair to you. It was wrong for me to expect you to keep seeing me after I said that."

"You didn't have the guts to break up with me. You made me do it."

I think back to that morning. I don't know where I'd found the mettle to leave, knowing I might never see him again. I remember the moment he grabbed me after I'd announced I didn't want to see him anymore. I'd never seen him react so effusively. Some sense of urgency had flared up in him and surged toward me. He'd lost control for a few moments, and it had given me hope for something that never came. I had walked out with legs shaking and lip trembling, holding back the floodgate of tears I'd let loose in my car at Marcy's.

"That morning. When I left for good. Your reaction stunned me," I say.

"I didn't want to give you up."

"Then you sent me flowers," I remind him.

"My feeble attempt at romance," he says with a laugh.

"But it didn't work."

"I was also devastated, V," he confesses. "I didn't realize how I felt until the moment you were leaving, and I reacted the way I did. It stunned me too."

"I could tell."

"You told me you loved me that day," he says.

I'm surprised he remembers my words.

"Yes, I did," I murmur. Had I really loved him?

Maybe I had.

"That's when I realized I loved you too. That morning. But I couldn't say it."

His words hang in the air. Did he just say that to me? Did I hear him correctly, or is my mind conjuring up the words I'd always longed to hear him say? My heart is throbbing in my ears. His words feel as fragile as spun glass.

"You don't have to say that," I say weakly.

It's too late, Brad. Too late.

"Yes, I do, and I should've said it then," he asserts. "And I still do. I love you, V, and I always have."

Chapter 29

I sit with the phone in my hand after we hang up. Brad had hung up abruptly. Had he said more than he'd intended, or had he been interrupted?

I'm sweating in the sun, and I fold up my lounge chair and go inside. I want so much to call Marcy and spill it, but I can't. Because I'll have to sort this out first in my head. Because I'm not sure how I feel right now. Because I don't know what to do.

I can't do anything. He's married. He's not going to leave his wife and I don't want him to. I think. I can't destroy a family. He has kids. Why didn't he say this to me when things weren't so complicated? Now it's too late. Isn't it?

What does he expect me to do with this? What does he want from me? He always loved me. This is validation that I wasn't deluding myself about what I believed was between us in the past. I always knew deep down on some level that he did. I wasn't an idiot to keep seeing him. It wasn't just sex. I *knew* it. I *felt* it. I felt he loved me, and I hadn't been wrong. That's what had kept me hanging in there, even though we only saw each other once a week, even though he never called me between dates. It was because, when we were together, I knew how he felt. The fervor he expressed said what he could not. I knew it deep down to the core of my heart that he loved me. And he has just professed that he still does.

Has he felt this way about me all these years? Have songs or movies triggered thoughts of me? Had he looked for me after I'd moved? Yet, he had married soon after our breakup. Had he been on the rebound? Does he feel he's made a mistake?

I reflect on the few brief relationships I've had since my move. They all pale by comparison. I hadn't felt the same level of ardor with anyone. Had I been subconsciously comparing others to Brad? Are we fated to be forever doomed to unrequited love?

Brad. Brad. Brad. I'd convinced myself I'd never loved him. Now I'm not sure what I'm feeling. How do you know if it's love or lust? And what if it's both? That would be too potent a combination to suppress.

He calls me back a few minutes later.

"Sorry I hung up," he says. "I had to..."

"It's fine."

"I want to see you."

"That's kind of impossible," I say.

"Why?"

"You live there, and I live here in different parts of the state," I remind him, glad for the distance.

"I have to go to L.A. for a meeting next week," he says quickly. "I'll buy you a plane ticket and meet you there."

"I can't. I work."

"Right. Well, fly out on Friday night and stay until Sunday. I'll work it out. I want to see you."

"Brad..." I say slowly, shaking my head on the phone.

"I want to see you," he insists.

"You know what will happen if we see each other," I say.

"I'll get you your own room, I swear," he says. "This isn't about sex. We should talk in person. We're having an important conversation that should be done in person."

"I don't think it's a good idea."

"This has nothing to do with my marriage. I'm not leaving my wife," he emphasizes.

"I don't want you to," I say.

"This is only about us. We need to talk."

Us. There is no us anymore, though I can't help liking the sound of it. I haven't been part of an *us* for a long time.

"Come down to L.A. Spend one night. We'll just talk," he coaxes. "Come on, V."

Who would've thought Brad would have to convince me to see him? I feel a bit of vindication. It's incredibly tempting, but how can I agree to this?

"I can't. I told Lacie I'd help her with something," I say grateful for the excuse.

"Okay. I'll see if I can change my meeting to the following weekend."

"This isn't a good idea," I object.

"Come on, V. You know you want to," he teases.

I smile. He's right. I do want to see him, but I'd be playing with fire. Oh, how I miss the fire between us. Is it possible simply to have dinner and talk? Luscious food and scintillating conversation. A bit of wining and dining. How fun to flirt and feel that torturous sense of longing. I need this.

"Maybe," I say. "I'll think about it."

"I can't wait to see you, V," he breathes into the phone.

"No," I say abruptly. "If I come down there, I have to have my own room, and we're just having dinner. Nothing more. Promise me."

"Whatever you want. Your wish is my command," he declares. "It'll be a mini vacation. I'll find a nice hotel, and we'll eat at an expensive restaurant. You can have room service while I'm at my meeting. Just think how relaxing it will be to have a break at the end of the work week. Let me give that to you."

It's sounding better and better. Room service at a luxurious hotel on him. If we can restrain ourselves, what's the harm? We wouldn't truly be doing anything wrong, would we? Just talking. I dismiss the little voice that warns me not to give in, not to trust him, not to do the wrong thing.

I let myself indulge in the fantasy. I see myself soaking in an immense tub, holding a drink in my hand, bubbles floating in the moist air around me. I see myself clinking my wine glass to Brad's over dinner, the two of us laughing and talking like old friends. We are old friends, really, nothing more. Why can't two old friends have dinner together?

"A mini vacation does sound appealing." I weaken.

"You deserve it," Brad says.

I do deserve it. I'd studied diligently in school, I'd married the first man who said he loved me, I'd been a good wife and mother, the best I could. And where had it gotten me? Floundering, often feeling like I was drowning. The things I wanted always beyond my grasp.

Brad and the dream of our life together had been maddeningly elusive. Those were such soul crushing days. All the times I cried over unpaid bills and fretted how I'd be able to afford things. How torn I'd been between my own needs and my kid's. I'd tried so hard to do the right thing for all of us.

But what I'd felt for Brad hadn't been an illusion. It had been real. Now I know that. And this man, who had been the center of my fantasies for a better life, but had been obviously out of my league, now he wanted me. It was flattering, to say the least. But it was still wrong.

"You're tempting me," I demur.

I'm enjoying this reversal. Brad trying to persuade me to see him. Brad imploring and cajoling. Me with all the power.

"Good," he says. "I swear I won't compromise your virtue."

I laugh.

"But seriously, we should talk in person, and I need a friend I can talk to," he maintains. "I could always talk to you honestly."

"Why?" I ask.

"I think because you always believed in me," he

199

answers. "You always saw the best in me."

I ponder this. "But what about your wife?"

"Let's not talk about her. This has nothing to do with her."

"Yes, it does," I counter.

"Fine. What about her?"

"This isn't fair to her," I argue.

"Look. Marriage is a complicated thing, as you know. We don't spend every minute together..."

"You work together."

"Yes, but she sells other houses. It can take me months to complete a house, so she does other deals. We often spend time apart. We don't question each other."

"Because you trust each other."

"We trust each other not to leave the marriage," he clarifies.

"What does that mean? That you each..."

"I don't know what she does."

"Don't you trust her? Are you saying you think she..."

"No, I don't think that, but who knows?"

I'm confused. "Are you insinuating...?"

"No. No. I'm saying our lives are very... separate sometimes," he says.

"I don't know what's going on between you, but I don't want to get in the middle of your marriage," I emphasize.

"That's what I'm trying to tell you in my very awkward way, V, that you wouldn't be. You don't have to worry about that," he says vehemently. "That's why I'm being upfront with you. I don't intend to leave my wife. There will be no messy complications. We need to set things right between us. I need to see myself through your eyes again."

I contemplate Brad's words. He needs to enhance his ego through the prism of my eyes. And I need to feel desired. We both crave this for different reasons.

I wish I could tell Marcy about all this. She'd never believe it. But I can't because I know what my answer is. I could never say no to Brad.

"Say yes," he says earnestly. "Say you'll see me, V."

"Yes," I whisper.

Chapter 30

I stop in at Luke and Serena's house before heading over to Lacie's. It's a small two-bedroom house with a large private yard. Serena has a sizeable garden in the back, and she shows me her vegetables and flowers.

She's taller than me, with light blonde hair and fair skin that almost appears translucent in the sunlight. She and Luke are striking together with his dark looks.

We spend some time sitting on their small back deck in the early morning sun. I take in the slightly floral fresh air while the sun caresses the bare skin of my arms. Soon it will be too hot to sit outside.

Luke is planning on building a gazebo in their backyard, and he asks me which spot I think is best. Their two dogs tear around the yard whenever one of us tosses a ball, and they almost knock me over as we walk around discussing the merits of each potential location for the gazebo.

"Well, I'd better go. I promised to help Lacie put together the crib," I say after a few hours of leisure. I hate leaving the quiet tranquility.

Luke walks me to my car while Serena pulls weeds from the garden. I marvel at how happy and well-adjusted my kids have turned out. As I become more mired in the past.

~ ~ ~

Lacie has already pulled everything out of the box, and parts are scattered all over the carpet in the baby's room.

"What a mess," she says as we stand surveying it. "But we just have to follow the directions."

"We can do it," I say, though I'm not so sure.

We sit on the carpet, and Lacie picks up the foldout with the directions. We work on it for about an hour and a half when Brandon comes home and helps us finish the last few steps. He pulls Lacie to her feet and places the mattress in the crib frame. We stand admiring our work. It almost matches the wood of the rocking chair.

"I just have to buy sheets," Lacie says, stretching her back.

"You need a stroller," I say.

"I need a bunch of things, Mom."

"I thought we could go shopping after your shower and buy whatever you don't get," I suggest.

"That'd be great. I can't wait to pick out all the little baby things." She smiles and rests her hand on the rise of her stomach.

"I'm hungry. I'll go make sandwiches," Brandon offers, heading toward the kitchen.

We meander down the hall and seat ourselves at the big island. Brandon works quickly and sets plates before us.

"Have you thought of any names?" I ask.

"We have some in mind." Lacie glances at Brandon with a smile. "If we can agree."

My phone rings and I check the caller ID before answering it.

"It's me," Marcy says.

"I can't talk. I'm at Lacie's. I'll call you when I get home," I tell her.

"Okay. Tell them hi. Talk later."

"Marcy says hi."

I set my phone on the counter next to my plate.

"We decided not to tell anyone the names until we agree," Lacie says.

Brandon is leaning on the other side of the counter sporting a toothy grin. Brandon is tall and lanky with light brown hair that always looks like he just got out of bed. He's laid back and mellow and easy to like.

Lacie is my height, and I wonder whether this baby will inherit her height or Brandon's. I guess it depends on whether it's a boy or girl, yet a girl could be tall and a boy could be short. I can't imagine what it will look like.

~~~

I call Marcy back when I get home and resist the impulse to divulge my recent conversations with Brad. She'd rightfully disapprove. I'm bursting to share this with someone, but there's no one I can tell.

I have no inkling how my kids feel about Brad. I'm not sure what their memories are, though I remember Lacie telling me he wasn't good enough for me when we broke up. Those words were the precise words I'd needed to hear.

"Wait. What did you say?" My thoughts return to my conversation with Marcy.

"I signed you up. I created a profile…"

"Don't you need a picture for the profile?"

"I have one. It's a few years old, but it looks fine. I wrote the about-me section for you. All you have to do is answer any guys who respond," she says. "I put your email on it."

"What did you do, Marcy!" I cry. "Why didn't you ask me first? Undo it. I don't want to meet any guys online."

"You said you would."

"No, I didn't. *You* said I would." I groan. "What have you gotten me into now?"

"Hey, you'll thank me later, and I told you I'll fly up there for your wedding," she continues blithely.

"Marcy, I don't want to do this. Take it down."

"Too late," she says merrily. "Go to your computer right now so you can see it."

"I'm going to kill you someday."

"No, you won't. You're going to thank me."

I bring my phone to the spare bedroom I use as an office, so named because I have a desk upon which my computer sits. I turn it on and enter my password. Marcy tells me the site and the password she created for me, and I search for myself. Then there I am, smiling in a photo in which she cropped herself out. My hair is a bit windblown, but I look friendly. I read the profile she's written, and it's fairly accurate. I probably couldn't have written it better myself.

"Do you like it?" she asks anxiously.

"Wow! I already have three responses."

"What do they say?"

I read her each one. One of them has atrocious spelling and I frown while reading it.

"Not bad to start," Marcy says.

"I'm going to close this profile down as soon as I figure out how," I inform her.

"Just give it a week or so. At least check out the guys on there. Some of them look pretty good."

"I'm not speaking to you right now."

I hang up and spend the next two hours perusing the men on the site. I send curt responses to the emails I've received and immediately feel bad. Oh well, you have to get used to instant rejections on this type of social site. I scroll through the profiles to see if anyone grabs my attention, but there's always something that curtails my interest, and I keep moving on to the next profile. This is an entire world of which I know nothing. I can see how people might want to try it, especially as you get older, and your options for meeting people narrow.

I see a few men who perk up my interest and one in particular whose picture and profile draw me. On the spur of the moment, I send him a short and sweet email. Then I shut down my computer and curse Marcy.

What on earth am I doing? I'm going to see Brad next weekend, and I'm searching on some singles site like I'm ordering vitamins from Amazon. And I'm about to turn fifty and become a grandmother. I have enough going on. I don't need to complicate things with internet dating. Apparently, I've lost my mind.

My thoughts wander to seeing Brad and looking into his blue-blue eyes once again. Our meeting at the airport had been so brief and unexpected, that I hadn't had much time to process how he looked or how I felt seeing him again. I'd concluded that I'm immune to him now, that I never loved him, that it had been lust that held me in its grasp, but, somehow, he's broken through my defenses once again. How does he always get what he wants? Including me.

It gives me a little thrill to know how much he wants to see me, to savor the words I'd hungered for almost fifteen years ago. He said he loves me and that he always has. Is this really love? Or am I too hurt or closed off to recognize it? Do we belong together? Has fate conspired to draw us back together?

But he's married. I don't want to help someone cheat on another woman. Us women have to stick together. Yet what if she's just like Brad? What if she bends the truth to her whims, just as he does? I don't belong in the middle of this. I should've said no. I shouldn't let people like Marcy and Brad talk me into things I don't want to do.

Brad has forwarded the email confirming my airline reservation. After work on Friday, I have two hours to get on a plane. Then I'll be face to face with him again. He sent me a link to the hotel. It looks posh and extravagant. I never thought I'd stay in a place like that. He has a lunch meeting on Saturday, which gives me the afternoon to lounge in my room. I can order room service and check out the amenities such as the gym or the spa or the pool. I can laze about and unwind.

His business must be doing well. He and his wife are a successful power couple. His parents must be proud. If they only knew. And what trouble lurks in paradise that makes Brad turn to me, or does he just want it all? A wife. A family. A "friend."

I recall how his touch had always sent shivers through me, the irresistible softness of his lips, the fierce lovemaking. I'd been out of control with him. It was almost scary. His voice, his skin on mine, the way he looked at me with hunger in his eyes. I feel weak just thinking about it. He could consume me—body and soul. I don't think I'll be able to resist. And why should I? Only Brad can make me feel like this. Only Brad can quench my longings.

I let my fantasies take me away to him. I envision all I wish could happen between us. I get it out of my system because it can't happen in reality. I can't surrender to him, though I yearn to. I'm not going to let it happen. He won't get what he wants this time.

Chapter 31

My suitcase is in the trunk of my car, and I've checked the big ticking clock on the wall and the time on my computer a thousand times by now while I work away in my little cubicle. As the time draws closer, my stomach twists more and more. Even though it's casual Friday at work, I've dressed nicely knowing Brad and I will go to a restaurant this evening when I arrive.

As soon as the clock strikes five, I log off my computer and hurry toward the exit. I smile and wave to my coworkers as casually as I can summon. I point my car toward the freeway. Darn! I forgot about rush hour. Time is tight and I drive as fast as traffic permits to the airport parking lot, hoping it's not too busy with weekend travelers.

I'm able to find a spot fairly quickly and jump on the shuttle to the airport. If all goes well, I'll make the flight. I weave through the long snaking lines at the security checkpoint. I run, pulling my carry-on suitcase behind me to the gate, which is all the way at the end of the row, naturally. Within five minutes, we're boarding. I just made it. By now I'm a nervous wreck, shaking with anxiety and anticipation.

The plane isn't full, and I wrestle with my carry-on to hoist it into the overhead compartment until a gracious older man helps me. This is what you deal with when you're short.

As soon as the beverage cart wheels down the aisle, I order a drink. I usually avoid drinking on an empty stomach, but my nerves need soothing. This calms me until the plane descends. Here I am, back at LAX, where our chance meeting set all this in motion.

Brad's waiting at the baggage claim. He gives me a big grin and I smile back. He is so familiar to me, and that's comforting in a way. I associate him with competence and composure and confidence. I trust in him to handle things, to take care of every detail.

"Let me get this." He takes the suitcase handle from me and leans into me saying, "I'm so glad you're here."

The tickle of his breath on my ear sends a tingle through me. I almost feel dizzy for a moment and words fail me.

"Let's get out of here." He leads the way and I follow. He's driven up from San Diego, and I notice his newer Camry is a hybrid. He places my suitcase in the trunk and opens my door, closing it once I'm settled. After he slides in and shuts his door, he turns to me.

"I can't believe you're here."

"I can't either."

"Are you hungry?"

"Starving."

"Good. I know a nice place we can go. The dinner rush will be cleared out by now. We'll go there first instead of the hotel. We'll check in after dinner," he says as he drives out of the parking lot. "How was your flight? Did you have any problems with parking or anything?"

"I almost missed the flight," I answer.

"Did we cut it too tight?"

"Rush hour."

"Ah. Right."

I feel numb. It's like we've fallen back in time and it's just another Saturday night. I try not to stare at his profile, which is almost the same sans mustache. His face is more handsome without it. His hair is a little thinner and a little grayer. He's definitely heavier, stouter, but his eyes are just as blue, his smile just as magnetic.

The restaurant has valet parking, and he hands over the keys. It doesn't appear crowded at this later hour. He asks the hostess for a booth, and we're led to a dim, spacious curved booth.

"Wine?" Brad asks as the server patiently hovers.

"No. I'll have a rum and Coke," I say to the server, deciding to continue what I had on the plane.

Brad orders a glass of wine, and we study our menus. I'm famished, but I don't want to eat a heavy meal since it's late. I order a salad and Brad does the same. I quickly take a few gulps of my drink as soon as it arrives and wait for the relaxation it will bring. My nerves are still jittery.

"Thirsty?" Brad raises his eyebrows.

I let out a sigh. "I feel much better now."

"Good."

"The airport is so stressful," I explain. "So crowded. Weekend travelers."

He nods. He's staring at me with a little smile, and I laugh self-consciously.

I lean forward. "What are we doing? Are we crazy?"

"We're just having dinner."

"You know what I mean."

"What do you mean, V?" He still has that mischievous little smile on his face.

I take another sip of my drink.

"This feels good, being here with you," he says.

"Are you going to tell me your wife doesn't understand you?" I say with sarcasm and instantly regret it.

"No, but she probably doesn't understand me like you do."

"Is that true? And I want to remind you that you're under oath." My drink is definitely hitting me.

"In some ways." He shrugs. "She gets my business side."

He takes a sip of wine without breaking his gaze.

"Well, I'm not interested in your business side."

Stop it, I tell myself. I just can't get ahold of myself around Brad, especially after a drink or two. I vow to shut my mouth.

He laughs at my remark and shakes his head.

I stir my drink with the swivel stick and fish out the cherry, which plops onto the table.

"Oops." I pop it into my mouth.

"You look exactly the same," he says. "I'm amazed some guy hasn't grabbed you."

"A few have, but..." I pause and allow myself to meet his eyes. "None of them measured up to you." That might be too much honesty, but I said it and it's true.

"No one measures up to you either, V."

"Then why did we break up?"

"You broke up with me."

"Only after you said you wanted to see other people..." A sense of boldness comes over me. "Because you already were."

"I don't think so."

"Oh, come on, Brad. You were already seeing your wife."

I chew on the end of my swivel stick.

"I think I started seeing her later," he insists.

I lift my glass to take a sip and discover it's empty.

"Where did my drink go?" I say with bewilderment.

The server places our salads before us.

"Another drink?" he asks.

"Yes. The lady will have another and another for me as well," Brad says.

"I don't want another drink," I say, watching the server walk away.

"Yes, you do."

"You always know what I want," I marvel.

"Ditto."

We eat in silence, and I finish another drink. I

stagger to the restroom while Brad orders dessert. I don't want dessert, but he insists we'll share it. I hold a damp paper towel to my forehead. It's difficult to contain myself. This always happens around him.

I return to see a huge brownie fudge sundae topped with a mountain of whipped cream. My eyes widen.

"I knew you'd like it," Brad chuckles.

It's the most sublime dessert I've ever tasted. The brownies are warm and the ice cream is creamy. The whipped cream melts sweetly in my mouth. Brad and I finish it, and I'm truly full and satisfied. I almost feel like I could fall asleep. I am now completely relaxed.

Brad pays the bill and we exit the restaurant. I feel pampered as he holds open the car door. It feels good to be treated well, and I remember that this was the way it always was when we dated. What a wonderful oasis he'd afforded me in the desert of deprivation that had been my life. I'm grateful to him for that.

He pulls up to a hotel that looms like a luminous mirage. Retrieving my suitcase, he stands it behind the car as he shuts the trunk.

"Okay. Let's go get you checked in," he says.

I sidle up to him. "I don't want my own room."

I can't help myself. I press my lips to his, craving the softness, the taste of him. There's smoothness above his upper lip where before there had been the tickle of a mustache.

"Are you sure?" he whispers.

"I knew what I was agreeing to when I said I'd come here." The truth of it registers as the words tumble from my mouth.

"I don't expect..."

"I know."

"There's no pressure."

"I know. What do you want?"

"I want you."

His words incite my fervor, and I can't think of anything I want more right then.

We enter the vast lobby. It has a high ceiling and beautifully tiled floor. Everything sparkles and shines. I stand off to the side while Brad speaks to the desk clerk. We don't say a word up the elevator or walking down the hallway. He inserts the key card and we enter the room. A small desk lamp is on and he barely gets the door closed before I'm pressing myself against him again.

I don't know how I thought I could resist him. He's been a perfect gentleman, and I'm the one who can't hold back. I tear at his clothes like a feral animal. We shed our clothing and make it to the expansive bed where we express the fiery passion that has overtaken both of us. It's been so many years since I've felt this way with anyone. I run my fingers over his skin, through his hair, and over his lips.

"Vera," he sighs. "How did I ever give you up?"

How had we ever given each other up? And how can we do it again?

Chapter 32

I wake up wearing one of his T-shirts and determine not to give it back. He's already dressed.

"I have to go to my meeting," he tells me.

I'm groggy and nod at him.

He laughs. "Okay, sleepyhead. Go back to sleep. Order room service when you get up. Do whatever you want and charge everything to the room. They have a gym and sauna. I'm not sure what else. Probably a spa. I'm going to a job site after the meeting. It may take a few hours. Will you be okay on your own?"

"Uh, huh."

"It looks nice out." He squints toward the heavy draperies. "There are some stores within walking distance, and I thought I saw a park."

"Okay." I haven't moved.

"See you later." The door closes behind him.

I roll out of the mussed bed and pull open the draperies. A flood of blinding light hits me and makes me blink rapidly until my eyes adjust. Below is the parking lot, and I watch Brad cross it and get into his car. I step out onto the small balcony that's drenched in sunlight and sit in one of the cushioned chairs. I sit out there for a while, soaking up the sun with my feet propped on the balcony railing. No one has a view of me in my scanty attire.

When more people walk across the parking lot, I withdraw inside. The room is large and modern. I order room service and unpack my suitcase. I put on one of the thick white terrycloth robes hanging in the closet.

After a breakfast of pancakes, English muffins, hash browns, and orange juice, I take a long hot shower and explore the hotel. I find the gym, sauna, pool, bar, restaurant, and gift shop. They have a plate of warm chocolate chip cookies in the lobby, and I take one before venturing outside to see what's around.

There's a small strip of shops nearby. I stroll in a bookstore, scanning the books for a while. A park is farther down the street, but I go back to the room. I'm not sure when Brad will return. Impulsively, I stop at the bar and order a Mimosa, which I carry back to our room on the eighth floor. I take my drink out onto the balcony. A wide stripe of sunlight falls across my legs as I rest my bare feet on the railing again.

I haven't allowed myself to reflect on what transpired. I feel too good to weigh myself down with remorse, but now my thoughts intercede, and I let myself acknowledge them.

I can't undo it, and it was totally my fault. Had he anticipated this? I should've known I'd never be able to resist Brad. All he has to do is look at me, and my resolve melts like an ice cube on a hot sidewalk. He seems to be the only one who can fulfill my emotional and physical needs so completely. Do I love him or is this lust? I just don't know. I decide to get his perspective when he returns. He said he's in love with me, but is he also in love with his wife? And where do we go from here?

~ ~ ~

I'm lounging on the bed with the TV remote in my hand, flipping channels when Brad returns.

"Exactly where I left you," he says, placing his black briefcase on the small desk.

"How was your meeting?" I ask.

"Productive. How about you? What did you do or did you not leave the room?" He surveys the rumpled bed. "I don't blame you. This is a nice room."

I describe my day and suggest walking down to

215

the park. I want to talk, though once outside, the noise of the traffic makes this a challenge. We walk briskly to the park and, once there, meander more leisurely. A breeze is rustling the leaves and we can hear the sounds of kids at the playground. We take a path away from the noise of the traffic and kids. I debate how to broach the subject, but Brad brings it up first.

"Are you okay with everything?" he asks.

"I'm not sure. Being with you feels good, but it's wrong." I try to articulate what I'm feeling. "This can't lead anywhere."

"Why does it have to lead anywhere?"

"I don't know. I mean, where do we go from here?"

"Wherever we want. We see each other whenever we can work it out."

"But... but what about your wife? Your family?"

"This has nothing to do with them. This is between us. Just me and you."

"But what if she finds out? You could lose everything," I emphasize. "Your family. Your business. Everything."

"How would she find out? She'd only find out if one of us told her and I'm not going to tell her."

"But you're lying to her."

"I'm not lying to her. I'm just not going to tell her." He stops and faces me. "This is how I see it. I have my family over here." He holds out his right hand. "And you're over here." He holds out his left hand. "These things are separate parts of my life that have nothing to do with each other."

"I don't know."

"Men can compartmentalize things. Think of it this way; let's say I have a good friend, Bob, that I hang out with. We go to games or hang out at a bar or play golf, whatever. We're really close. I tell Bob things I don't tell my wife. It's a whole separate type of relationship."

"Okay," I say slowly.

"It has nothing to do with her. He fills certain needs she doesn't fill. I do different things with him, confide in him. Not everyone can fill all your needs."

"Uh, huh."

We begin walking again.

"We all have many relationships in our lives, and they don't cancel each other out," he argues. "That's reality."

"Does this mean I'm Bob?" I ask.

Brad grins. "I guess you're Bob."

"Except your wife doesn't know about Bob."

"She doesn't need to know about Bob because it has nothing to do with her or my relationship with her."

"Do you love your wife?"

He stops and looks at me with disbelief. "Of course I love my wife."

"Wouldn't you be upset if she had her own Bob?" I continue on the path.

He lags for a few moments before he catches up to me. "Okay, I *would* be upset. I get your point."

I stop and face him. "So, what now?"

"That's up to you, V," he says. "I don't want to stop and I see no reason to, but if you can't handle this, I get it. I'm the one taking a risk. You lose nothing by seeing me."

I deliberate this. He's right. I'm only risking my conscience. But now I have a big secret, something I can't tell Marcy or Lacie or Luke. A big dirty secret.

Chapter 33

We go out to dinner at an upscale restaurant, the sort Brad had gotten me used to when we were dating. We have a sumptuous meal, and again I can't resist the temptation to order a few drinks. I hardly ever drink anymore, and it seems so indulgent sipping a drink with dinner. Once again, Brad orders a sinfully delicious dessert that we share. He makes me feel pretty and sexy and desirable. I haven't felt this way in years. In fact, I'd forgotten how alive it makes me feel. I'd obliviously settled into a rut, but now a chasm of yearning has opened that can only be filled with Brad.

Again, I find it impossible to suppress my impulses once we're in our room. I revel in the exquisite bliss of the moment and tell myself this will be the last time. This will not be a regular thing. I sleep like a rock afterward in the large bed.

I'm not distraught over saying goodbye to Brad at the airport, which amazes me. Maybe this one weekend has satiated me, and I don't *need* him anymore.

I contemplate the weekend as I sit on the plane staring down at the fluffy white clouds. I hadn't meant for it to happen this way. In fact, I'm not sure what I'd expected to happen. Did he anticipate I'd behave this way? Did he count on it? Does he know me better than I know myself?

Okay, so now I've gotten it out of my system. It doesn't have to happen again, but since it already has, what's the difference if we do it again? This outlet seems essential.

I've always done everything right and look where it's gotten me. Alone with no excitement in my life. Sure, Lacie's baby will be here soon, but I need something for myself. Bits of guilt snag at my buoyant mood, but Brad's right. I'm not the one doing anything wrong. Yet a sense of female loyalty looms for his wife. But what if she's also doing her own thing? It's not my fault that their marriage is lacking. I don't know what's going on between them.

I think of Marcy. Boy, would she be mad at me for being the other woman. I don't like that term. I'm not competing for Brad.

It's late afternoon when I arrive home on Sunday after the short flight. Brad had tried to hand me a hundred-dollar bill to pay for parking and any other expenses I may have incurred, but I didn't accept it because it doesn't feel right.

I get some laundry going and log onto my computer. I have seven messages from guys on the singles site. I skim through them. Two of them look appealing. I might meet them. That will get Marcy off my back. I reply to each of them and debate whether to delete my profile. There's not much harm in leaving it up for now.

~ ~ ~

Later in the week, I meet a guy at a coffee place. It initially feels awkward, but we begin a casual conversation after a while. He's nice enough, but my feelings are tepid. There's just no spark. He tells me I'm more attractive than my photo and wants to meet again. I stammer, not sure what to say.

"I... I have a few other guys to meet," I say.

How do you kindly reject someone, especially when he doesn't deserve it?

"Okay. How about if I give you my number and you can call me?" He writes it on a napkin and hands it to me.

I smile and quickly escape. I'm no good at this dating thing. Next time I'll have something prepared that doesn't sound heartless if I'm not interested.

Lacie's best friend throws her a large shower. I've never met most of these women who are friends, former classmates, and coworkers. I carpool there with Luke's girlfriend, Serena. We're both introverts and are overwhelmed by Lacie's raucous friends. Serena is a quiet person and smiles easily. She's made a diaper "cake" for Lacie out of rolled up diapers with teething rings, rattles, and small toys attached. It's cute and clever. I wonder if she and Luke will ever have a baby.

Lacie receives lots of cute outfits that make us ooh and aah, a highchair, a few mobiles, a few books, two gift certificates, and various other items. No one has given her a stroller. That will be on me. Somebody also bought a giant teddy bear that delights Lacie. She jokes about throwing Brandon out of bed and cuddling with the bear. I sit with a stuffed penguin in my lap, taking pictures with my phone. Serena documents the gifts on a pad of paper next to me. Lacie has a great time, and it's a fun day.

The following weekend, Lacie and I head to the mall where we spend her gift certificates, and I buy a pricey car seat that attaches to a stroller frame. I didn't even know they made things like that, but it's brilliant and efficient. We choose outfits and blankets and socks. They're so tiny I can't imagine a little human fitting into them.

~~~

I meet the other guy at a bar not too far from my house. This is better because we can have a drink and feel more at ease. I'm in a weird mood and keep making snide remarks that he finds amusing. I'm actually enjoying myself. Justin works in HR for a large company and is low key. He has kind eyes and light shaggy hair. We laugh a lot during our conversation, and I leave with a favorable impression. Maybe I'll see this one again. He's no Brad, and I don't feel any passion for him, but I'll probably never find that with anyone else.

Brad has been texting me every few days. Then I get an email with flight information. He hasn't even asked me if I want to see him again. He knows me too well. He knows I'll get on a plane again to meet him. He knows I can't say no, and I suspect he feels the same inability to resist me. So, it seems I'm going to keep seeing him until... What? Forever? I don't know, and I don't want to think about it.

Again, I go to work with a suitcase in my trunk and drive straight to the airport after I get off work. Again, I park at the same shuttle lot and get on the plane. And tingle with exhilaration at the thought of seeing him again. This time I know what to expect. He'll wine and dine me before I ravage him. He'll spoil me and I'll bask in his attention. We can't get enough of each other. Again, little bits of remorse will snag at my bliss and I'll ignore them. How can I so flippantly sleep with another woman's husband? I don't know how I can do it. I never would've thought I'd be capable of getting into a situation such as this.

"How long are we going to do this?" I ask him at dinner.

"Do what?" Brad looks at me innocently with his blue-blue eyes.

"You know. See each other?" I lower my voice and look around as if people can tell what we're doing.

He shrugs. "As long as we want."

"Aren't you happy with your... Julia?"

"Sure I am. This has nothing to do with her."

I hate when he says that.

"It sort-of does."

"No, it doesn't." He takes a sip of wine. "This is

totally separate from my relationship with her. In fact, it makes me a better husband because I'm happier."

"That makes no sense." I shake my head.

"I think we're good for each other."

I can't help agreeing, but that doesn't make it right.

"I guess I'm still your friend, Bob," I say stirring my drink with the swizzle stick.

He grins. "You're still Bob. I put you in my phone by that name."

"Too bad I can't see Marcy while I'm down here," I say wistfully.

"Why can't you?"

"How would I explain being here? I've hardly talked to her on the phone because I don't want to lie to her."

"You don't have to lie. Just don't tell her."

"She's too perceptive. She'll know I'm not telling her something," I say. "Anyway, I can tell her I met one of the guys from the site. Did I tell you she signed me up?"

"She signed you up? Don't you have to sign yourself up?"

"She did the whole thing for me," I say. "I didn't want to, but she just did it, created a whole profile and everything."

"And you met some of these losers?" he asks.

Do I detect a hint of jealousy? I like that. Let him know what it feels like.

"*We* met online," I remind him.

"That's right. We did," he confirms. "So, who's my competition?"

"I met two guys. One of them was nice. I'll probably see him again," I say nonchalantly.

"Why?"

"Why?" I repeat.

"Isn't this enough for you?" he asks. "I try to give

you everything you want."

"You do, but I..."

"Oh." He reaches in his pocket. "I won't get to see you for your birthday."

He places a small silver box on the table between us. I let out a little gasp. He's never bought jewelry for me before. How I'd longed for this type of intimate gift that I could wear all the time, reminding me of his feelings. I picture him at a jewelry store perusing the items, choosing something special for me.

"Fifty, right? A milestone."

"Yes, I'm going to be fifty. I can't believe you remembered." I reach slowly for the box and lift the square lid. It contains a delicate gold chain with a small gold heart. In the center is my birthstone.

This isn't like Brad, sentimental and romantic. Knowing him, it's an expensive necklace. I put it around my neck where it rests coolly against my skin.

"You do have my heart, V," he says.

"Brad," I murmur. "Thank you. It's beautiful."

And my heart opens a little more.

Chapter 34

Brad has just taken a shower. For some reason, it amuses him to shake his wet hair at me like a dog and sprinkle me with droplets of cold water while I'm still lounging in bed in his T-shirt.

"Stop it!" I shriek.

He laughs and tosses the towel on the bed.

"Oh, crap," he says when his phone rings. He looks at me and shakes his head.

I stare at him blankly.

He puts his finger to his lips.

I nod. His wife is calling.

"Hi," he says. "No, I just got out of the shower... I don't know how productive it was... Well, I don't think they're going to come up with the money... I told them that... Yeah... Right..."

He's pacing the sunlit room naked. I watch him mesmerized. The flex of his leg muscles, the sag of his stomach, the drips on his shoulders. He slicks back his hair with his fingers and flashes a tight grin at me.

I think of her on the other end, having no idea her husband just got out of bed with another woman this morning, that I'm viewing his naked body right now, that I'm just as familiar with it as she is.

"What did the electrician say? ...What's the delay? ...I'll talk to them when I get back... Okay, well, ask them... Okay... I didn't mean... That's not what I said... Right..."

He glances my way. I should get up and go into the bathroom to give him privacy, but I can't make myself move. I want to hear what he says to her. It sounds like there's tension between them. I can hear it in his defensive tone.

"We'll talk about this when I get back... I know... How are the kids? ...Can I talk to them? ...Where are they? ...Okay, when I get back... That's good... What did they offer? ...Did they say anything about the carpets? ...Good... Sounds like a done deal... That'll free up some money for the other house..."

I get out of bed and wander over to the sliding glass door leading out to the balcony and stand silently, looking down at the glare of the sun on the cars below. The trees in the park beckon in the distance. We should take a walk down there. It's a nice day.

Brad is behind me, wrapping his arm around my waist and pulling me to him.

"Okay... I will... Tell the kids hi. I'll be home soon."

He hangs up. "I hope that wasn't too weird for you."

"It sounds like you sold a house."

"We did."

We. But I didn't hear him say he loves her or misses her. It sounded almost like a business call. Maybe that's how it is after being married so long, but I wonder about their intimacy or lack of. Does he miss her? What is their marriage like?

He kisses my neck. He rarely does that, and I automatically respond. His kisses set the hairs on my neck on end, and his damp hair brushes my shoulder, making me tremble. His hands roam over my body, under the T-shirt, down my stomach.

"You just got out of the shower," I say.

"I don't care."

Talking to his wife appears to turn him on. Is it because what we're doing is wrong? Is he getting back at her for some slight? In some twisted way, this call has turned him on, and I give in even though I feel impassive. His lovemaking is intense, a little aggressive.

Afterward, we lay sweating on the bed. His hair has left areas of dampness on the sheets and

225

pillows, which are now in disarray. A pillow is on the floor along with the T-shirt. A long ray of sunlight stretches over my thighs. My stomach reminds me we haven't eaten breakfast yet, but I'm drained of energy and remain motionless.

"It would be a tremendous turn-on if we had a three way," he says as we lay there.

"Three-way?" I raise my head. "With who?"

"Well, my fantasy is my wife, but she'd never do something like that," he says.

"Is that what you were fantasizing?" I ask.

"Yeah. Does it bother you?"

"No." I contemplate this a moment. "Is she pretty?"

"Yes," he says. "Like you."

"But she's not open to certain things?"

"No, she's a little uptight sexually."

This is interesting. I'm curious about her. Every fragment of information falls into the puzzle that forms the bigger picture. What am I doing here? Fulfilling his sexual needs, or does he love me as he claims? As well as I know him, I still can't fathom what's truly in his head and his heart. Sometimes I see genuine affection in his eyes when he gazes at me. At least I think I do, but am I confusing this with desire?

"So, what do you think?"

"About what?"

"About a three-way."

"Seriously?" I wrinkle my nose.

"No? I thought you were up for anything," he says.

I turn onto my side, facing him.

"I'm here for *you*, Brad, because of my feelings for you. Not because I want crazy sex, even though we have this amazing chemistry. I'm just trying to analyze what I really feel."

I have no need to play games and hide my

226

feelings. He can't hurt me like before. I'm not as fragile. I've achieved a level of detachment, perhaps by necessity. He says nothing, and I can't read him.

"And what you really feel for me," I add.

"You know how I feel," he answers.

"I think I do, but..." I pause. "You told me you love me, and you always have. So, I don't know how..."

Say it! I scream inwardly.

"How you can stay married to her when you feel..."

"I'm not leaving my wife," he says adamantly and sits up.

"I'm not asking you to." I sit up too and watch him get dressed. "I just want to know where I fit in all this."

"Don't make it complicated."

"I'm not trying to make it complicated." I dress as well. "I just want to clarify things for myself."

"There's nothing to clarify," he says with irritation. "This is what it is. Right here. This is what it is."

"Just sex?"

"No, of course not." He sighs heavily. "Yes, I love you, V, in a certain way. It's different with my wife. You love people in different ways."

"You love me in a noncommittal way."

"I am committed to you, to us, in the way we are right now," he says.

Whatever that means. It's maddening how vague he is.

"So, it sounds like I'm free to meet guys on the singles site then," I say breezily.

I notice him stiffen.

"None of them is you," I assert, because it's true.

He turns and fixes those blue eyes on me intently. "Just don't stop, V. Don't stop seeing me."

"What if I start seeing someone?"

"It has nothing to do with us."

"Not if I get into a relationship," I say. "I'm not going to keep doing this if I meet someone."

"Why not? He doesn't have to know. What we have is separate."

"Brad." I shake my head at him. "I won't do that. Trust is important in a relationship, and I'd want honesty."

"Be honest with yourself about what *you* want." He points at me. "Be honest with yourself."

"That *is* what I want. A real relationship with commitment."

"Is that why you're shopping for guys?" he asks. "I thought you were happy being single. Your friend is the one who signed you up. She doesn't know what you want. You don't need some guy."

I shrug. "That's true, but Justin was..."

"Justin?" He raises his eyebrows.

I'm beginning to enjoy this. This is obviously getting to him.

"Justin was nice and I'll probably see him again."

"I don't think Justin can give you what I can."

"In some ways, but he can give me something you can't." I pause and wait for him to ask.

He gives me an annoyed look. He's going to be stubborn and refuse to ask.

"He can give me time. He can give me a commitment."

"Oh, so you and Justin are a big deal now." He grabs his wallet off the desk and shoves it in his pocket.

"No. I've only met him once, but he's available. I can call him whenever I want and see him anytime," I answer.

"I thought you didn't care about commitment."

"I don't with you because that's the reality, but maybe I do want an actual relationship someday. I'd like to have that option."

The necklace sparkles on the end table by the bed. It softens me and I go over and pick it up. I put it around my neck and grasp the little heart.

"Thanks for giving me your heart." I smile tenderly at Brad.

He gives me that warm smile that melts me a little. My insides soften and send a tiny flutter of exhilaration rippling through me. Oh, how he gets to me.

"But I want more," I say weakly.

"You have me, V," he insists. "You have as much of me as I can give you."

Chapter 35

Marcy calls me on my birthday, which is a Monday. I've just gotten home from work and have changed into sweatpants and Brad's T-shirt, though I'll have to change again soon.

"Happy birthday, stranger," she says. "Why haven't you returned my calls?"

"Just busy," I say. "I don't have much time. I'm meeting the kids for dinner."

"That's cool. The big five-oh, huh? Man, you're old." She laughs.

"You're right behind me," I remind her.

"Whatever."

"Thanks for the card."

We send each other funny cards every year. The sillier the better.

"You're welcome."

"I wanted to tell you that I met a few of those guys."

"From the singles site?" she asks with interest. "Did you like them?"

I don't tell her I have since deleted my profile. It was too much work keeping up with the daily emails I was getting, and most of the guys didn't spark my interest.

"Well, I didn't feel anything with the first one. He was nice, but you know."

"Yeah. Got to have chemistry."

"I liked the second one, though. Justin."

"Justin. Vera and Justin. I like it. What do we know about him?" she asks.

"He's divorced. No kids."

"No kids?"

"No. He works in HR. He's taller than I like."

"You like the short guys," she states.

"That's because I'm short."

"Anything else?"

"I only met him once, but I might see him again. We had a good time, laughed a lot," I say.

"Ooh. I'm jealous. I want to get dressed up and go on a date like a real grown up."

"Tell Doug to take you out."

"It's not the same," she whines.

"How are you guys doing?"

"Oh, you know."

"What's going on?" I can hear it in her voice.

"You never believe me," she says.

"What? Is Doug cheating on you again?" I roll my eyes.

"See? You never believe me."

"That's because Doug would never..."

"My coworker saw them."

"Saw who?"

"Doug with some woman."

"Did you ask him about it? There's probably a good explanation."

"I'm going to go through his wallet and look at his phone," she says.

"Marcy, don't do that," I implore. "Just ask him about it."

"I don't want to give him time to hide the evidence. Oh, I should check his emails too."

"Marcy, give Doug the benefit of the doubt for a change."

"Ha!" she cries suddenly. "I got you!"

"You were joking?"

"Yes, silly. I trust Doug. Most of the time, anyway. I know I'm lucky."

"It's taken you long enough."

"I know. But you're right. He'd never cheat on me. He knows I'd divorce him in a New York minute, not to mention I'd kill the slut I caught him with."

"That's a little harsh," I say. "Maybe it wasn't her fault."

"Any woman who sleeps with a married man deserves the wrath of his wife. That's all I can say," she says vehemently.

I bite my lip. I can't defend this imaginary woman too much or Marcy will get suspicious, yet I feel the need to. Things aren't always black and white. What's my excuse? Love? Closure? Would Marcy ever understand if I told her? Probably not. This makes me sad. Now there's a secret between us.

"I should go," I say. "I have to get ready for dinner with my kids."

"Okay. Have a wonderful birthday," Marcy says.

As soon as we hang up, I call Justin. I get his voicemail. I almost hang up, but then leave a brief message. Done. Now the ball is in his court. If he calls, he calls. If not, no big deal.

I change and head over to Lacie's for my birthday dinner. I smell it as soon as I enter the house. Lacie has made lasagna, just like I used to make. I never make it anymore because it's too much work for just me. She's also baked garlic bread, and the aroma wafts tantalizingly through the house.

"It smells delicious!" I exclaim. "You shouldn't have gone to so much trouble."

Lacie is eight months pregnant and tires easily.

"It's for your birthday, Mom. I remember all the times you made us lasagna. It was always so good," she tells me, giving me a hug. "Anyway, Brandon's going to clean up."

"That's right. Happy birthday." Brandon leans down to give me a hug too.

"How do you feel? What did the doctor say?" I ask Lacie.

"Everything's fine." She waves her hand.

Luke and Serena arrive shortly after me. Luke holds a potted plant, and Serena carries a cake she's made from scratch. I peer at the lettering on the pink frosting.

"Happy Birthday Mom," it says.

"It's chocolate with strawberry icing," Serena says as she sets it on the counter.

"Wow, that sounds scrumptious," Lacie says.

"This is for you, Mom," Luke indicates the plant. "Happy birthday. I'll put it here so you won't forget it." He places the plant on the floor by the front door. It has delicate purple leaves that look like butterflies.

"I love it," I say. "I've never seen one of those before. It's so pretty."

"Isn't it? I have one too. Indirect light." Serena hugs me after Luke. "Keep the soil moist."

I reach up and play with the necklace that Brad had given me.

"Is that new?" Lacie asks as she slices the bread.

"Yeah." I say nothing more and no one asks.

We have a leisurely meal peppered with light conversation. The lasagna is filling. I don't think I'll have room for cake, but everyone has a small slice. Serena and I saunter into the baby's room with Lacie, who wants to show us how she has it set up while Luke helps Brandon clean up in the kitchen.

For my birthday, Lacie has bought me a frilly top that I'd admired when we'd gone shopping. She also gives me a small decorative crock pot. This is good for meals for one.

"I use mine all the time," she tells me.

"I have one too," Serena says. "I throw veggies from the garden into it."

I envision how it would be if Brad were here with us today. Would he have taken all of us out for dinner? Would he be comfortable sitting here at Lacie's house? I don't know. Then I picture Justin with us. I don't know him very well, but he seems more casual and would probably fit in anywhere.

~ ~ ~

At the end of the week, I see Justin again. We go out to dinner. I can't help comparing him to Brad. Justin is less sure of himself and klutzy. He can't get the server's attention, and we sit at a noisy table at the back by the kitchen. This would never happen with Brad, who would calmly ensure that everything went smoothly. I view Justin through a more discerning eye than the first time we'd met. I note the flow of our conversation, how often he speaks of himself or asks about me, how intelligent he seems, how witty and clever, his political views, his feelings about children. This is important. I'm about to become a grandmother.

"I feel like you're interviewing me," he says.

He's perceptive.

"I guess I am," I laugh. "We're on our second interview. We're interviewing each other."

"Let's not be so solemn. Let's just enjoy ourselves," he says.

Good response. I like him more and more.

"What are you hiding?" he asks.

"Huh?" I look up at him with astonishment. How could he know I have a secret?

"You keep turning the conversation back to me."

"Do I? That's because I already know all about myself. I want to know more about you." I smile.

"You have a Mona Lisa smile," he tells me. "You're a woman of mystery."

"How did you know I was in the CIA? Are you my contact? What's the secret password?" I laugh again.

He grins. "Okay, Agent 009, the password is ketchup, and while you're at it, could you pass it to me?"

And the mood is light once again. I couldn't be silly like this with Brad. Everything is so serious and polite with him I realize for the first time.

But there's not the same insane magnetism with Justin. In fact, my attraction to Justin is mild. Perhaps it could grow as I get to know him, and it's better to be drawn to the whole person rather than indulging in a purely primal hormonal urge.

Surely, there are other things that draw me to Brad. I admire him in many ways. I feel safe with him. My needs are attended to, even when I'm unaware of them. He indulges me.

Yet I'm aware of everything I do or say around him. I always feel I'm aspiring to his world, that I must meet some standard, that I don't quite belong. Not as much as in the past, but I've always been striving to prove that I'm good enough. But maybe I hadn't had to prove it to him. Maybe it had been myself I was trying to convince.

Chapter 36

"Hey, Bob." Brad likes our secret joke.

I smile into the phone. Brad has called me during lunch time at work. He knows what time I eat and sometimes calls or texts me then.

I'd been straightening the expanding lending library in the lunchroom, which now encompasses two small bookcases. Many of my coworkers have thanked me for the idea, and I'm proud of this minor accomplishment.

"My wife is going out of town for a few weeks with the kids," Brad announces. "You should come down here."

"When?" I ask.

"Next weekend," he says. "I'll get you a room at a hotel here."

I push open the door to the parking lot behind the building and walk towards my car for privacy. My car is parked in the shade, and I open the door and sit sideways on the seat.

"Where is she going?" I wonder.

"To Colorado to visit her parents. She's goes once or twice a year."

"You don't go with her?"

"Sometimes, but we have some projects I have to keep an eye on," he explains. "Why don't you take off Friday and come down for an extra night?"

"I'll have to check with my boss."

"Okay. Let me know right away so I can make the reservation."

"Okay."

"V, I really want to see you." The earnestness in his voice makes me tingle with anticipation.

I sit, dangling my feet onto the asphalt after we hang up. I'll have to break a date with Justin and ask if I can have Friday off, which will be fine with my supervisor. I know I'll have to stop seeing Brad soon. It's not fair to Justin, even though things haven't turned physical or serious yet, but this thing with Brad is holding me back. I feel torn. Am I ready to give him up? I shouldn't keep seeing him if I'm dating someone else, especially if things get intimate. But can I give him up? I don't want to just yet.

Then it occurs to me that I could see Marcy if I fly down to San Diego. I'll just have to work out how to coordinate it without her finding out that I'm visiting Brad. I need to see Marcy. It's been too long.

I ask for Friday off and Monday for good measure. That way I'll have more time to work with. I'm not sure how I'll divide up my time between Marcy and Brad. My mind whirls with possible scenarios as I begin madly texting.

Got Fri & Mon off, but want to see Marcy while I'm down there, I text to Brad.

Will be able to visit you next weekend. Does that work for you? I text to Marcy.

Have to cancel next Fri. Will be visiting my friend in San Diego. Fri after? I text to Justin.

Sounds good. Have fun, Justin texts back.

Yes! Can't wait to see you! Text me details, from Marcy.

OK. Will book flight and call when I get a chance, from Brad.

I don't know how I'm going to coordinate my visits with Marcy and Brad without making her suspicious. I'll also have to lie to her. Should I just spill it? She's my friend. She'll get it. No, she won't. I don't want to spend our limited time dealing with the maelstrom my confession will spawn. No, I'll have to come up with something. I'll have to lie to my best friend. The truth will have to wait.

The best way to do this is to visit Marcy first. I can fly in on Friday and see her that night and all day on Saturday. I'll tell her I have to fly back that night. Then I'll have the rest of the time with Brad. Excitement still ripples through me at the thought of seeing him. It's always been that way. I don't want to give that up. It's too exquisitely thrilling.

I'll tell Marcy I'm taking an Uber from the airport to the hotel and she can pick me up there. Then I'll tell her I'll take an Uber to the airport to go home. She'll probably insist on picking me up or driving me to the airport, except she hates the airport, so I can probably convince her otherwise. Ugh! So many complicated details to coordinate, but it will be worth it to see her. I truly miss Marcy.

Brad emails me the flight info as usual. We discuss the merits of my plan at length when he calls that night. We go over different scenarios, but mine works best. I can't go from being with Brad to visiting Marcy. I'll have to see her first.

"You mean I'll only get you one night?" he complains.

"Two nights. Saturday and Sunday nights," I remind him.

"Okay. I suppose I have to share you with Marcy."

He acts wounded, but I can tell he's not too torn up about it. If I can pull this off, it will be a crazy fun weekend.

~ ~ ~

I fly out on a bright Friday morning. After we land, Brad picks me up and takes me to the hotel. He didn't want me to be too close to the airport, otherwise I'd be hearing the sounds of planes taking off and landing all night. This is something I wouldn't have thought of.

We only see each other briefly. He notices I'm wearing the necklace he bought me and gives me a

238

smoldering look.

"I'll see you tomorrow night," he says. "Text me when you're back at the hotel or if you need anything."

"I will."

Marcy tells me she and Doug want to take me out for a belated birthday dinner. She says it's the perfect excuse not to cook and to have a few drinks. They pick me up in the hotel's lobby.

"Vera!" Marcy shrieks when she sees me, and we hug tightly.

"How can you afford this place?" she asks, peering around the lobby as we go outside to get into the idling car.

"There was a special rate," I lie. "I always wanted to stay in a nice place like this."

"You could've stayed with us, you know," she says. "You could've saved some money. This must be expensive with the flight and everything."

"I know, but I'm treating myself," I answer. "It's my birthday present to myself."

"Nothing but the best," Doug says from the driver's seat.

"That's right," I say from the back seat.

They take me to a restaurant they've recently discovered. It's a little run down, but it's cozy and inviting and the delectable aromas make my mouth water. But I can't help comparing the ambiance to the upscale places at which Brad and I dine.

"The food is good, and it's cheap," Marcy says as we view our menus.

We order sourdough bread and drinks along with our meal. My drink is strong, and I feel the effects immediately.

"Happy birthday," Marcy toasts.

"You look exactly like you did at thirty," Doug says.

"Thanks," I say with a wide smile. Doug is

awesome.

"Fifty is the new thirty," Marcy toasts again.

"Remember when you thought you were so old when you turned thirty?" I remind Marcy.

"Oh, my God. I was depressed for weeks. I thought my life was over." She giggles.

"Fifty is nothing," Doug declares. "Just wait till you're eighty. You'll wish you were fifty again and think how young that was."

"Don't even say that number to me." Marcy points her finger at him.

"Which one?"

"Any of them."

I watch them and think how cute they are together and how lucky they are to have each other. Could I feel that with Justin? Do I *want* that with Justin? I don't know. Right now, my feelings toward him are tepid. I picture Brad being here with us. He'd be looking on with mild amusement. He never loosens up or really laughs, except at movies. He doesn't do crazy silly things. His family has always been too proper and formal. His wife could be like that too, for all I know. But he might eventually learn to unwind more with me. It might be just what he needs. Someone to loosen him up.

What am I thinking? It will never happen. Our relationship is a side thing for him. He'll never commit to me fully. Maybe he's right. This is the ideal arrangement for us because we fill the need to express passion with each other. Living together day after day probably wouldn't work. Would it?

Marcy clinks my glass again. "To friends."

"To friends." I smile at her fondly.

I love this woman. She's been my closest friend for decades. We've seen each other through tough times. We've had laughing fits together. We've shared our insecurities and know each other's weaknesses. We know everything about each other.

Well, almost. Now I've lied to her, but I don't see how I can disclose the truth. I'll have to tell her. Just not yet. Not in the thick of things with Brad.

The three of us talk and laugh and reminisce for hours. Marcy orders shots for me and her. Doug shakes his head and sticks to beer. After the shot plus my strong drink, I'm sufficiently buzzed. They invite me back to their house, but I'm a little too inebriated and just want to fall into my big comfy bed back at the hotel.

Doug says he's okay to drive and puts Marcy in the back seat where she tips over and falls asleep. I climb into the front seat and buckle up.

We drive silently through the busy streets bustling with weekend traffic. I lean my head back against the neck rest and almost fall asleep.

"You should come over for breakfast," Doug suggests. "What time is your flight?"

"In the evening. I could come for breakfast and hang out."

"Why aren't you staying till Sunday? Marcy would love to spend more time with you."

"Oh." I attempt to remember what I'd told her. "I wanted to take a quick trip before the baby. You know Lacie is due any time now. She wants me to help her get ready."

I hope that sounds plausible. My mind is too hazy to come up with anything else.

"Well, next time stay longer," he says. "And stay with us. You don't have to pay for a hotel."

"I will." I promise.

"Can you tell Marcy doesn't get out much?" He nods toward the back seat.

I smile. "You should take your poor wife out more."

"I will. She worries about money too much." Doug smiles at me as he pulls up to the entrance to the hotel. "I'll pick you up tomorrow morning at ten.

Does that work?"

"Yup." I suddenly feel too groggy to expend my breath on more words.

He jumps out to come around and get my door. I take a few long moments to get up the energy to exit the car. He stands patiently and extends his hand. I grasp it, and he tugs me out onto the pavement and right up against him. We stand for a few seconds, frozen with surprise. Then he wraps his arms around me into a clumsy hug.

"It was good to see you, Vera," he whispers in my ear and our lips meet lightly.

My brain jolts to consciousness as I watch the car pull away. What was that? Did I imagine it? The chill of the evening air sharpens the dull edge of awareness, and I question my distorted memory. That did not just happen. That would *never* happen. I must be hallucinating. What the heck did Marcy make me drink?

I drag my heavy body inside the lobby doors and up the elevator. I must be totally misinterpreting it. Doug would *never* do anything like he just did, or I imagined he did. Or did I? Was it my fault? What is wrong with me? I'm turning into some sort of femme fatale.

Chapter 37

I awaken with a dry mouth and thudding head. I hadn't had that much to drink. What a lightweight I am. I use the bathroom and drink down a whole glass of water. I also feel famished. I check my phone.

What time do you want me to pick you up? Brad texted a half hour ago.

Breakfast with Marcy. Will let you know, I text back.

I find a package of crackers from the plane in my purse and quickly get those into my stomach before jumping in the shower. The shampoo has a lovely floral scent, and I linger a little too long, savoring the soothing heat of the shower.

By the time I get down to the lobby, I'm almost ten minutes late. Doug's car is parked off to the side of the entrance. I adjust my glasses on my nose and cross the pavement to his car. The breeze feels cool, ruffling my damp hair.

"Hey," I say, pulling open the passenger door and sliding in. "Sorry I'm late. The shower felt so good."

"That's okay." Doug gives me a tight smile. "Marcy wanted to make pancakes, but she's got a raging hangover."

"Oh, no." I frown. "Then I probably shouldn't come over."

"Yeah, I told her I'd stop here and tell you on my way to the store for orange juice. That's supposed to help with a hangover. She feels terrible because she wanted to spend more time with you before you left."

"That's okay," I say. "She drank a lot last night, but it was fun."

"How are you?"

"I have a little headache, but I'm fine."

"Listen." He stares straight ahead. "I don't know what happened last night. I would never..."

"I know," I say. "We all had too much to drink."

"I don't think you realize..." He pauses.

"Realize what?"

"How pretty you are." He gives me a slight smile. "I always had a little crush on you."

I shake my head. I don't want to hear anything like this from Marcy's husband.

"Don't say another word, Doug. You love Marcy."

"I love Marcy with every fiber of my being."

"I've known you since high school."

"You were pretty then, too."

"I always thought you were kind of cute," I confess.

"Cute?" He looks at me with a grin.

"Yeah. But you were Marcy's."

"Always," he says. "So, don't say anything to her about last night. You know her. She'll blow it up out of proportion. It wouldn't be good for either of us."

"Agreed." I watch a couple rolling their suitcases across the parking lot. "So now we have a little secret."

"We do. We could blackmail each other."

I turn toward him. "Tell me the truth, Doug. Have you ever cheated on Marcy?"

He groans and my heart sinks.

"When? Is it over?"

"No. I never have. Give me a little credit." He gives me a smirk. "Sure, I've had a few flirtations, and I was really tempted once when she kept accusing me. I thought, 'Why not? She already thinks I am.' But the truth is, I don't want anybody else. Not even you, Vera."

"Not even me?" I tease.

"Not even," he says, shaking his head. "Remember when she made you spy on me that one time, and we had drinks at that tavern by my work?"

"Oh, yeah."

"She was so mad that we had drinks."

"She was?" I try to recall.

"That's when you were dating that guy. That one who was rich or something."

"Brad."

"Yeah. She told me you couldn't break up with him because the sex was too good."

"She did?" I blush and turn away from him. "I can't believe she told you that."

"I'm just saying I get it. It would be hard to give that up."

"Did she tell you I ran into him at the airport a while ago?" I ask. "I had to go to L.A. for training for work, and I ran into him when I was waiting for my flight home."

"That must've been strange after so long. Was the old chemistry still there?"

"Yeah, it was, but he's married now."

"That's too bad."

"Anyway, he lives here, and I live up north."

"You're not tempted to meet up with him for lunch or something while you're here?"

"I can't. He's married." I can't look at him.

"Didn't you just meet some guy on one of those sites online?"

"Yeah, he's okay." I shrug.

"Well, if it's not right, it's not right."

I've hardly thought about Justin since I got on the plane. Even though I enjoy my time with him, I don't miss him. I don't think about him. I don't hunger for him.

I look at Doug with fondness. If I could only combine Doug and Brad, I'd have the perfect man.

"Marcy's lucky to have you, Doug," I say.

"Thanks," he says. "Any guy who doesn't appreciate you is crazy."

"Thanks." I look toward the entrance to the

245

hotel. "I might as well go take advantage of the complimentary breakfast."

"Do you want some company?" he offers.

"No. Go home and take care of Marcy." I open the car door and step out. "Tell her I hope she feels better."

"I will," he answers. "And say hi to Brad."

"I will." I freeze as our words sink in and look at him wide eyed.

"I thought so." He nods.

"I... I..." I stammer.

"Don't worry. I won't say anything to Marcy," he swears.

"Does she..."

"No."

"How did you..."

"Just a feeling. I could tell by the way you acted talking about him, and I thought it was weird you weren't spending the entire weekend with us. You still have the same chemistry, huh?"

I get back in the car without closing the door. "I haven't felt this way with anyone else. He's not going to leave his wife or anything, and I don't want him to." I stare at my hands in my lap. "I know it's wrong, it's just that..."

"I'm not judging, Vera. Things are complicated sometimes."

Tears well up. I hadn't realized all I'd been holding in. I remove my glasses and fish for a tissue in my purse.

"I feel so horrible if I let myself think about it, but I can't stop myself. It's like he fills this need in me."

"You just have to let it run its course."

"You think so?"

"I don't know. I don't know anything about this stuff, but it sounds like it to me."

"What's wrong with me that I'd do something

246

like this?" I dab at my eyes with the remnants of a tissue.

"Don't be so hard on yourself." He pats my shoulder.

"Do you think I can ever tell Marcy?" I ask. "I hate lying to her."

"And face the wrath of Marcy?" He laughs. "At your own risk. I don't think she'd ever forgive you."

"But she knows how things were between us. She knows how I felt about him," I protest.

"Yeah, and you know how she is about this subject. This is her trigger subject. She'll just go off on you and probably never speak to you again."

"But I share everything with her," I whine softly.

"You might have to keep this one to yourself."

We sit silently, each in our own thoughts, for a few minutes. The entrance to the hotel is getting busier as guests come and go. I watch them impassively.

Doug breaks the silence. "Did Marcy ever tell you we went to counseling?"

"No." I turn to him and raise my eyebrows. "When was this?"

"It was a long time ago. It must've been right after you moved."

"Did it help?"

"I think so. It made her understand that her constant accusations could push me away," he says. "You know, we both have our issues, stuff from our childhoods. I need validation…"

"Who doesn't?"

"Yeah, and she has her insecurities."

"How long did you go?"

"About a year or so. I think it helped us understand each other better. Everybody's screwed up. We just have to learn to overlook each other's craziness."

"I'm surprised she never told me," I say,

wondering what else we haven't shared with each other. "I probably need therapy to help me understand why I can't resist Brad."

"I think you go for guys who can't commit. The less he wants to commit, the more drawn in you are. Think back to all your relationships. Try to see the patterns. I bet if he left his wife, you wouldn't want him as much."

"He wasn't married the first time I was involved with him."

"But he still wouldn't commit to you."

I contemplate this. "We always want what we can't have."

"The grass is always greener," Doug says.

And we all have secrets.

Chapter 38

I mingle in the dining room with the other guests at the hotel. The buffet line is long and I stand patiently deep in thought. I'm astounded that Doug guessed my secret. How could he pick up on it when Marcy hasn't? Somehow, we'd started talking about Brad, and my feelings must've been obvious. If Marcy ever comes to the same conclusion, she'll be furious with me. I vow to tell her when it's over. This can't go on forever, especially if I keep seeing Justin. But why hadn't she told me years ago that they'd gone to therapy? I'm hurt that she hadn't confided in me, yet I have no right after what I've kept from her. We all have secrets.

I choose a croissant and an English muffin and hash browns. Comforting carbs. And orange juice. I should get something in my stomach before I see Brad. I sit by myself and text him.

An hour?

I wait, but no response. I still have a mild headache and go back up to my room to wait for him. I sit out on the balcony, but it's bathed in shade. My hair is still wet and makes me shiver. I don't see any shops or a park I can walk to, so I sit on the bed and flip through the TV channels. An old sitcom catches my eye, and I watch it while I continue to reflect.

I text Marcy, *Hope you feel better.*

She texts back, *Sorry! I feel like poop. Talk soon.*

Finally, a text from Brad. *See you in 20.*

I'm not sure what he has in mind for today. It's going to warm up, and we could stroll around somewhere or go for a drive.

I'm standing outside wearing my sunglasses when he pulls up. That familiar little thrill rushes through me.

249

"How was breakfast with your friend?" he asks.

I find it annoying that he either doesn't remember her name or won't say it.

"Marcy wasn't feeling well, so I ate here," I respond.

"She's sick?"

"We had some drinks last night at dinner and she has a hangover," I clarify.

"Do you have a hangover?" He glances at me as he pulls onto the busy street.

"Just a little headache," I answer. "Where are we going?"

"I thought I'd show you the house I'm working on."

I perk up. "I'd like to see it."

I'm eager to tour this house. He's never taken me to any of his jobs before. I'd only gotten to see the house he'd been living in when I'd met him. Why hadn't he ever shared this with me before? Why hadn't I asked?

I debate whether to mention what transpired with Doug, the brief kiss, the conversation where he'd guessed my secret, but I don't want to give Brad cause to disparage Doug. I toy with bringing up Justin to spark his jealousy again, but I remain silent. I'm tired and the sun coming through the windshield is making me feel drowsy.

I used to live in this area, but it's gotten more built up, and it's no longer familiar. There are stores and strip malls and parks everywhere. We drive past a huge playground overrun with kids beside a recently built housing development.

"I don't recognize anything," I lament.

"There's been a lot of new construction, which is good for me," Brad says. "The market is good right now."

"I bet."

He turns onto a residential street and pulls into

the driveway of a two-story house in a pleasant neighborhood. The front lawn is torn up, and the outside is half painted.

"We'll get all this done next week." He gestures to the outside of the house.

"Does anybody live here?" I ask.

"No. This is one I bought to renovate and sell."

He opens the front door with a key, and I follow him inside. It smells of paint.

"You should've seen it when I started. It was very dated," he says. "Most of the inside is finished now."

"I like the floors."

The plank flooring beneath our feet stretches out luxuriously into the living room.

"Most buyers like this look," he tells me.

I wander around. Long black streaks splay across the white kitchen countertop, the stainless-steel appliances gleam, and black pendant lighting hangs over the large island. The cabinets are a clean white and the backsplash is a black and white herringbone pattern.

"Wow," I say.

"You like it?"

"It's beautiful."

"Come see the rest of it."

He leads me through the house, pointing out his improvements. The walls are painted light colors and there's new carpeting in the bedrooms. Both bathrooms are being completely redone.

"I wish you could work on my house," I say with admiration.

"What's your budget?" he asks.

"Zero." I shrug.

"I couldn't do much with that," he teases.

I think about my little house and picture Brad fixing it up for me. It definitely needs updating. I could probably paint some rooms myself and get new furniture. The flooring could be replaced in addition to the countertops and appliances. Someday.

"We're going to make a quick stop at my house," he interrupts my daydreams. "I have to change out of my work clothes, and you can see the deck I just built."

"Okay."

He locks up and we get back in the car. His house. Where he lives with his wife and kids. I must admit I'm curious.

"What about your neighbors?" I ask when we pull into the driveway.

"We don't know them that well, but I'll say you're a client if it comes up."

The landscaping is trim and neat in the small front yard, and I follow him through the front door into a tiled foyer.

"You can look around," he says at my reticence. "I'll go change and then I'll show you the deck in the back."

I roam into the living room. There's a large L-shaped couch and big screen TV affixed to the wall. There are two lounge chairs facing the TV. Throw pillows are scattered, and a blanket is draped over the back of the couch. This place looks more lived in and casual than the house he had when I met him. Two bookcases stand side by side against the wall, filled with framed photos and books. I gravitate to the photos.

A large silver frame holds their wedding photo. I finally get to see what Julia looks like. Just as I suspected, she's a pretty blonde, curvier than me, the quintessential California girl. She's slightly taller than Brad, though I can't tell if she's wearing heels underneath her wedding gown from which flows a long train curved artfully to one side. She and Brad are smiling happily. They pose in another photo with his parents standing rigidly by his side and a couple

I assume to be her parents next to her. I view pictures of his two sons, who resemble him, and more casual family photos.

"Come look at the deck." Brad startles me when he reappears.

I dawdle behind him, taking in the hallway and dining room with its large oval table. He opens the sliding glass door and we step onto a tiered deck. The yard smells of fresh wood and mowed grass. Along the cedar fence is a section sporting small bushes and plants.

"It looks good," I say. "I like the different levels."

"Thanks. I've done a lot of work since we moved in. It was a mess. No plants, mostly dirt."

"You looked so happy in your wedding photo," I remark.

"I was. I never said I wasn't happy," he answers.

"You're risking all this," I remind him. "To see me. Aren't you afraid of losing it all?"

"That's my problem," he answers. "You don't have to worry about it."

I shake my head.

"Hey," he comes over to me. "You know how I feel about you."

I wonder if I do.

"I didn't think it would bother you to come here," he says.

"I guess it makes it more real to see those pictures of your family."

"Don't worry. Nobody's going to get hurt," he says. "Come inside. I want to show you something and then we'll go."

He tugs my hand gently. He never takes my hand, and I let him lead me back into the house, away from the living room. I trail behind him down the hall to his office. I'm amazed to see he has the same desk and the same old filing cabinets.

"Look."

He holds up the miniature house I'd bought him for his birthday years ago.

"You still have it," I say with delight.

"Of course I do. It's my good luck charm." He grins.

The little house triggers memories of when he was my world, when I'd count the days until Saturday, when I thought he was my salvation, when we'd sit in the family room eating ice cream out of the same container, the little wine buzz I'd get at dinner, throwing the ball for Coco, hearing the thump of her tail on the floor when we'd wake up in his king-sized bed. I melt with affection for him.

He's giving me that little smile that lights up his eyes and makes him irresistible. His blue-blue eyes are staring right into me and setting me afire.

"Brad," I say breathlessly.

We still have this intoxicating effect on each other and nothing else seems to matter. All the little details like wives and kids fall away, and there's just us standing there staring at each other with a whirlwind of tempestuous desire. He's got that hunger in his eyes right now and I can't move. I can't look away. I can't think.

"V," he murmurs.

I barely hear it, but the sound vibrates through me like a melodic musical note. He is the Pied Piper, and I am helpless but to follow. He is Superman and Romeo in one. His gaze is mesmerizing, liquifying my insides while my will evaporates in the heat of his eyes.

He suddenly brushes past me and I follow. He's in the next room sweeping throw pillows off the full-size bed. He looks up at me. "Guest room."

"No. Not here. This is your house."

He approaches me and pulls me to him.

"Come on, V. I can't wait any longer," he implores.

I kiss him because I can't resist his tantalizing lips. He returns my ardent kiss, making me dizzy, but he's impatient and tries to coax me toward the bed.

"No." I pull away. "Not here, Brad. I mean it."

He runs his fingers through his hair. "Okay. We'll go back to the hotel."

So much for taking a walk or meandering through shops before dinner. We have to touch each other. We have to abate the crest of passion that surges within us whenever we're near each other. There's no use trying to fight it.

As soon as we're back in the car, there's a sense of relief. Being in Brad's house where he lives with his family is just too strange. It's like I could sense the energy of his wife and sons in the rooms. I felt like an intruder, and claustrophobia had grips me.

Remorse weighs on me like a cement block on my chest and my headache flares up. How can Brad be so detached? He talked about being able to compartmentalize, but how can he kiss his wife after being with me? I'll have to be the one to do it. Break it off. Maybe this will be the last time. But I need this last time.

I look at his profile as he drives. Can I give him up? I don't know. And then what? Justin? I feel no excitement about seeing Justin. He'd be a good friend, but that's probably not what he wants. Will I ever be able to feel this way about another man?

I hear my phone go off in my purse. Someone is sending me a text. Probably Marcy. I pull it out and look at the screen.

Where are you? I've been calling. I'm in labor. I need you.

"Oh, my God!" I cry out.

"What is it?" Brad demands as the car swerves slightly.

"Lacie's in labor. I need to get home!" I shriek.

"Oh, my God."

"Calm down," he says. "The first one takes a long time. How long has she been in labor?"

"I don't know. I'm texting her."

I'm in CA visiting Marcy. Will take the next plane. I'll be there! How long have you been in labor?

"Don't panic," he says.

Three hours.

"She's already been in labor three hours," I fret. "I *have* to be there. She needs me. I *have* to be there, Brad."

"Okay. There's lots of time. We'll grab your stuff, and I'll get you on the next plane. You'll be there in time," Brad promises me.

What if I'm not? I can't let Lacie down. I just can't. I'll never forgive myself if I'm not there for her.

Chapter 39

I trust in Brad. He knows how to calmly and efficiently get things done. I race to my room and throw my stuff in my suitcase while he settles the bill at the front desk and checks on changing my flight.

I'm on the verge of hysteria as he speeds to the airport. He speaks to me in a soothing tone while my mind is racing. Is this going to be my punishment for this Brad debacle? I've been selfish and what we've done is wrong. I should've known it would blow up in my face. Why doesn't it blow up in his face?

But is it wrong if you're in love? And is this love or something else? I keep returning to the fact that we were together *before* he ever met her. He was mine first. My mind is spinning in circles.

I vow to tell Marcy the truth. I need her advice and support. There's no doubt she'll be mad at me for keeping this from her and for doing it in the first place, but her strength will help me break it off. I hope.

Besides, she has her own secrets. Was she ever going to tell me about going to counseling with Doug? Why didn't she tell me at the time? We used to share everything, and now we have secrets from each other. Melancholy drifts down around me. Moving away divided us more than I'd realized.

Brad is busy navigating the traffic. He's not a good husband, but he's not a bad person. He was good to me when we were dating. He works hard. He usually does the right thing. I understand why things didn't work out before. I was too dependent and insecure. Now I'm stronger and more confident. New and improved. But the old feelings are still there. Will we ever be able to resist each other? Am I his weakness as he is mine?

"I wish we would've had more time together," I say to Brad at the airport.

"Next time." He waves his hand at me.

He assumes there will be a next time, yet I'm not so sure. But I can't think about that now. I must get to the hospital. Lacie needs me. Nothing else matters right now.

"Go be a grandmother," Brad says with a sweet smile.

My head is pounding, and I'm tense during the entire flight. It's the longest flight ever. It takes an eternity for the shuttle to get me to my car. My mind won't stop whirring. What a disaster of a trip. Marcy drank too much, Doug cracked my deep dark secret, and I hardly had any time with Brad. And he paid for everything. And Doug and I kissed. What on earth is going on? It was all like a bad dream. I should've never left town. I'd be with Lacie right now.

It's dusk by the time I get my car. I drive straight to the hospital and run down the maze of hallways looking for Lacie's room. My stomach is growling incessantly and I ignore it.

Please let me get there in time, I plead over and over.

Brandon is exiting the room up ahead. He sees me. "There you are." He looks tired.

"How is she?" I gasp for air.

"She's doing fine. It's just taking a long time. I'm going to get something to eat. Want something?"

"Yes. Anything. Whatever you're getting," I blurt before pushing aside the curtain and bursting into the room.

"Mom!" Lacie cries out.

I take in the tiny, dimly lit room. Lacie looks distraught. I grab her into a big embrace and hang onto her for a few minutes. It doesn't matter how old your kids are, your maternal instinct kicks in when they need you.

"How are you? What did the doctor say?" I ask.

"I'm tired and hungry and thirsty. This baby is taking forever. It's already been about ten hours, and they said I was hardly dilating," she tells me. "Brandon fell asleep, but then he went to get something to eat."

"I saw him. Are you dilating now?"

"Yes. The doctor said it won't be too much longer, but that could still be hours." She groans and sinks back into the pillows. "You were visiting Marcy?"

"I never would've gone if I'd known. I didn't think you were due for weeks," I say brushing her hair off her forehead.

"It's about twelve days before my due date. The doctor said it's close enough. Were you early with us?"

"I was actually a little late with both of you. That's why I thought you'd be late too."

"I hope the baby's okay," she worries.

"It's not too early. The baby will be fine," I assure her.

I straighten her blankets and hand her a cup of ice chips before settling beside her and grasping her hand. *Please let this baby be okay.*

"Did you let Luke know?" I ask.

"Yeah. They were out hiking somewhere." She puts her hand on her stomach and furrows her brow. "Oooh."

I watch the monitor and wish I could ease her pain. It's unbearable to see my children hurting.

"Okay, that one's over. Why don't you try to get a little sleep between contractions if you can?" I suggest. "I'll be right here."

Brandon returns with a sandwich that we share while Lacie dozes. I try to eat one-handed, not wanting to let go of her hand. Brandon times the contractions until he reclines in the chair in the corner where he naps, and I sit watching it get darker outside.

My phone is in my purse across the room. I want to text Marcy and let her know Lacie's in labor, text Brad and tell him I made it, and text Luke and see if they're coming to the hospital, but those texts will have to wait. I sit silently thinking until the doctor comes into the room with a flourish.

"How are we doing?" she asks cheerily.

Lacie rouses and Brandon stirs.

"This is my mom," Lacie tells the doctor.

"Nice to meet you," she says briskly. "Will you be in the room for the birth?"

"Yes. I want her here," Lacie answers.

She has another strong contraction and moans softly. We watch the monitor. It's a big one.

"Good. You're moving along. Let me check."

The doctor examines her and Lacie grimaces. My phone goes off and Brandon hands my purse to me. I fish out my phone and see a text from Luke.

We're here.

"Luke's here. I'll be right back," I tell Lacie, releasing her hand.

Brandon moves to my seat and kisses her forehead before taking her hand.

"They can come in and say hi," Lacie instructs. "Then I don't want them in the room."

I go out and find Luke and Serena in the waiting area at the end of the hall. It's fully dark outside, and the lights of the buildings twinkle like stars in the darkness. A half-moon hangs in the sky. There are a few other people in the waiting area pacing nervously or standing in front of the huge plate-glass window staring out into the darkness.

Luke and Serena jump up when they see me approach.

"Did it happen?" Luke asks anxiously.

"No. Come say hi to Lacie and then you guys can

260

wait out here," I say.

I stay in the waiting area and text Marcy. *At the hospital. Lacie's in labor. Hope you're feeling better.*

Then I text Brad. *Made it. Hasn't happened yet.*

I sit with my phone in my hand. I probably shouldn't have texted Brad. He's most likely home with his family. I usually wait for him to contact me first. Oh, well.

Marcy texts back right away, and my phone startles me. *I'll be fine. Let me know when you're a grandma! Take pictures.*

Luke and Serena are only gone a few minutes.

"Poor Lacie," Luke says. "That looks awful."

"They don't call it labor for nothing," I smile. "I better get back in there. I'll let you know when it happens. It could be awhile."

Things finally speed up a few hours later. I stand on one side holding Lacie's right hand and Brandon holds her left while the doctor keeps up a steady stream of encouraging words. Lacie is squeezing my hand so tight, I fear she might break some bones, but I don't dare extricate my hand and break her concentration.

One final forceful push and the baby is born as Lacie falls back against the pillows sweating and exhausted. The pressure on my hand loosens, and I glimpse dark hair.

"It's a girl!" the doctor exclaims.

Lacie has tears streaming down her face. My own tears roll down my cheeks, and Brandon's eyes are also moist. Brandon cuts the cord and we hear her first cries. The nurse whisks her off to clean her up and swaddle her in a pink blanket before placing her on Lacie's chest.

A floodgate of love has opened, and I can hardly believe my eyes as I peer into her little face. She has thick wisps of dark hair, and I see dark eyes when she blinks at us.

"She's so small," Brandon marvels.

"She's beautiful," Lacie says.

"What's her name?" I ask.

They haven't shared any names with me, even though I'd asked many times. Lacie always told me they couldn't agree.

She chokes up as she says, "Sofia."

Sofia was my mother's name. She passed away when Lacie was eleven. When my father died five years earlier, she had turned all her attention to spoiling her grandchildren. They have wonderful memories of their time with Grandma Sofia.

"That's a great name." I wipe tears from my eyes.

"Annette is her middle name after Brandon's mother," Lacie says softly. "Do you want to hold her?"

"Let Brandon hold her first. I'll go tell Luke and Serena. Can they come in the room?"

The nurse has finished cleaning up and tucks Lacie in with a clean blanket as Brandon takes little Sofia. His face radiates pride. I'm so glad I made it here in time and could share in this moment.

"Yeah, Mom. They can come in," Lacie says. "Uncle Luke and Aunt Serena."

"Can I hold her for a minute before I get them?" I ask.

"I'll get them. You can hold her," Brandon offers.

I'm aching to hold that little bundle. Brandon gently transfers her to my arms, and I gaze into Sofia's tiny face. Her eyes flicker open for a split second, and she squirms inside the blanket. Then she settles into a serene expression. Total bliss envelopes me. She's the most perfect little thing I've ever seen. Overwhelming love swells within me for my new granddaughter.

Chapter 40

I get home too late to call Marcy. I'm overjoyed, exhausted, and starving. I eat a piece of toast to still my growling stomach and fall asleep instantly. The day comes quickly after a deep sleep. I call Marcy before they discharge Lacie and Sofia.

I'm still on cloud nine. The sun hides behind some thin clouds before it breaks out and saturates the yard with brilliant light. The lawn has a few brown patches, but the bushes are a vibrant green. I stand outside on the patio, taking in the fresh air as I wait for her to answer.

"Congratulations, Grandma!" Marcy screams into the phone. "I bet she's gorgeous."

I had texted her the details the night before, along with pictures.

"Oh, Marcy. Sofia is the cutest little baby in the world," I gush.

"I can't wait to see her."

"Does that mean you're thinking of visiting?"

"Only if you know somewhere I can stay. Know anyone with a guest room?"

I laugh. "That'd be great. We didn't have enough time when I was down there."

A pang of regret at my deception snags at my euphoria for a moment. I should tell her. I can't wait any longer. Doug took it well, but I know Marcy. She will not. But wait a minute. She also has a secret. Not as disgraceful as mine, but, nevertheless, a secret she's kept from me.

"You know I'm always on your side, right? Even if you did something terrible, I'd be on your side."

"Yeah. Why?" She sounds hesitant.

"Well, Doug and I were talking before I left when he came over to the hotel to tell me you had a hangover."

263

"Okay, I'm sorry about that. I don't know why I drank so much. I don't get out enough. Are you still mad at me?"

"No, I'm not mad. I would never judge you. I'm just wondering how you guys are getting along."

"We're getting along fine," she says. "Why? What did Doug say? Why are you're asking me this? You just saw us. Everything's fine."

"Do you think it helped when you went to therapy years ago?"

"Yeah, it was…" She stops. "Wait a minute. Did Doug tell you about that?"

"Why didn't you ever tell me?"

She sighs heavily. "I guess I felt embarrassed because of my issues, and I do have my issues, but now I have to kill Doug in the worst way I can think of."

"Don't be mad at Doug. He's great. I wish I had my own Doug. You're lucky, Marcy," I say. "But did it help?"

"Well, according to everybody in the world, I'm too distrustful. You know why."

"Yeah, I do, but Doug said he has issues that come from his childhood too."

"He did?"

"Sure. He's a rational guy."

"Okay. I won't kill him, but you have your issues too. You always go for the wrong guys."

"You're right and that's actually why I brought this up. I do go for the wrong guys… like Brad." I wait for her reaction.

Two squirrels are chasing each other around the trunk of a large tree and up into the branches before leaping onto the fence and scampering along the top.

"That jerk. That's the only reason I'm glad you moved away because you didn't have the willpower to stop seeing him," she says.

"And I still can't resist him." I wait again.

"Then it's a good thing... Wait... Did you say... You didn't..."

"I don't want you to hate me, Marcy. You know I loved him, and I could never say no to him, and I was with him first, anyway. Doesn't that count for something?"

"I knew it!" she shrieks in my ear. "I just knew it!"

"You did?"

"You have no self-control. What is wrong with you? He's married, Vera."

She's screaming at me, and I hold the phone away from my ear.

"Marcy..."

"He's using you. Can't you see that? He's never going to leave his wife."

"I don't want him to."

"Now you're making no sense. Then why would you..."

"I guess it felt unfinished, and I wanted to see if I still felt the same. It's weird. I don't know if I love him anymore, but we still have this strong attraction. I can't tell if it's love or..."

"It's just sex, you know."

"I don't know what it is. He looks at me and... I've never felt this way before. Maybe it is love. I've been trying to sort it out."

"What about what's-his-name? The one you met. Justin."

"I feel nothing for him," I admit. "You can't force it. You can't say, 'Oh, this guy is right for me, so I'll fall in love with him.'"

"I'm really mad at you."

"I know."

"Furious. I might have to hang up."

"Don't. Please. I need your support."

"I'm not supporting this."

"I want to stop. I want to stop seeing him."

"Seriously?" Her tone is doubtful.

"Yes. I almost missed seeing Sofia born because I was still there. Brad had to get me on an earlier flight. That would've been the worst thing ever."

"Hmm. This is beginning to make sense. That's why you were at that expensive hotel. Did he pay for that?"

"Yes. He paid for everything, and I was trying to combine seeing you and him."

"I can't believe this."

The sun feels hot, and I step into the shade of the house.

"I've been feeling so guilty. I mean, I think about his wife and kids more than he does. He says he can compartmentalize. You know, like they're in one box and I'm in another, like he can separate things in his head."

"So, he wants to have his family and his cake too. And you're the cake."

"He doesn't feel guilty, or at least he doesn't act like it, but I told him I'm surprised he's willing to risk everything just to see me. They work together, so if she ever found out, he'd probably lose everything."

"Maybe he does care about you."

"He said he loves me."

"He did?" Her voice goes up an octave. "He never said that before."

"I know. He never said it when we were together the first time, but he told me he's always loved me."

"He said that? Then why didn't he marry you in the first place?"

"Because I was such a mess. I was. I don't blame him."

"I hate him. He's the one I should kill in the worst possible way."

"I'm not sure what to think. I'm so confused, Marcy."

"How many times have you seen him?"

"A few."

"Oh, my God, Vera."

"I know."

"I still don't get why you'd do this if he's not leaving his wife and you don't want him to. What's the point? It can't lead anywhere."

"I can't even explain it."

"How can you do something this awful, Vera? How could you do this?" Her voice is getting louder. "I can't believe... that's it." She hangs up.

At least I told her. I hope Doug will stick up for me, and she cools off sooner rather than later. It may take a long time for her to speak to me again. If she ever does. I can't stand it when we're mad at each other. And I didn't even confess the worst part. That I was in Brad's house. Where he lives with his wife. That would really freak her out.

My Brad predicament still perplexes me. The thought of him sends a shiver of excitement through me. Yet I will have to give him up. This will be so very difficult because I don't want to stop seeing him. It gives me something delicious to look forward to. Otherwise, my life returns to the same old boring routine.

Except there is little Sofia. She is the new joy in my life.

Chapter 41

When Lacie and Brandon take Sofia to meet his parents in Arizona, I get on a plane to see Brad again. Marcy hasn't spoken to me since I disclosed my dirty secret, and I tell myself I'll call her when the deed is done, when I've told Brad it's over. She'll be more likely to forgive my indiscretion.

At first, I resolve not to see him again and do it over the phone, which is what I should do, but I convince myself the decent thing to do is to break up in person. I swear to myself I won't sleep with him. I'll break up with him in a dignified grown-up way. But who am I kidding? I want to see him. I need to see him. I need him.

I ended it with Justin easily enough. I texted him and told him I was sorry. I just wasn't into dating at this time.

He sent a pithy text back. *Whatever.*

I am a heartbreaker. I am a wanton woman. I am a femme fatale. I am carnal. I am a slut. But only for one man.

I ache to see Brad. I don't know if I'll be able to do it, break it off. My will weakens with every mile that zips by in the air. Marcy's right. I have no willpower. I deserve her ire.

I think of his lips, his tongue, his fingertips, his eyes, the words he utters during our tumbles. It's too good to give up. Why did I ever agree to see him in the first place? Now I'm caught in this web of insatiable desire. For him.

What am I doing? I said I'd stop. I've sworn to myself. I almost missed Sofia's birth. I never would've forgiven myself. I've been given another chance, and, again, I'm making the wrong choice. I agonize during the entire flight, giving myself pep talks and listing all the reasons in my head to break it off. As I'm speeding toward him above the clouds.

I don't know how I found the fortitude to break it off years ago. I think back and can't recall how I did it. I only remember how devastated I was. I'd driven straight to Marcy's and cried my eyes out. It had taken weeks, months, forever for the ache in my heart to fade.

As usual, I melt like butter the minute I see him at the baggage claim. He never hugs or kisses me hello. He leaves me in a constant state of yearning. He takes my suitcase from me and heads off through the throng. I hurry behind as we weave our way toward the exit until we step outside and cross the traffic to the parking lot.

Once I'm safely seated in the car, he places my carry-on in the trunk, and we head into the Friday night traffic. He always asks about my flight and I always say everything was fine.

He drives unperturbed through the L.A. traffic, even when someone cuts him off. I like that it doesn't faze him, unlike my ex-husband. Brad is always composed, always considerate, always cognizant of how to deal with any minor problem that arises. Do he and his wife fight? I can't imagine him yelling. He's a good listener. He remembers little details. He's intelligent and informed, though we disagree on politics and probably other things. He's nice to everyone, the desk clerks, the servers, the valets, the hostesses. I've seen him buy a sandwich for a homeless man. Yes, Brad is just about perfect, except for one tiny little thing. He cheats on his wife. Oh, and sometimes he's dishonest in business. Let's not forget that.

I go over all this in my mind as Brad navigates to the restaurant where I intend to order a strong drink or two.

"You're quiet," he says.

He's observant, too.

"Just thinking," I say.

"About?"

"You. You and me," I answer honestly.

"You know I missed you."

It's the way he says it. *You know* I missed you. Not *I missed you.* His phrasing adds a little layer of detachment. Okay, so his biggest fault, other than the lying, cheating thing, is his emotional detachment. That's a big one in my eyes.

"Tell me what you like about me," I say.

He looks at me with raised eyebrows. "What I like about you?"

"Yeah, what is it that draws you to me?"

"I think you know." He briefly squeezes my thigh.

"Is that it?" I regard the car with tinted windows next to us at the traffic light.

"Not at all," he answers.

"Then what else do you like about me?" I persist. "What was it about me you liked when we first met? I'm curious."

"Okay." He makes a turn into the parking lot of the restaurant. "Let's go in and then I'll answer your question."

I wait until we're seated and scanning the menu. We've been to this place before. The food is excellent. I wait until I've taken a big gulp of my drink. Liquid courage, they call it, but for me it will more likely break down my defenses. I take a breath, but he answers before I can ask again.

"You're a good person," he says. "Better than me. You're kind and caring. You loved Coco as much as I did."

I smile wistfully at the mention of Coco. "But what drew you to me?"

"Have you looked in a mirror?" He chuckles. "You've gotten better looking as you've gotten older. You have more character in your face."

"Thank you. I think." But I wasn't fishing for compliments. I sincerely wanted to understand. "What else?"

"More?" He tilts his head in thought. "You're smart, smarter than you give yourself credit for." He leans forward. "But more than anything..."

I lean forward eagerly.

"I trust you. I can tell you anything and you..." He looks off into the restaurant a moment. "You never judge me. You respect me." He laughs. "You feed my ego."

I sip my drink, studying his face.

"Does that answer your question?"

"Sort of, but doesn't that describe a lot of women?"

"Not in that combination. No." He shakes his head. "Our... *visits* sustain me. It's brutal out there, in the world of business. You don't know who you can trust. You don't know if people are trying to rip you off or acting like your friend because they want something from you. You, you're not like that. You have no agenda. I can relax with you and be myself."

"But don't you feel that way about your wife?"

Maybe it's a low blow, but it had to be asked. For a brief second, a wounded look flickers across his face and I feel chastened.

"Why else would you marry her?" I shrug.

His expression hardens. "That has nothing to do with us."

The server appears and pretends he hasn't overheard.

"Do you still need a few minutes?" he asks.

Brad takes a sip of his wine while I order and then gives the server his order. We both watch him walk away before we look back at each other.

"Here's the truth, Vera," Brad says solemnly. "I have feelings for you. I've always had feelings for you." He takes another sip of wine. "Things are

271

complicated in my marriage. When you've been married a long time, things change, they evolve, not always for the better."

"Okay."

"I'm not unhappy, it's just that you give me something I don't get in my marriage. You fill some need, and, obviously, I fill a need for you, otherwise, we wouldn't both be sitting here."

"Like Bob." I nod and look down at the tablecloth. A bit of remorse tugs at me for giving him a hard time when he was opening up to me.

"Yes, like Bob," he says gently. "So, let's not try to second guess this or analyze it. Let's just accept it and enjoy each other. Life is short. Take what you can get."

I smile at him. "Thanks for honestly answering my question." I take a few more sips of my drink.

"We can go to a movie later," he says. "After we get you checked in at the hotel. Unless I wear you out." He gives me a sexy grin.

He often leaves me speechless, and I scramble to change the subject.

"It was interesting seeing the house you were working on," I say.

"I sold it. Only four days on the market. I got above asking."

"That's awesome."

"No movie tonight? There was one that looks good. Maybe tomorrow."

"I also found it interesting seeing your family photos at your house," I continue. "It surprised me you'd take me there."

"I had to change out of my work clothes. Why don't you just say what you want to say?" He sounds annoyed.

I shake my head. "I have nothing to say. I was thinking about stuff on the plane and I..." I smile fondly at him. "I missed you. This is just tough sometimes."

"I know, V." His tone has softened again.

Suddenly tears threaten to spill from my eyes. I grab my drink and take a few slugs.

"Vera," Brad says soothingly. "Things are better this time. I know it's not exactly what you want, but it's pretty great. I look forward to seeing you, and I can't wait to get you alone."

And then I glimpse something my heart has kept hidden. My abrupt emotional surge precipitates this revelation. I must've known on some level all along. It's always been lurking on the edges, ever since we'd first met. He'd captivated me from those first moments. I could never resist him. I could never say no to him. That's because I truly love Brad. I love him too much. I love him so much I can't let him go.

The server delivers our meals. The food is sublime, and I almost lick my plate when I'm finished devouring every morsel. Brad has ordered me another drink and a decadent dessert to share. We feed each other and laugh, and I wipe his chin with my napkin.

"I know how you are when you drink," Brad says as we drive to the hotel. I can hardly keep my hands off him. He certainly has me figured out.

The thought that this may be the last time, if I get up the nerve to break it off, to which I cling in my inebriated state, makes my craving for him more urgent.

"I keep thinking it can't get any better," Brad says as he's sprawled on the bed afterwards.

I just can't get enough of him. Is it because he holds back? This is the only time he allows himself to express his emotions and, when he lets it out, it's explosive, intoxicating, overwhelming, and satisfying without completely satiating me. He doles out just enough to keep me coming back for more and more. I'm addicted to him. Is there a twelve-step program for love? Is this love?

I wake up in the middle of the night and go to the bathroom without turning on the light. Then I crawl back into bed and cuddle up to him. I don't care if he doesn't like it. I fall into a deep, blissful sleep this way.

Chapter 42

I open my eyes with new determination and find myself alone in bed. I hadn't been able to say what I'd planned the night before. I'm not even sure what to say now, except that I must stop this. I don't know how, but I must. The weight of my conscience presses on me and is becoming increasingly unbearable.

"I ordered breakfast from room service," Brad announces when he steps out of the bathroom.

His hair is wet, and he has a towel around his waist, which he lets drop when he opens his suitcase.

"Do you have a meeting or something?" I ask.

"No. I'm all yours today." He turns to me and his smile lights up the dark places inside me.

I extricate myself from the twisted blankets and get out of bed. There's a long sliver of light escaping from between the heavy drapes, and I pull them open. The parking lot is active. People are getting in and out of cars. It's another balmy day in L.A. I admire the tall palm trees gently rustling above the pavement. This is a wealthy area. You can tell by the cars and the way people are dressed in whites and creams, with expensive watches and jewelry glinting in the sun.

I take a long hot shower and find breakfast waiting when I emerge. Brad is sitting on the balcony. Per his flawless manners, he hasn't touched his breakfast yet. I throw on a soft white terrycloth robe and sit at the little table in the corner of our room where the food waits under round plastic covers. Brad is reading the real estate section of the paper and brings it to the table. We eat silently until he sets it down and asks me what I want to do today. I suggest driving around Hollywood.

He makes a face. "Boring and too much traffic."

"I want to see the celebrity mansions," I implore.

"They're just big houses," he says. "Let's go walk along the beach. We can walk on the Venice boardwalk or down by the water."

"Okay."

The traffic is a nightmare, and it takes much driving around to find a parking space, but once we venture out by the ocean, a peaceful feeling settles over me. There's something about the rhythmic waves and the salty smell, the caw of the seagulls and the warm sand beneath my bare feet that makes all the stress seep away.

We stroll barefoot down the beach in our shorts and sunglasses. Couples pass us holding hands. I bend to pick up seashells, but they're all broken, and I toss them into the waves.

A young man passes by, staring at me until he gets further down the beach. I peek at him over my shoulder.

"He probably thinks you're someone," Brad says.

"You mean like a movie star?"

"Yeah."

"I don't look like a movie star," I protest.

"You're pretty enough to be one."

"I don't think so." I'm not voluptuous enough. Or tall enough. Or blonde enough. Or graceful enough.

Another couple meanders by holding hands, and I notice Brad's hand dangling by his side as he stares out at the waves. What's he thinking about? I saunter over and take his hand, tugging gently. He walks with me, letting me hold his hand for a few minutes until he pulls it away to check his phone.

I plop down on the sand while he walks further down the beach to make a call. It's hypnotic watching the waves tumbling onto the shore, depositing white foam on the sand and swiftly receding, only to do it again and again. My sunglasses deepen the blues of the water and sky that meet in a hazy line at the horizon. The reflection of the sun bounces and shimmers in the choppy vastness of the ocean while seagulls swoop and glide above it.

Brad is a bit agitated, which is unlike him. At least as far as I know. Maybe I don't know him that well. I only see what he wants me to see, and he has always limited my view.

He walks back and sits beside me on the sand.

"Everything okay?" I ask.

"Yeah." He gives me a tight smile. I can't see his eyes through his sunglasses.

I wonder if it was his wife. I wonder about a lot of things with him. Was he seeing other women years ago when we were dating? Did his wife overlap with me? Is he honest in business? Why would he bring me to his house? Why am I here? What does he really feel for me?

"I don't think you love me," I say evenly. "I think this is just sex."

"Vera..."

"It's okay, Brad. Let's call it what it is." I'm still staring straight ahead at the blue of the ocean instead of the blue of his eyes.

"You know how I feel about you."

"I've been trying to sort out how I feel about *you,* but this is really all there is between us. There will never be more. This is all it will ever be."

These words drop in the chasm between us, the words that have fought their way out of me to be acknowledged and now feel like cinders on my skin.

"You knew what you were getting into." His voice is edged with a hint of anger. "I told you from the beginning I would never leave my wife."

I face him. "I can't be detached. I can't do it. I

277

think I love you but in some twisted dysfunctional way."

"What we have is exactly what we need from each other. Why ruin it? We're both getting what we want out of this."

"I'm not getting what I want. I want more." I turn my gaze back to the horizon.

"I can't give you more than this."

"I know."

We sit for a few minutes. He doesn't understand me or what I want, and this gives me a numb strength. All my emotions have been wrung dry, and I just feel sad, profoundly sad.

"What do you want me to do?" he asks. "I can try to see you more often. Will that make you happy?"

"I feel empty," I say. "I feel empty inside."

"I don't know what you want me to say."

"You've always kept your distance. Even when we're together, I feel this distance."

"I'm not a touchy-feely person. I don't let my emotions affect me," he says. "You've always been too emotional."

"I don't know what I expected. I assumed things would be different this time."

"They are. This is the best possible arrangement," he says. "We'll never find what we have with anyone else, this incredible physical connection that we have."

"But I want more than that. I want an emotional connection too."

He shakes his head. "I don't think what you want exists. Take what you can get in life."

"I deserve more than this. More than just weekends," I retort. "And your wife deserves more too."

"You know nothing about her or my marriage."

"Then tell me. Do you have an open marriage?

278

Do you each do whatever you want? Is that how it is?"

"This has nothing to do with my marriage. This is between me and you," he says emphatically.

"But it does. I'm right in the middle of your marriage," I say. "I don't think I can do this anymore. I don't feel good about it. It's wrong."

"I told you, Vera. You're not doing anything wrong. I am and I can deal with it."

"I'm helping you cheat on your wife. I don't know. Maybe she cheats on you too. But I don't want to be in the middle of it."

My fist is clenching sand, and I let it sift through my fingers. A wave is rolling toward us and looks like it may reach us, but I don't move. I watch impassively as it comes within inches of my feet.

"V," Brad moves closer to me. "Come on. Don't be like this. We had such a good time last night."

He's very persuasive, and I'll cave if he kisses me. But he won't. He never kisses me first.

"I need you, V," he says softly. "It's so good with you. I think about you all the time."

"You do?"

"Yes. I'll be working or see the little house you bought me on my desk, and I can't help being turned on."

Turned on. That's all he thinks about me. Sex seems to be the foundation of our relationship, not that that's a bad thing. We crave each other on a deep primal level, and if that's all we wanted from each other, that would be fine. If he weren't married. If that's all I wanted. But he is married. And I want more.

"You get turned on whenever you think of me?"

"Very turned on."

"I feel the same," I profess.

"That's good."

"Does anyone know about me? Have you ever

279

told anybody? Your friends? Your brothers?"

"Nobody."

I consider this. I hadn't told anybody until Doug had guessed and I'd confessed to Marcy, who was no longer speaking to me.

"You're my secret," he murmurs.

I pull away and glare at him.

"I'm your *dirty* little secret. That's what I am, Brad. Your dirty little secret."

I get up and brush the grains of sand from my shorts. I turn back the way we came and march down the beach. He jumps up and follows.

"Let's go get something to eat. We'll have a few drinks," he suggests.

I keep walking, trying to get my thoughts together. I have one more night with him. One last night.

"I'm glad you told me how you feel," he says. "I'm glad you got it out. Now the air is cleared."

We walk briskly past the couples holding hands, past the families, past the kids throwing a frisbee, past the seagulls picking at trash. I say nothing the entire way to the car and he says nothing more.

"Are you mad at me now?" he demands once we're inside.

"No. I'm just deciding what to do."

"Let's talk over drinks." He backs out of the parking space.

"I want to go home," I declare.

"Your flight is tomorrow. Don't make me change it. Let's just finish this weekend, okay?"

I agree because it's unreasonable to expect him to pay to change the flight on my whim, but I fear my resolve will quickly erode. He has that effect on me. Still, I vow that this will be the last time.

"I don't know what I can do to prove to you how important you are to me," he says.

"I know I am." I stare out the window at the

traffic.

"Do you want me to drive through Hollywood?" he asks. "We can do whatever you want. I'll fight the traffic for you."

"No. Let's go eat."

I really want a drink, but I know what happens when I drink. And so does he. What does it matter at this point? I look over at him. I'll miss you, Brad.

Chapter 43

Our lovemaking is slow and sensual instead of frenzied and crazy like it usually is. Brad holds me more, looks into my eyes more, kisses me more fervently. Is he expressing what he feels or trying to give me what I want? I suspect the latter.

"I love you, V," he says afterwards. "I do whether or not you believe me."

"I believe you," I whisper in the dim light of the lamp on the desk.

I believe he thinks he does. He also thinks he loves his wife. Maybe he doesn't know what love is. Maybe I don't either. But this isn't it. Or are we entangled in an impossible situation? What if I'll never feel this way again? I can't dwell on that.

I have trouble sleeping. Brad is snoring lightly beside me. My thoughts tumble in my head, twisting and turning until I can't keep them straight. If I follow my heart, I'll keep seeing Brad. If I follow my head, I'll stop.

I slip out of bed and get a quarter out of my purse. I can barely see it as I flip it in the air and it bounces on the carpet, jumping underneath the desk. Down on my hands and knees, I reach around in the dark for it. I'm careful not to turn it.

"What are you doing?" Brad asks sleepily.

"I dropped something."

I've finally lost my mind tossing a coin in the middle of the night. I scurry into the bathroom and turn on the light holding my eyes closed a moment telling myself I already know my inevitable decision. There's only one choice, but I'm curious to see what chance dictates.

I open my eyes and squint in the bright light until I can make out the coin. Tails. Stop seeing him. Two out of three? No, the coin has spoken in its wisdom.

I climb back into bed. Brad stirs and turns over, away from me. I am alone in the darkness, drifting on a cold sea. Deeper and deeper I sink till I'm drowning. There's moistness on my pillow that has dripped from my eyes. I try not to make a sound.

~ ~ ~

When I awaken, Brad is studying me. He rarely lingers in bed, but he's watching me sleep. It seems he's been deliberating as well. For a fleeting second, I wonder if he's about to break up with me. He likes to be the one with the power.

"I want to visit you next time," he says. "Let me come to you for a change."

"You want to visit me?"

"I want to see where you live, and I can help with your house. At least, I can advise you about what you can do to increase the value."

"I'm not selling it."

"Right, but you want to keep it updated, so when you're ready to sell, you get the best price. Don't you want to get a bigger house someday?"

"No. Then I'd have to clean it."

He shakes his head at me. "Okay. Then we could fix it up for you."

I picture Brad in my house. I try to see it through his eyes. I picture him eating with me at the small round dining table I never use and sitting on my couch watching TV in the evening. I envision him in my bed and waking up with him, going to my favorite breakfast place, the one I never go to because I don't like to go alone. There's a bush in the front yard I'd like to move to the side of the house. He could do that for me.

But then I think about his unsuspecting wife and know that he's just feeding me a fantasy, that playing house wouldn't be real, that I have to stop buying the dreams he doles out keeping me hooked.

"That'd be great, but I don't think so," I say reluctantly, letting the alluring dream slip away.

"Why?"

"Because this has to be the last time, Brad."

I'm proud of myself. I said it and it can't be unsaid. I throw back the blankets and swing my legs onto the floor. I cross the room and pull open the drapes, drenching the room with sunlight.

"That's bright." Brad momentarily covers his eyes before getting out of bed.

I'm wearing his T-shirt and turn to look at him. What will he say to persuade me to continue seeing him? Or will he let me go?

"I'm really tired of this game," he says.

"What game?"

"Whatever game you're playing with me." His tone is filled with irritation. "This is the way it is. You just have to accept it and deal with it."

"I know."

"Okay. Fine then."

"I appreciate... everything," I say. "I truly do. I'm not trying to give you a hard time."

"Okay, let's get breakfast before your flight." He checks his watch. "We can go to the airport from the restaurant."

I pack my things. Brad has ignored the implications of my statement. But I meant it. He'll realize it soon enough. This is the last time. If I can stay strong. I will stay strong. I will.

He takes a quick shower. I'll take one when I get home. I'd like to have a last leisurely breakfast. I drink down a glass of water hoping that will still my grumbly stomach. I dress comfortably to travel and don my glasses. I'll have much to ruminate about on the plane. When I get home, I'll call Marcy and inform her that I ended it.

All the Little Secrets

Brad has dressed and is putting on his socks when there's a knock on the door.

"Room service."

"Did you order breakfast?" I ask, walking toward the door. "I thought you wanted to eat at that restaurant..."

"They must have the wrong room," he says.

I pull the door open. A short, plump blonde woman is standing there. I don't see a cart with food. She must be a guest looking for her room, but she pushes past me. How rude.

"You have the wrong room," I say after her.

Then I see Brad's face. I've never seen him look so shocked, so vulnerable, so stupefied. I'm completely bewildered. Why does he have this look on his face?

He says a single word. "Julia."

It takes a moment for my mind to register that this is his wife. My hand is still resting on the door handle. She turns to look at me, and I can't move, let alone speak.

"So, this is her," she says to Brad.

She looks around the room taking in the unmade bed, my suitcase standing upright, Brad's open on the bed, his shoes by his feet, the towel slung over the desk chair.

"It's not what you think," Brad says quickly. "She's a colleague. I was giving her a lift to the airport."

Julia puts her hand on her hip. "Yeah, right. You must think I'm really stupid."

I'm not sure what to do or say. Should I try to back him up? I can't find my voice or the right words. I keep silent. I'm not a good liar.

"You do remember I have a nanny cam in the house, right?" she says to Brad.

A shock wave rushes through me. She knows I was in their house. She *saw* me in their house. My

285

mind struggles to recall what she may have witnessed. What did we do? What did we say? I'm still frozen like a statue.

"As usual, you're jumping to conclusions," Brad says. "You're so distrustful, Julia. She's in the industry. That's why she was at the house. And why is there a nanny cam there? You don't trust me?"

I have to admire his skill at deception. His indignation is an effective tactic. But what transpired at his house? Memories float up to my consciousness. We kissed in the guest room. I think that was all. What did we say? Thankfully, we hadn't had sex or there'd be a video out there. I can't imagine the repercussions of a video. I shudder at the thought.

"That's right. I don't trust you," Julia says vehemently. "I had a nanny cam installed in the guest room because remember when my sister visited with the baby?"

I can see the memory dawning on his face. "That was a few years ago."

"I never took it out because, you're right, I don't trust you, Brad. Not since the last time."

Last time? There was a last time? I'm not the only one? I try to wrap my head around this news.

She turns to me. "You're not the first one, you know. He's done this before."

"Julia..." he says with exasperation.

I look at him. I'm sure my expression reflects hurt and disappointment and disbelief. He meets my eyes with a defeated look. I feel completely betrayed. Now it seems more likely than ever that he'd cheated on me those many years ago when I'd trusted him with my heart. It's becoming clear that this is who he is. A liar and a cheater. How could I have been so gullible, so naïve, so blind, so manipulated?

I let go of the door handle and push it closed, anger propelling me into the room.

"When did you meet Brad? And how?" I demand. I must know once and for all.

"Excuse me?" Julia gives me a withering look.

"Vera. Don't say anything," Brad cautions.

I ignore him. "I think we may have overlapped years ago," I explain.

"Really?" She glares at Brad and turns back to me. "We met at a real estate seminar here in L.A. Let's see. When was that? I was living here, and I used to drive down for brunch. He told me he'd just broken up with someone. Was that you?"

"Probably," I say, glancing at him, but he doesn't meet my eyes. "Except we hadn't broken up."

"Is that true, Brad? Did you cheat on her with me? You're unbelievable." She shakes her head.

"Are you done, Julia?" Brad puts on his shoes.

"Have you been seeing him all these years we've been married?" she asks me incredulously.

"No. We broke up back then."

"How did you hook up again?" she asks.

"Vera, don't answer," Brad orders.

"We ran into each other not too long ago."

"Sounds like we're even then. Oddly enough." She gives a little laugh.

"I guess so," I agree.

"Did he tell you he was divorced or something?"

"No," I answer. "He told me he loves you and would never leave you. I... I probably needed closure. I've never done anything like this before. I'm sorry." I shrug weakly.

"He said he wouldn't leave me for you?"

"He said he wouldn't. He said he still loves you," I affirm.

"Did he?" She stands staring at Brad, who refuses to look at her as he finishes packing.

"I should..." I grab the handle of my suitcase with a clammy hand. I feel the pressing need to escape. I've finally gotten the answer to the question that has plagued me all these years. It was Julia who I heard on Brad's answering machine that early morning. I'm sure of it.

"They'll have a shuttle to the airport," Brad says to me.

"Where do you live?" Julia enquires.

"I live up in Northern California."

"You came all this way to see Brad?"

"She used to live here. She has friends here," Brad interjects.

"I'm so sorry," I say again to Julia and roll my suitcase to the door, bumping against the desk and into the wall before making it out to the empty hallway.

"She's pretty, but not as young as the other one," I hear Julia say to Brad as I close the door behind me.

Thankfully, she's not a violent person. I stand for a moment, trying to take a few deep breaths. I'm shaking uncontrollably. I've never been such a nervous wreck in my life. I walk rapidly down the carpeted hallway to the elevator, then down to the lobby. I tell the desk clerk Brad will check out shortly and will pay the bill and ask for a shuttle to the airport. He informs me it will be about forty minutes, and I sit in one of the upholstered chairs by a large window in the lobby to wait.

I can't stop trembling. A drink would relax me, but the bar isn't open yet. I'm shaken and dazed. My heart is pounding, and my breathing is shallow. I'm panicky and nauseous, though I have nothing in my stomach. A headache throbs in my temples.

I wonder what's transpiring up in the room. Will she forgive him? Again. How often has this occurred? I wish I'd asked her, but what does it matter? Brad will most likely be able to talk his way out of it. Apparently, he has before. He could tell her I'd pursued him. He could say it was just this one time. He could keep denying it.

But she'd caught him. On the nanny cam. Smart woman. She'd traveled to his hotel room to catch him, and she had. That took guts. She wasn't at all what I'd expected. I'd pictured a gorgeous, sophisticated ice queen. But she was just a regular woman married to a cheating husband.

Chapter 44

I call Marcy a few days later, after I've recovered somewhat from the shock of it all. Sleep has eluded me for two nights while I toss and turn and then have disturbing dreams from which I awaken with no specific memory. I need to talk to somebody about all this trauma. I need to talk to Marcy.

"I'm not speaking to you yet," Marcy says when she answers the phone. "Unless you've broken it off."

"I did," I state and relate the whole sordid scene in detail.

"Oh, my God," she keeps exclaiming.

"You were so right," I say. "I should've listened to you."

"And I should've told you about the therapy we went to. I just felt... I don't know, so exposed, like all my faults were under a microscope, like all my insecurities were being shoved in my face. I just couldn't deal with it," she shares. "It dredged up a bunch of stuff from my childhood."

"You know I'm always on your side," I assure her.

"I know. I shouldn't have been so judgmental about your situation. You were in love, and you do stupid things when you're in love."

"How's Doug?"

"I don't hate him." She laughs. "I don't know if I'll ever get over feeling like I can't trust him one hundred percent, but we've hung in there together for a long time. He puts up with my paranoia."

"You're lucky to have such a great guy," I say sincerely.

"Yes, I am."

It strikes me as ironic that she hadn't trusted Doug while I'd trusted Brad. How wrong we both were. She'd trusted too little, and I'd trusted too much, and we'd each seen the clarity of each other's circumstances, yet not our own. We believe what we want to believe.

And now I'm emotionally exhausted. I'm glad to be back home and out of the drama. That ugly scene has cured me of my addiction to Brad once and for all. I'll always miss him and what I believed we had, and I may never feel the same about anyone ever again, but, right now, I'm thankful for the peace and quiet and solitude of my little haven tucked far away.

~~~

During the week, Brad's number comes up on the caller ID, and I'm too curious not to answer.

"V..." His voice fills my ear and sends a warm tingle through me.

"Brad..." I murmur, reacting automatically to his familiar voice.

"I'm sorry about that... fiasco at the hotel," he says. "I didn't remember the nanny cam."

"It could've been worse. We could've..."

"I know."

"So, what happened?" I'm dying to know.

"What do you mean?"

What do I mean?

"What happened after I left? How is everything with Julia? Did she forgive you?"

"What does it matter?"

"It matters a lot. She took it pretty well, considering, but I guess you've been through this before."

"Don't pay any attention to what she said. She was exaggerating."

"You haven't done this before?"

"Things are different with you," he says. "I know that was unpleasant, and I'm sorry you had to go through that, but I promise it won't happen again."

"Brad, are you and Julia still together?"

"We're... Our marriage isn't perfect. She made me look like the bad guy, but there are issues you're not aware of."

"Like what?" I believe I have a right to this information since he put me in the middle of it.

"I'm not going to get into that." He lets out a heavy sigh. "She thinks we should go to counseling."

"That's a good idea. It helped Marcy and Doug."

"Who are Marcy and Doug?"

"My friend, Marcy, and her husband."

"Oh, right."

"Is it true that there were other women besides me?"

"Julia tends to get jealous and exaggerate. She imagines things."

It sounds like Marcy, except I don't think Julia imagined anything. I think she was right. Brad was always out for himself. I can see it so clearly now. He went after what he wanted, despite how it affected others. He was arrogant enough to think he deserved whatever it was. Funny, I'd never seen his arrogance before.

"She didn't imagine me," I point out.

"Let's not talk about Julia or my marriage."

"Tell me the truth, Brad. Were there other women besides me?" I ask again.

"Look. I didn't call to argue. I just wanted to apologize. You didn't see me in the best light, but you know me, V," he says adamantly. "Don't buy into all the paranoid accusations."

"I need you to be honest with me, Brad. When we were dating, were you seeing Julia at the same time?"

"Honestly, V, I don't remember. What's the difference now, anyway? You and I... We have this connection. We always have. You *know* me."

"I don't feel like I do anymore," I say flatly.

"Okay. Fair enough. Let me make it up to you. Let's..."

"Are you serious? Are you seriously suggesting..?"

"Come on, V. Don't be like this."

"I can't do this. I'm not going to see you anymore. She's not going to let you out of her sight, anyway. I don't see how..."

"Trust me. I can..."

"I told you before she came to the room that it was over and I meant it. I don't want to be in the middle..."

"Don't be hasty, Vera. Don't overreact."

I take a deep breath before I respond. "I can't respect someone who lies like this. I feel like I don't even know you. I didn't know you were capable of such... dishonesty."

"That's pretty harsh." He sounds wounded.

"I miss the Brad I thought I knew," I say wistfully. "I miss what I thought we had."

"What we have is real. It's real, Vera."

"I think it was real the first time we dated, but maybe I'm wrong. Maybe it was never what I thought it was."

"Vera..."

"I'm sorry, Brad. I hope you work on your marriage or get a divorce or whatever is best for both of you. I just can't talk to you anymore."

I hang up on Brad. I never would've thought that was possible. I'm no longer drowning. It had all been a desperate delusion I'd clung to like a lifeboat. I'd wanted it so badly I'd refused to open my eyes.

And now that my eyes are open, what I see is not so bad. I see harmony and tranquility. There's no more turmoil, no deceit, no secrets. There's no more frantic sex that I'd mistaken for love. I'd never felt quite satiated because it wasn't substantial. It had always left me wanting more. Love is comfortable, not frenzied. Sure, I crave passion, but I also yearn to hold someone's hand and cuddle up to them at night. I want the comfort of love, not the chaos.

I'll have to discern why I've chosen men who withhold, men who take more than they give. Otherwise, my old patterns will continue to emerge, and I'll go round and round getting dizzier and dizzier until I no longer recognize something good when it flashes before me. I may never find that nugget of gold in the dust. I may keep running after fool's gold.

I thought I loved Brad wholly. I thought he was the answer to all my problems and the man who would heal the past. I'd believed with an urgency that consumed me. That fire that he stoked inside me wasn't love. That burning desire wasn't for him. It was for something he was unable to give me. And now the fever has finally broken.

It's not his fault. He has his own failings. I don't hate Brad. I hope he learns to tap into his emotions to enrich his relationships. I hope he learns about trust. I hope he learns to differentiate sex from love, and I hope I do too.

I don't know Julia. Maybe she has the same issue as me. She chose a man who wouldn't give himself completely to her, someone who withholds bits of himself for other women. I know how it feels and I wish her well.

~ ~ ~

Luke and Serena come over and help me move the bush from the front yard to the side of my house. Now it has a place to stretch out and grow. Serena and I spread bark in a few areas around smaller plants, and we push a few giant sunflower seeds into the soft soil where they can grow tall and I'll be able to see them from my window.

I marvel at how compatible Luke and Serena are. I can see how wonderful it is when you find the right person, someone who complements you and supports you and appreciates who you are. I'm glad my kids have found that. Someday, I might find it for myself, but I don't feel any rush. I'm happy and content with my life as it is.

I visit Lacie often to see little Sofia. I hold her in my arms, and she looks up at me with her big brown eyes and fills my heart. She kicks her little feet and waves her fists. She coos and smiles and yawns. I wish her all good things in the life that's ahead of her. I wish for her to grow up strong and smart and to know that she is loved so very much.

I call Justin and apologize to him for being abrupt. I divulge that I had been in the midst of a complication with someone from my past. He admits that he's having trouble getting over his ex. We talk for a long time, and by the end, we've become friends. We laugh and agree that we're both too screwed up for a new relationship, but we could each use a friend.

~ ~ ~

This is not a story about romantic love. I thought it was at first. I thought I was deeply, passionately in love with Brad. I believed it with all my heart and soul. Because I wanted so much for it to be real. But it was a mirage, an illusion, a fantasy.

I built Brad up into the ideal man. I saw only what I wanted to see. There were traces of the real Brad, but I ignored them because they marred the dream. He couldn't have lived up to my idyllic vision of him, the fairy tale hero of my life. It wasn't his fault I didn't see him or my own shortcomings.

We're conditioned to pair up, but it's not right for everyone. Maybe if I stand still and listen to my inner voice, I'll know what's right for me. There's nothing wrong with filling your life with a different kind of love, that of family and friends. The love that grows from truly knowing those in your life and sharing yourself with them. True friends like Marcy, and Doug too, who accept you and have your back, and family who bolster you with love and support and are right there in your life. Sometimes you forget they're there. Yet they provide the solid foundation from which you can build upon.

And there's one more person whose love is often dismissed but who is the most important of all. This person is the hero of our story. This is the one we take most for granted. Maybe this is a love story after all. The story of loving yourself.

~ ~ ~

Exclusive short story!

Sign up for the Book Bird newsletter and receive *The Interviews*

What's it like to be a fictional character? D. Thrush "interviews" the female protagonists of her books and then lets the male characters have their say. She said/he said! It was a little weird for D to hear some of their unexpected responses, not to mention the two who crashed the interviews uninvited! You don't have to be familiar with them to enjoy their thoughtful responses and lively banter.

https://landing.mailerlite.com/webforms/la
nding/m8v0s5

Why sign up? You'll find value in every newsletter whether it's freebies, sales, contests, inside news, info on new releases, or the opportunity to read ARCs (Advanced Reader Copies) and give your input on titles and covers. You'll only hear from me about once or twice a month and will be able to contact me directly. Join us and don't miss out on the fun!

Acknowledgments

The most important thanks go to you, the reader, for spending the time reading my words. I can't tell you how much it means to me to share what I write.

For the first time, I used a Beta Reader team who read ARCs (Advanced Reader Copies) to give me early feedback and help improve this book. Most of these readers replied to a request sent to my newsletter list. These volunteers read it quickly, caught careless errors, and provided thoughtful feedback.

Heartfelt thanks go out to Nick Iuppa, a supportive fellow indie author; Princess Sally Dagger, the first to volunteer to read it; Carolyn Shelley, who was so persistent through glitches to download the ARC; Sheridan Lee, who finished the book so quickly; Judy Knox, who also persisted through annoying glitches to download the ARC; Autumn Reid, for her suggestion to go back to the beginning; and Lisa Cesena, who has been my friend forever and says I always make her cry.

Thank you for catching errors in the original draft and giving me honest, detailed feedback that helped to improve this story. Your contributions and suggestions have been invaluable. And all of you also volunteered to read the first draft of the sequel. Now I just have to write it!

From the Author

I hope you enjoyed **All the Little Secrets**! The idea came to me after an old boyfriend and I got back in touch after many years. I had been a struggling single mother like Vera. Though the rest of the story is pure fiction, I thought it'd be an interesting dilemma. Most of my female characters make a journey from insecurity to realizing their power, which is, perhaps, the life journey I've taken myself. I hope Vera inspires you, and you'll want to continue her story in the next book coming soon!

If you enjoyed this book, please post a rating or brief review on Amazon and/or Goodreads. I appreciate every one and it helps readers decide whether to read this book. Thank you! Here's the link to leave a review on Amazon:
http://www.amazon.com/review/create-review?&asin=+B08QGBW7FB

Finish the story with **Little Secrets Revealed**! The description and first chapter are on the following pages.

Each of my novels explores family and friendship, love and romance, relationships and life, and finding your power!

~*~*~*~*~*~*~*~*~*~*~*~

Little Secrets Revealed
Sequel to *All the Little Secrets*

Love, lust, or friendship? Vera finds herself involved in romantic entanglements once again. Justin is a good friend. But does love begin with friendship and can it exist without passion? And is it possible to be friends with newly divorced Brad, the man she thought was The One? Or is there a third choice? As Vera struggles to recognize true love, she delves into a search for inner peace with crystals and a psychic whose predictions begin to come true.

https://www.amazon.com/dp/B092SVKGXP

https://www.amazon.co.uk/dp/B092SVKGXP

Enjoy the first chapter next!

Chapter 1

A lot has happened in the last year. I hit some milestones when I turned fifty and became a grandmother. Both events signified the passage of time and the uncontrollable rollercoaster of highs and lows life can whisk you along on. Otherwise, my life is like everyone else's. Work and family and routine. Except for one little thing that transpired last year.

I had an affair with a married man. My life was ruled by secrets and deceptions, and I let my better judgment be swept away by passion.

I never thought I was the type of person who would become involved in a situation such as that. I'm too nice and honest. And I wouldn't want to do that to another woman. I know how it feels to doubt yourself.

But there it is. I did it. So why did I do it? I'm still trying to determine that. My excuse was that he was a man I'd been madly in love with about fifteen years before. He had been The One and my dreams and fantasies of an idyllic life had swirled around him when I was a struggling single mother. Yet, of course, it had been doomed to crash under the weight of my expectations.

But then, there he was, standing before me like an apparition I'd conjured after fifteen years had dulled the edges of heartache. Running into him had been a shock after so long as the old longing simmered beneath the surface. I tried to resist. I really did. But he'd handed me his business card, which teased with the temptation of having his phone number.

Distance assured safety while curiosity compelled me. Talking on the phone was healing, and the next thing I knew I was on a plane heading

301

500 miles south to see him. Just for dinner and friendship, I promised myself. Ha! I could never say no to Brad. I could never control my hormonal urges around him. He drew me like catnip. I was the one who pounced on him. I couldn't help myself. Perhaps he knew that about me.

Yet, at some point, I gathered the strength to break it off. For the second time. I simply couldn't lie to everyone anymore. My kids didn't know I was flying south every month or so. And my best friend, Marcy, my best friend in the world, didn't know. We had always told each other everything. A friend like that is worth all the gold on the planet. It was awful to lie to her.

But I soon discovered she had her secrets too, though not as shameful as mine. She and her husband, Doug, had been to marriage counseling. I don't know why she didn't tell me about it at the time. She was probably embarrassed because most of their issues stemmed from her unfounded suspicions that Doug was serial cheating on her. Her father had cheated on her mother and destroyed her ability to trust. All our subconscious issues come from our childhoods, don't they? But now you see why I couldn't tell her I was involved in an affair with a married man. I was the other woman, the enemy. She was angry when I finally confessed, even though it had nothing to do with her, but she eventually forgave my indiscretions,

And now all that is behind me. I haven't seen Brad since his wife barged in on us at the hotel, and I haven't talked to him since shortly after, despite my curiosity about what ultimately became of them.

I've moved on. I'm completely over him and see all the insanity with clarity. It's apparent how pathetic I'd been, how humiliating it was to be so easily manipulated. He said he loved me, but I don't think he knows what love is. There's a good chance

I'm just as clueless. I've resolved never to let myself get sucked in again like that. Ever.

Now I have my little granddaughter, Sofia, to enjoy. She learned to walk about a month ago, and she's so funny to observe staggering around like a tipsy drunk. She has a fierce determination when she wants something. She's persistent. She'd drag herself across the floor for a toy before she began to crawl. She's strong willed like her mother, Lacie.

Lacie and I spend more time together now because I babysit whenever she and Brandon need a break or have to go somewhere or I convince them to let me take Sofia for a few hours. I love her squirmy cuddly body and the transparency of the emotions that burst from her. I'm seeing the world through her eyes, and it's amazing when you look around. Bugs fascinate her. When was the last time you watched an ant or a bee or a butterfly? She's a pure bundle of delight and has shown me the world anew.

I see my son, Luke, and his girlfriend, Serena, more often as well since she's been helping me with my small garden. She's a quiet, peaceful person with a competent green thumb. It calms me simply being around her. I've made more of an effort to get to know her. It's challenging when you're both introverts.

After all the emotional drama last year, I vowed to remain single. I've never chosen relationships wisely. After reading a few self-improvement books, I understood how dysfunctional I am. I may just be hopeless, and I accept that.

Marcy came to visit from southern California, where I used to live, after the baby was born. We had a great time cementing the bonds of our friendship and talking at length about our issues. We're great at analyzing each other and less skilled at evaluating ourselves. But I absolutely adore her and her husband.

One little secret I can never reveal to her is the kiss I shared with her husband, Doug. It was completely inadvertent. We'd both been drinking, and I don't think it was an actual kiss. I think we brushed lips as we hugged while Marcy was passed out in the back seat of their car. My memory is hazy, and I'm not sure who instigated it, but no, it wasn't really a kiss at all. Doug is like a brother to me. I'm sure it was just a brief brush of the lips, an accidental encounter of our bodies that involved our mouths. It sounds so wrong, but, trust me, it wasn't as bad as it sounds. Doug would never and I would never.

Things like this make me wonder what is wrong with me. See? This is why I have to remain single. After the fiasco of last year, I promised myself that I would. Possibly forever.

I'm better with friendships. Those I can handle. Justin and I have been hanging out more often. I met him on a singles site last year when Marcy signed me up without my consent. I don't feel much chemistry with him, but we have fun when we're together. We like to laugh and joke, as friends do.

That reminds me that Brad used to call me Bob sometimes, when he wasn't calling me V, short for Vera. He gave me this whole speech justifying his infidelity with the example of having a friend named Bob who filled certain needs his wife didn't. He put me in his phone as Bob, which amused him. But I suspect I filled other needs that Bob would not have.

I feel completely relaxed around Justin because there's no pressure like in a relationship. I never realized before how aware of every little thing I am with someone I'm dating. I obsess about what I'm wearing, how I look, what I say. It's exhausting. There's none of that with Justin. How liberating. Why hadn't I considered being platonic with men before?

We go to movies or out to eat or even do a Costco run together. It's nice having a guy friend. We can be totally honest with each other, and I can get a man's perspective. I told him about Brad and he told me about his ex, Madelaine, who wanted to be called Madelaine, not Maddie. He used to call her Mad to piss her off.

Sometimes he dates and tells me about it and asks my opinion. I feel zero jealousy, which reinforces the fact that we're just friends, and it's absolutely perfect this way.

I have random dreams about Brad. I don't know if I'll ever get him completely out of my head. This is something I admit to no one. It's mine to deal with, though I can't help savoring these dreams. When it was good between us, it was *very* good. The best. And I'll never have that with anyone again. But my eyes are open now. He's a liar and a cheater. He's selfish and arrogant. I feel for his wife.

~ ~ ~

Justin picks me up to go out to dinner. We arrive at our favorite Mexican restaurant and order our usual meals. He gets a Margarita and I sip on a Pina Colada, which I can't get enough of since I had one with Doug at a tavern last year. Marcy had insisted I follow her husband after work to see if he was cheating on her. I don't how she always talked me into her schemes, but, of course, Doug had seen me, and we'd ended up having a drink together. I wish I could find my own Doug.

Justin always looks a little disheveled. He has light shaggy hair and usually manages to get food on himself. He reminds me a little of Doug because they're both easygoing. I bet they'd hit it off.

"How was your date?" I ask him.

Justin has seen someone a few times, and things seem to be going well. I don't mind as long as we can still be friends. This is my big worry. I don't want to lose his friendship.

"I like her, but why do women always try to rush things?" His eyebrows go up in consternation.

"Why? What's she doing that's too fast?" I'm sipping my drink through a wide paper straw. It occurs to me I could be a sugar addict, especially when it's mixed with alcohol.

"There are a few red flags." He leans forward.

"Like what?" Red sauce is dabbing at his light blue Henley shirt from his plate. "You need to... You've got..." I indicate his shirt and pull his plate away from the edge of the table.

"Oh, man. This is one of my favorite shirts." He dips his napkin in his water glass and rubs at it furiously.

"So, what did she do?" I bring him back to the topic at hand. I can't remember her name.

"For one thing, she doesn't like that we're friends."

"You told her about me?"

"Yeah. I said we're platonic, and then she asked if you were pretty and what you look like."

"How did you describe me?"

He tosses the wet napkin on the table. "I said you're short and have dark hair and that you're attractive."

It was interesting to hear how a man summed me up. Then I smile. "You think I'm attractive?"

"Oh, don't give me that coy smile, Vera. You know you're pretty. Guys probably fall all over themselves gawking at you," he says with a grin.

"Someone thought I was a movie star once." I exaggerate the time Brad and I were walking along the beach and a man stared at me as we passed. Brad said it was because he thought I was *someone.*

"It gives me cred to have an attractive platonic friend."

"Except she doesn't like it."

"No, she doesn't."

"What else happened?" I ask.

"She wants us to cohabitate."

"Already? You haven't even..."

"Yes, we have."

"You didn't tell me that."

He shrugs. "Sex is a whole other topic."

Yes, it is. I suck down the rest of my drink. "How was it? With her."

He looks at me sideways. "Can we talk about this?"

"Sure. Why not?" I focus on my meal now that my drink is gone.

"Well." He takes a bite of food, and I wait while he chews. "It's good. It's satisfactory."

"Satisfactory?"

"It's only been one time, and the first time can be a little awkward."

I nod. Sex had been the best from the first time with Brad and every intensely satisfying time after. Stop thinking about Brad!

"Potential?" I ask.

"I think so. She has a good body."

"You never mentioned that."

"I've only seen it recently."

"Oh." I'm not sure how to respond. We've never talked about sex before. It's a little weird.

"So now she thinks we should cohabitate."

"What do you think?"

"I don't know her well enough."

I give him a look.

"Fornicating with someone doesn't mean you know them. Living together is a whole other commitment."

"True." I glance at Justin and wonder what it

would be like to have sex with him. Is he a good lover? It's been a long time. I always was a bit carnal, and Brad had certainly brought that out in me.

But no, Justin and I are friends and that's it. What would it be like having detached sex? It would probably feel empty like it had with Brad when he only gave me so much of himself and then withdrew. How maddening that had been.

Stop thinking about Brad!

I sigh. I'll always compare everyone to Brad. My thoughts are doomed to keep circling back to him. Another involvement might break the cycle, but let's not be that drastic. Would hypnosis help?

Love, lust, friendship. Does it all overlap? Can you find it in one person? I wish I could unravel this paradox.

https://www.amazon.com/dp/B092SVKGXP

https://www.amazon.co.uk/dp/B092SVKGXP

May your life be filled with great books!

Printed in Great Britain
by Amazon

71626681R00180